EGMONT PRESS: ETHI

Egmont Press is about turning writers into successful authors and children into passionate readers – producing books that enrich and entertain. As a responsible children's publisher, we go even further, considering the world in which our consumers are growing up.

Safety First
Naturally, all of our books meet legal safety requirements. But we go further than this; every book with play value is tested to the highest standards – if it fails, it's back to the drawing-board.

Made Fairly
We are working to ensure that the workers involved in our supply chain – the people that make our books – are treated with fairness and respect.

Responsible Forestry
We are committed to ensuring all our papers come from environmentally and socially responsible forest sources.

For more information, please visit our website at
www.egmont.co.uk/ethicalpublishing

THE
STONE
LIGHT

KAI MEYER

THE STONE LIGHT

Translated by Anthea Bell

EGMONT

EGMONT

We bring stories to life

First published in Great Britain 2006
by Egmont UK Limited
239 Kensington High Street, London W8 6SA

First published in Germany 2001
under the title *Das Steinerne Licht*
by Loewe Verlag GmbH, Bindlach, Germany

ISBN 978 1 4052 1640 1
ISBN 1 4052 1640 9

1 3 5 7 9 10 8 6 4 2

A CIP catalogue record for this title is available from the British Library

Typeset by Avon DataSet Ltd, Bidford on Avon, Warwickshire B50 4JH
Printed and bound in Great Britain by the CPI Group

CONTENTS

SON OF HORUS

Far below the great wings of the obsidian lion, the landscape stretched away like a sea of ashes. Vermithrax's black stone body could have been almost weightless, gliding beneath the thick cloud cover. The girl on his back felt that she had only to stretch out her arm to touch the cotton-wool underside of the clouds.

Merle clung to the winged lion's mane with both hands. Vermithrax's long coat was stone, like the rest of him, but for reasons that she did not understand his hair felt soft and supple – just one of the many marvels present in the great weight of the lion's obsidian body.

At this height the wind was keen and very chilly. It cut with ease through Merle's red cape and the coarsely woven calf-length dress that she wore under it. The hem of the dress had slipped up above her knees, exposing her legs to the wind. By now the goose pimples on her thighs seemed as natural to her as her rumbling stomach and the pain in her ears from altitude and the cold air. At least her sturdy leather shoes protected her feet from the chill, which was not much comfort in this desperate situation as she watched the empty landscape moving away many metres below them.

Two days ago, Merle had escaped from her native city of Venice on the back of the winged lion Vermithrax. Together they had broken through the Empire's encircling ring of besiegers and set a course flying north. Since then they had seen nothing under them but a devastated wilderness. Empty, ruined cities with scorched walls rising as jagged outlines to the sky; abandoned farms, many destroyed by fire or crushed into dust beneath the feet of the Egyptian armies; villages inhabited only by stray dogs and cats; and of course those places where the earth seemed to have been turned upside down, churned up, devastated by powers a thousand times stronger than any ox-drawn plough.

Only nature opposed the brute force of the Empire, and many meadows were bright with springtime green, flowering lilacs rose above the remains of walls and the trees were putting out dense, lush foliage. Their strength and life were in stark contrast to the abandoned farms and settlements.

'How much longer?' asked Merle gloomily.

Vermithrax had a voice as deep as a well-shaft. 'Half a day less than at noon today.'

She didn't answer that, but waited for the spectral voice inside her to speak up, as it usually did when Merle needed comfort or just a few encouraging words.

But the Flowing Queen kept silent.

'Queen?' she asked hesitantly.

Vermithrax had become perfectly used to the way Merle occasionally talked to someone he could neither see nor hear. He soon realised when her remarks were not meant for him.

'Isn't she answering?' he asked after a while.

'She's thinking,' were the words that came through Merle's lips, but it wasn't Merle who spoke them. The Flowing Queen had taken over her voice again. By now Merle had learned to tolerate this bad habit, although at heart it annoyed her. For the moment, however, she was glad to get any sign of life at all out of the Queen.

'What are you thinking about?' asked Merle.

'You human beings,' said the Queen, and changed back to the thought-voice that only Merle could hear. *'How it could come to this. And what makes a man like the Pharaoh do*

'. . . *do such things as that?*' She had no hand of her own to point to the desolation on the ground, but Merle knew exactly what she meant.

'But is he? I mean, is he a man? After all, he was dead until the priests brought him back to life.'

'*A man may rise from the dead. That doesn't mean he has to spread war worse than the world has seen for a long time over all the countries on earth.*'

'For a long time?' Merle was surprised. 'Do you mean there was once another war when someone almost conquered the whole world?' For with the exception of Venice, whose days were numbered, only the Tsarist Empire had withstood the attacking Empire of the Pharaoh for the last three decades. All other countries had long ago been overrun by armies of mummies and swarms of scarab beetles.

'*They tried. But that was thousands of years ago, in the age of the sub-oceanic civilisations.*'

The sub-oceanic civilisations. The words echoed on in Merle's mind long after the Queen's voice had died away. After freeing the Flowing Queen from the hands of an Egyptian spy, she had begun to suspect that the Queen herself, that strange creature, was a survivor of the

Sub-Oceanic Realms, which were said to have been unimaginably powerful. But the Queen had denied it and Merle believed her. It would have been too easy an answer.

No one could fully understand a being like the Queen, not even Merle, who had been closer to her than anyone since they fled from Venice together.

Merle shook off these ideas. Thinking of Venice meant thinking of Serafin, and that hurt too much just now.

She gazed intently ahead over Vermithrax's black mane. The jagged rocks of high mountains rose before them. For some time the country below had been hilly and now it was rising ever more steeply. They would soon reach the mountain range, and their destination was supposed to be beyond them and not far away.

'There's snow!'

'What did you expect?' asked the obsidian lion, amused. 'You can see how high we're flying. It's going to get a good bit colder before we come down on the other side.'

'I've never seen snow before,' said Merle thoughtfully. 'People say there hasn't been a real winter for decades. And no real summer either. Spring and autumn just somehow seem to merge.'

'Looks as though nothing much has changed while I was

held prisoner in the Campanile.' Vermithrax laughed again. 'Human beings are always complaining about the weather from dawn to dusk. How can so many minds think so much about something they can't change anyway?'

Merle had no answer to that, and the Queen took over her voice again. 'Vermithrax! Down at the foot of this mountain . . . what is it?'

Merle gulped, as if she could simply swallow the unwelcome influence controlling her tongue. She immediately sensed the Queen leaving her mouth. For a split second, it felt as if all the blood were draining away from her tongue and cheeks.

'I can see it too,' she said. 'A flock of birds?'

The lion growled. 'Rather large for a flock of birds. And much too dense.'

The dark shadow hovering like a cloud above part of the mountainside was sharply outlined. It was still several thousand paces away and, by comparison with the gigantic rock formations in the background, its dark shape standing out against the slopes didn't look particularly impressive. But Merle already guessed that it would not seem the same once they came closer to it. Or once the thing came closer to them.

'Watch out!' called Vermithrax.

He lost height so abruptly that Merle felt as if her guts were being pressed up and out through her ears. For a moment she thought she would be sick. She was about to say something sharp to the obsidian lion when she saw why he had made the manoeuvre.

A handful of tiny dots was swirling around the large outline: bright specks glowing in the light of the setting sun as if someone had scattered gold dust over a landscape painting.

'*Barques of the Sun,*' said the Queen inside Merle's mind.

They've caught us now, thought Merle. They've barred our way ahead. Who'd have guessed we were still so important to them? Yes, she was the bearer of the Flowing Queen, the guardian spirit who had lived in the waters of the lagoon and protected Venice from the Egyptian conquerors. But that was all over now, and the city was doomed to fall into the power of the tyrants for good.

'*This meeting must be a coincidence,*' said the Flowing Queen's voice in Merle's thoughts. '*It doesn't look as if they've noticed us.*'

Merle had to agree. The Egyptians couldn't have caught up with them so fast. And even if they had succeeded in alerting some of their fighting forces in this region, Egyptian vessels would certainly not have been waiting for the fugitives in front of a snowfield, clearly visible from afar.

'What are they doing here?' asked Merle.

'The large ship must be a Gatherer. One of their flying mummy factories.'

Vermithrax was now flying just above the treetops of a dense forest. Occasionally he had to swerve to avoid the tallest of the pines and firs, but apart from that he was making straight for their adversaries.

'Perhaps we ought to change course,' said Merle, trying not to sound too terrified. But her heart was racing. It felt as if her legs belonged to a rag doll.

A Gatherer. A real, genuine Gatherer. She had never before seen one of those Egyptian airships with her own eyes, and she could have done without the experience. She knew what the Gatherers did, she even knew *how* they did it, and moreover she was only too painfully aware that every Gatherer was captained by one of the Pharaoh's much-feared sphinx commanders.

Not a cheerful prospect.

And there was worse to come.

'There's a whole squadron of Barques of the Sun flying around it,' said Vermithrax tonelessly.

Merle too could see now that the golden dots were the smallest flying units of the imperial fleet. Each of the crescent-shaped Barques of the Sun had room for a troop of mummy warriors and the high priest whose magic kept the barque moving and airborne. If the Egyptians noticed Vermithrax and his rider, sunset was their only hope. The darker it grew, the more slowly the barques moved through the air, and once night fell they couldn't be flown at all.

But blood-red light was still flooding the slopes of the mountain range, and the sun had only half sunk behind the summits in the west.

'Let's change course,' Merle repeated, more urgently this time. 'Why don't we swerve aside and fly round them?'

'If I'm not much mistaken,' said the Queen through Merle's mouth, for her words were meant for the lion too, 'then this Gatherer is on its way to Venice to take part in the great battle there.'

'Always supposing there is one,' said Merle.

'The Venetians will surrender,' said Vermithrax. 'They were never particularly brave. Present company excepted.'

'Thank you kindly.'

'Vermithrax is right. There probably won't be any fighting. But who knows how the imperial armies will treat the city and its people? Venice has defied the Pharaoh for over thirty years.'

'But that was your doing!'

'To save you all.'

They were now only a few hundred metres from the Gatherer. The Barques of the Sun were patrolling at a great height above them. Their golden armour-plating reflected the light of the setting sun, making them glow red in the evening light. Merle could only hope that from above the obsidian lion was invisible in the shadows among the treetops.

The Gatherer was a mighty construction, shaped like a three-sided pyramid with its tip flattened. At the top of the pyramid, and surrounded by battlements, was a wide observation platform with several structures on it. These structures in turn rose towards the centre and thus themselves formed a kind of spire. Merle could see tiny figures behind the battlements.

The woods thinned out as the terrain rose slightly. Deep furrows in the forest floor were clearly visible, a labyrinth of trenches still not entirely overgrown after all these years. Bitter battles had once been fought in this place.

'*There are people buried here,*' said the Queen suddenly.

'What?'

'*The land below the Gatherer — a great many dead must have been buried there during the war, or it wouldn't be hovering on the spot over a single place.*'

And indeed the mighty hull of the mummy factory was hanging absolutely motionless above a meadow of tall grass bending in the evening wind. At any other time it could have been an idyllic picture, a calm and peaceful place. But now the Gatherer cast a menacing shadow. It was hovering no more than the height of a Venetian palazzo above the meadow.

'I'm going to land,' said Vermithrax. 'They'll see us without the shelter of the trees.'

No one contradicted him. The obsidian lion came down on the outskirts of the forest. A jolt ran through Merle as his paws touched the ground. Only now did she realise how her bottom was aching after such a long ride on the stone lion's back. She tried to move, but it was almost impossible.

'*Don't dismount,*' said the Queen. '*We may have to take off again in rather a hurry.*'

And there's another cheerful prospect, thought Merle.

'It's starting.'

'Yes . . . I can see that.'

Vermithrax knew no more of the Empire and its methods than Merle and the Queen had told him after freeing him from the tower prison in the middle of the Piazza San Marco, but he uttered a deep growl. His mane bristled. All of a sudden his whiskers stood out so straight that they might have been drawn with a ruler.

First of all the leaves on the trees around them withered, fading as fast as if autumn had decided to start its work a few months early and finish it within minutes. The foliage turned brown, shrivelled and dropped from the branches. The spruce tree under which they had taken shelter lost all its needles, and Vermithrax and Merle were instantly covered with a brown cloak.

Merle shook herself and looked up at the Gatherer. They were not directly under it, thank heaven, but close enough for her to have a good view of its entire underside.

The gigantic surface was suddenly covered with a network of shining, dark yellow lines running in all directions, describing angles that followed no recognisable pattern. But there was a dark, circular area half the size of the Piazza San Marco left in the middle. Merle had to cling even more tightly to Vermithrax's obsidian mane when the ground suddenly shook as if in a strong earth tremor. Several trees quite close were uprooted and tilted over, pulling others up with them and crashing to the ground among dense, swirling clouds of leaves and conifer needles. For a moment Merle found it difficult to breathe, the air was so full of dry splinters of wood and debris from the withered leaves. When her eyes stopped streaming, she saw what had happened.

The meadow above which the mummy factory was hovering had disappeared. The earth was churned up as if an army of invisible giant moles had been at work. The glowing network of lines no longer clung to the underside of the Gatherer, but had frayed into a countless number of blazing strands and hooked lines of light, none of them shaped like any of the others. They were all pointing down, with their ends approaching the devastated ground and pulling something out of it.

Bodies. Gaunt, grey corpses.

'So that's how they get their mummy warriors,' whispered Vermithrax, in a horrified voice that sounded as if it would fail him at any moment.

Merle tugged at his mane. She had looked away, she

couldn't bear to watch what was happening before her eyes any more. 'Let's go!'

'*No!*' said the Flowing Queen.

But Vermithrax felt as Merle did. They must get away from there. Away from the suction exerted by the Gatherer before they themselves were caught on one of those shimmering hooks and hauled up into the mummy factory, where slaves and machinery would make them into something full of a *different* kind of life, imbued with docility and obedience and the will to kill.

'Hold on!' he roared.

The Flowing Queen protested out loud, using Merle's voice, but the obsidian lion ignored her. His wings carried them up into the air like the wind. Executing a daring manoeuvre, he turned east towards the approaching darkness. At the same time he shot forward, even though all the Barques of the Sun and the high priests had noticed them at this very moment.

Merle was clinging so tightly to Vermithrax's mane that her arms disappeared into it up to the elbows. She bent low over his neck so as to offer less air resistance and avoid the Egyptians' missiles. She hardly dared look up, but when at last she did she saw that half a dozen Barques of the Sun had fallen out of the formation around the Gatherer and were in pursuit of them.

Vermithrax's plan was as simple as it was suicidal. He guessed there must be weapons in the mighty hull of the Gatherer that could easily shoot a flying lion out of the sky, but if he made for the Barques of the Sun, then the commanders on board the Gatherer might think twice about aiming at a target in the middle of their own people.

It won't work, thought Merle. Vermithrax's plan would have been a good one if they had been dealing with ordinary adversaries, the kind of people the winged lion had known in the days before he had been a prisoner of the City Guard of Venice. But the Barques of the Sun were manned by mummy warriors, every one of them only too easily replaced, and even a few priests could probably be sacrificed.

When Vermithrax too realised that, he cursed. Only a little way in front of them a wooden bolt the length of a man whirred through the air, fired from one of the hatches in the Gatherer's hull. The mummy factory itself was too heavy to give chase, but its weapons were menacing and travelled a long way.

Merle felt sicker than ever as Vermithrax kept swerving

sideways, performing agile manoeuvres that she wouldn't have thought possible given his heavy stone body. They swooped up and down, often in such swift alternation that Merle soon lost all sense of what was above and what was below. Even the Queen seemed to be affected.

Once Merle looked back. They were now almost level with the observation platform at the top of the pyramid, and there were several figures standing behind the battlements. Merle could see their robes and their grim expressions. High priests, she suspected.

Just below them stood a particularly striking man. He was a good head taller than the rest and wore a billowing cloak that looked as if it were woven of pure gold. His hairless skull was covered with a network of golden threads, like lines engraved on a brooch by a goldsmith, and his hands were clenched grimly on the top of the battlements.

'*The Pharaoh's vizier,*' whispered the Queen in her head. '*His name is Seth. He is high priest of the cult of Horus.*'

'Seth? Isn't that the name of an Egyptian god too?'

'*The priests of Horus were never famous for their modesty.*'

Merle felt as if the man's eyes were looking across all that distance and straight into her brain. For a split second it was as if the Queen were groaning in pain inside her.

'Are you all right?' she asked.

'Turn away! Please . . . don't look into his eyes.'

At that moment a whole volley of bolts raced over them and away. Two struck Barques of the Sun flying close to the lion. Smoke rose from one as it went into a spin and fell in an irregular spiral. The other dropped like a stone and smashed to pieces on the ground, with a firework display of iron splinters. The other Barques of the Sun immediately retreated out of range of the hail of shots coming from the Gatherer.

This was the chance Vermithrax had been waiting for.

With a great roar, he plunged down into the depths. Perched on his back, Merle screamed as the ground came closer at lightning speed. She already saw herself lying shattered beside the wreck of the barque.

But a few metres above the rocks Vermithrax halted his dive, soared above the ground and up over the top of a steep precipice, and then plunged into the depths again, with the wall behind him and out of the Gatherer's direct line of fire. Now they had only to deal with the four barques that would surely follow them over the top of the rock at any moment.

The Flowing Queen had recovered from the vizier's penetrating gaze. *'I know why I chose Vermithrax for our flight.'*

'Because you didn't have any choice.' Merle could hardly hear her own words; the wind tore them from her lips like scraps of paper.

In her mind, the Queen laughed: a strange feeling. It seemed to Merle as if she herself were laughing, but without any effort on her own part.

The lion began flying horizontally again, and crossed a maze of crevices in the rock before finding one broad enough for him to dive into. Volleys of shots came from the left and the right, this time steel balls fired from guns mounted on the prows of the Barques of the Sun. But none was close enough to be dangerous. Splinters of stone rained down on them from all sides. Sparks flew up when ricochets skidded over the walls, driving furrows into the rock.

Only a little way down, the shallow ravine into which they had dropped narrowed; its walls were just far enough apart for Vermithrax to race through at a low level. Two Barques of the Sun had followed him into the rocky labyrinth, while the other two glided on above the maze of crevices, waiting for the obsidian lion to emerge again. It wasn't hard for Vermithrax to fly around sharp angles and curves, while the long Barques of the Sun had to slow down at every bend if they were not to collide with the rocks.

Now the ravine below them was filling up with water. It was the arm of a stream or mountain lake, coming to a dead end here. Vermithrax followed its course and soon they were flying fast above a river. The rock walls drew further apart here and gave the Barques of the Sun enough space to manoeuvre. But Vermithrax still had a good start, and the two barques above the crevices hadn't spotted them yet.

'We can't keep flying so low forever if we want to get to the other side of the mountain range.'

'First we have to survive, right?'

'I'm only trying to plan ahead, Merle, that's all.'

Merle found it hard to concentrate at this speed, with death so close behind her. They might have escaped the Gatherer, but the Barques of the Sun were still after them.

'Vermithrax!' She bent down to the lion's ear and tried to shout above the sound of the wind. 'What are you planning to do?'

'Sunset,' was his brief reply. From the tone of his voice

she realised that he was closer to exhaustion than she had thought. It hadn't entered her mind that even a creature like Vermithrax might simply run out of breath.

The current below them was flowing faster. Merle saw that the water no longer glowed red, as it had been doing only a few minutes ago, and only reflected the shadowy rock faces. The sunset glow had gone out of the sky too and it was turning violet blue.

She could have shouted out loud with relief. Vermithrax was right; his plan was working. He had tricked the Egyptians. The Barques of the Sun were left behind. Merle imagined the crescent-shaped airships returning to the Gatherer at snail's pace, crippled by the fading daylight, useless as scrap metal.

The river flowed faster, became more turbulent and above all louder, and soon a white crest of foam appeared before them, stretching over the entire width of the waterway. There was nothing but darkness beyond.

With a roar of delight, Vermithrax soared over the waterfall, and all at once the ground dropped to 100 metres below them. The obsidian lion maintained their height, so that Merle could see far over the land at the foot of the mountains, across forests and meadows slumbering in the darkness of approaching night. The lion's wings were beating more slowly now, but he continued unwaveringly on his course. Merle stared down in silence at the landscape passing by for a long time before she turned to the Queen again.

'What do you know about this Seth?' she asked the voice inside her.

'*Not much. Followers of the cult of Horus called the Pharaoh back to life over thirty years ago. The high priests of the Empire have been drawn from their ranks ever since. It's said that even then Seth was their leader.*'

'He didn't look all that old.'

'*No. But what difference does that make?*'

Merle wondered how she could explain to a timeless being like the Queen that a man's appearance normally gave some idea of his age. If it didn't, it could mean one of two things: either he wasn't showing his true face, or he looked like a man but wasn't really. At least, not a mortal man.

As Merle did not attempt to answer the question, the Queen went on. '*The priests of Horus are very powerful. It is they who really determine the fate of the Empire. The Pharaoh is just their puppet.*'

'So you're saying that if Seth is the chief high priest of Horus, and vizier to the Pharaoh as well, then he's –'

'*The true ruler of Egypt. Yes, certainly.*'

'And the world.'

'*I'm afraid so.*'

'Do you think we shall meet him again?'

'*You'd better pray we don't.*'

'Pray to the Flowing Queen? Like the whole of Venice is probably doing at this moment?' She regretted her words the moment they were out, but it was too late to take them back now.

Over the next few hours the Queen kept silent, and retreated to the furthest corner of Merle's mind, spun in a cocoon of her own cool, strange, god-like thoughts.

They crossed the mountain range a little further east without encountering any more adversaries.

A time came – it must have been after midnight – when they saw the other side of the mountains ahead of them in the grey, icy starlight and now at last Vermithrax allowed himself to rest. He landed on the peak of an inaccessible needle of rock, a place just wide enough for him to lie down and let Merle climb off his back.

She hurt all over. For some time she doubted whether she would ever be able to walk again without aching in every bone and muscle at each step she took.

In the dark she strained her eyes for any sign of pursuers, but she could see nothing suspicious anywhere. Only a bird of prey circled in the distance, a falcon or a hawk.

No sound rose from the wide expanse of country at the foot of the mountain range, not even the cry of an animal or the flutter of birds' wings. Her heart contracted and a sense of uneasiness came over her. With eerie certainty, she knew that nothing still lived down there. No human beings, no animals. The Egyptians had robbed the place even of its dead to man their galleys, the Barques of the Sun and their engines of war.

She sat down on the edge of the tiny plateau and stared into the night, lost in thought. 'Do you think Lord Light will help us?' It was the first time in hours that she had spoken to the Queen and she wasn't really expecting an answer.

'*I don't know. The Venetians brutally mistreated his envoy.*'

'But they didn't know what they were doing.'

'*You think that makes a difference?*'

'No,' said Merle sadly. 'Not really.'

'*Exactly.*'

'But Lord Light did offer to support Venice in the city's struggle against the Empire.'

'*That was before the bodyguards killed his envoy. And anyway, it's not in human nature to make a pact with Hell.*'

Merle smiled humourlessly. 'Oh, I've heard some very different stories. You really don't know all that much about human beings.'

She leaned back and closed her eyes.

In the year 1833 the English explorer Professor Burbridge had discovered that Hell was far from being just an old wives' tale. It really existed: it was an underground region below the earth's surface, and Burbridge had led a series of expeditions there. He came back from the last one alone. Much of what he had seen and experienced was set down in documentary records and had been taught in schools until the beginning of the Great War. But there was no doubt that this was only a fraction of what he had really discovered. Rumour said that the rest was too dreadful and horrifying to be made public. Such claims were supported by the fact that no one else had ventured to make the descent in the years since Burbridge's last expedition. Only after the outbreak of war had signs of life from those lower regions surfaced again, finally culminating in the offer made by Lord Light, the ruler of Hell and a figure steeped in legend, to help the Venetians in their struggle against the Pharaoh. But in its arrogance and self-satisfaction, the City Council had declined any help. Merle herself had witnessed the murder of Lord Light's last envoy in the Piazza San Marco.

And now Merle, the Flowing Queen and Vermithrax were on their way to ask Lord Light in person for help in the name of the common people of Venice — not its councillors. The question was whether, even if their mission was successful, they would arrive in time. And who was to say that Lord Light wouldn't treat them exactly as his envoy had been treated in Venice?

The worst of it was, however, that they had no option now but to follow in Burbridge's footsteps and go down into the abyss. And none of them, not even the Queen, had any idea what they would find there.

Merle opened her eyes and looked at the sleeping Vermithrax. She was tired out herself, but her feelings were still in too much turmoil for her to rest.

'Why is he helping us?' she whispered thoughtfully. 'I mean, you're the Flowing Queen, so in a way you're a part of Venice – or the other way around. You want to protect what's yours. But why Vermithrax? He could just fly back to his own kind in Africa.'

'*If he found any of them still there. It isn't only to the north that the Empire has spread.*'

'You think the other talking lions are dead?'

'*I don't know,*' said the Queen sadly. '*Perhaps. Or maybe they have simply moved on, gone somewhere so far away that the Egyptians won't find them for a while yet.*'

'And Vermithrax knows that?'

'*Perhaps he guesses it.*'

'Then we're all he still has left, aren't we? His only friends.'

Merle put out a hand and gently stroked one of the lion's stone paws. Vermithrax made a soft purring sound, turned on his side and stretched all four paws out towards her. His mouth quivered with every breath he took, and Merle could see his eyes twitching under their closed lids. He was dreaming.

She wrapped her cape more tightly round her body to protect herself from the chilly wind and then nestled very close to Vermithrax. He purred again with well-being and began to snore softly.

The Queen is here, she thought, because she and Venice somehow belong together. Neither can exist without the other. But what about me? What am I doing in all this?

Her closest friends, Junipa and Serafin, her master, Arcimboldo, and of course Eft too were all still in Venice, exposed to the dangers of the Egyptian invasion. Merle herself had been found as a baby, floating in a basket on the canals, and brought up in an orphanage; today the thought that she had no parents to worry about was for once reassuring.

Not that it was quite as simple as that. Some day she'd find out what kind of people her mother and father had been. At some point she was sure she would.

Lost in thought, she took the magic hand-mirror out from under her cape. Its surface was water which did not spill out of the frame whichever way up you held it. If Merle put her arm into the water she sometimes felt a soft, warm hand clasping her fingers on the other side of the mirror, right inside it. The water mirror had been in the basket beside her when she was found. It was her only link to her parents. The only trace she had of them.

And there was something else in the mirror too: a milky film constantly flitting across the surface. A phantom had escaped from one of Arcimboldo's magic mirrors and taken up residence in her little hand-mirror. Merle would have loved to get in touch with it; the only question was how. Serafin had told her that the phantoms in Arcimboldo's mirrors were people from another world who had managed to cross into this one – but without guessing that here they would only be phantoms, shapeless, misty forms caught inside mirrors.

Serafin . . . Merle sighed inaudibly.

She had hardly even come to know him properly before they were separated by the city councillors' bodyguards. They'd spent only a few hours together, difficult, dangerous hours in which they had saved the crystal flask containing the essence of the Flowing Queen from an Egyptian spy. Yet although they knew so little about each other, she missed him.

She fell asleep thinking of Serafin's smile and the mischief in his eyes.

In her dreams, she thought she heard the cry of a falcon. She was woken briefly by a gentle draught passing over her face and a smell of feathers, but there was nothing anywhere close, or if there was it hid itself in the darkness again.

THE MASTER THIEF

The church clocks of Venice had struck midnight some time ago. Deep darkness lay over the city and the waters of the lagoon. The streets were empty of human beings, with nothing moving in them but stray cats out hunting for prey, unimpressed by the threat of the Empire.

All was still on the bank of the narrow canal – eerily still. Serafin sat on the stone bank swinging his legs. The soles of his feet were just above the water. The street lined with buildings that had led him here was narrow and gloomy, ending in this cul-de-sac at the waterside.

Not so long ago he had brought Merle to this place to show her the strange reflections on the surface of the water. Reflections that ought not really to exist at all, and could be seen only between midnight and one in the morning. They were of the buildings on the bank of the canal, yet they did not reflect reality. There were lights in many of the windows that you could see in the water, although the buildings themselves were dark and deserted. Now and then something moved on the water, as if reflecting passers-by who weren't there – or not in *this* Venice, the city where Serafin and Merle had grown up. But there were rumours that a second Venice existed in another world, perhaps even a dozen Venices, or hundreds of them.

Serafin gloomily crumbled a small loaf into the water, but no fish came up to take the unexpected treat. Now that the Flowing Queen had been driven from the lagoon by the poison of the Egyptian high priests, few fish were to be seen swimming in the canals. Instead, seaweed grew in the water, and Serafin wasn't the only one to think that there was more of it every day. Dark green strands, shapeless and twisted like wet cobwebs. It was to be hoped that they hadn't really been spun by one of the great sea-spiders no one had ever seen, but that were said to live out in the Mediterranean where the water was deepest, in the ruins of the Sub-Oceanic Realms.

Serafin was feeling terrible. He knew that Merle had escaped from Venice on the back of a stone lion, and even in his present mental turmoil he was glad of it. At least no danger from the Egyptians threatened her at the moment – always supposing she had been able to get through the

Empire's besieging ring around the city without being captured by the Barques of the Sun.

Nor was it just that he was afraid of the coming invasion. Fear of the Egyptians went deep, yes, but in a strange way — a way that unsettled Serafin — he had accepted it. The conquest of Venice was inevitable.

No, something else preyed on his mind, would hardly let him sleep and made him restless by day. His stomach felt like a hard knot that wouldn't let him take nourishment. He had to force himself to eat every morsel, and even then he didn't always succeed. The crumbs of bread on the water beneath him were his supper.

He was anxious about Junipa, the girl with the mirror-glass eyes. And of course about Arcimboldo, the old man who made magic mirrors in his house on the Outcasts' Canal. It had been Arcimboldo who took Junipa and Merle from their orphanages to be apprentices in his workshop; Arcimboldo who — as Serafin had only recently discovered — had come to an agreement to deliver up Junipa very soon to Lord Light, the ruler of Hell.

Serafin had confronted Arcimboldo with what he knew, and the mirror-maker had answered most of his questions.

These days Arcimboldo seemed a defeated man. He had been secretly delivering his magic mirrors to Lord Light for years. Time and again he had met Talamar, Lord Light's envoy, to hand over new mirrors, and when one day Talamar had made him a very special offer, Arcimboldo, after long hesitation, had agreed. He was to restore the blind Junipa's eyesight with the aid of his magic mirrors. A noble action in itself, and afterwards Junipa had learned to cope with her new powers of vision a little more easily every day.

But that wasn't all.

Lord Light had not brought the frail Junipa to Arcimboldo's attention purely out of selfless kindness. Serafin had had to press the old mirror-maker for some time before he finally learned the whole story.

'Junipa can see in the dark too with her new eyes,' Arcimboldo explained over a glass of tea one night, as the moon shone into his workshop through a skylight in the roof. 'Merle may have told you so already, but it doesn't end there.'

'End?' asked Serafin, intrigued.

'A time will come when the magic mirror glass I used to replace her eyeballs will make her able to see into other worlds. Or rather, to see through the *mirrors* of other worlds.'

After a long silence, Serafin finally found words again. 'Worlds like the ones reflected on some of the canals at midnight?'

'You know about that? Yes, those and other worlds besides. Junipa will look at the people living there through their mirrors and they won't even notice. She will watch kings and emperors making decisions of state in their mirror-lined halls, and she will see heavily laden ships reflected in the water of distant oceans. That is the true power given her by the mirror-glass eyes. And that's what Lord Light wants.'

'Surveillance, you mean? That's what he's after. He doesn't just want to know what's going on in this world, he won't be happy until he knows everything. About all the worlds there are.'

'Lord Light is curious. Perhaps we should say avid for knowledge? Or interested in everything?'

'Unscrupulous and vicious is what I'd say,' replied Serafin angrily. 'He's exploiting Junipa. She's so happy that she can see — and she has no idea what's really behind it.'

'Yes, she does,' Arcimboldo contradicted him. 'I've

talked to her. She knows now what power she will have one day, and I think she has accepted it.'

'Has she any choice?'

'Lord Light leaves none of us any choice. I have none either. If I hadn't taken his gold, the workshop would have had to close long ago. He's bought more magic mirrors than anyone else since the guild expelled me. But for him I'd have had to send all my apprentices back to their orphanages, and Merle and Junipa wouldn't have come here in the first place.' The little old man sadly shook his head. 'Serafin, believe me, I don't mind what happens to me. But the children . . . I couldn't allow that.'

'Does Junipa know where she'll be going?'

'She guesses there's more than I've said. And she must also surely guess that she won't stay here with us forever. But she doesn't know about Talamar and Lord Light. Not yet.'

'But we can't let it happen!' cried Serafin, almost knocking his tea over. 'I mean, we can't simply let her . . . well, let her literally go to Hell.'

Arcimboldo did not reply, and now Serafin was sitting here by the canal trying to find a solution, think of answers, devise some way out.

If Venice had been a free city, if there had been no threat to it from the Egyptians, he might perhaps have been able to escape with Junipa. He had once been one of the most skilful master thieves in Venice – he was familiar with places and paths which most Venetians didn't even know existed. But the besieging ring of the Empire's forces had closed in on all sides to a distance of only a few hundred metres from the city, a hangman's noose of galleys, Barques of the Sun and thousands of warriors. There was no way out, and hiding from the powers of Hell *and* the Egyptians somewhere with Junipa would be pointless. They'd be found sooner or later.

If Merle had still been in Venice, perhaps they could have thought up a solution together. But he had seen her with his own eyes flying over the Piazza San Marco on the stone lion's back – across the lagoon and away from the city. And for reasons that he did not understand himself, he doubted whether Merle would be back soon enough – from wherever she was – to save Junipa from her fate.

And where, indeed, was Merle? Where had the lion taken her? And what had become of the Flowing Queen?

The reflection from that other world faded as a nearby church clock struck one, followed by the chimes of several more. The hour after midnight was over, and with it the brightly lit windows on the water suddenly disappeared. Now there was only a vague reflection of the dark facades of the buildings on the surface of the canal, a copy of reality.

Serafin sighed softly, stood up – and leaned forward again at lightning speed. There was something in the water, a movement. He had clearly seen it. Not a reflection from either this or the other world. Perhaps a mermaid? Or a large fish?

Then Serafin saw a second movement, and this time his eyes followed it more easily. A black outline was gliding along in the canal, and now he saw yet a third. Each was about five metres long. No, they were definitely not fish, even if they had a rather shark-like shape. And most definitely not mermaids either. They were pointed at the front and were the same breadth all the way along, about the size of a large tree trunk. Nor did they have any fins, as far as Serafin could see in the dark water.

The last outline was gliding along just under the surface of the water, not as deep as the others, and now the moonlight was refracted from it. No doubt about it – metal! That settled the question of where it had come from. Only magic could move objects made of iron or steel through the water, apparently as light as a feather. Egyptian magic.

Serafin took to his heels. The surrounding buildings came right down to the water, so he couldn't follow the canal directly. To follow the three underwater vessels he would have to go a long way round. He quickly ran back along the blind alley, turned several corners and finally reached a piazza that he knew only too well. Forty paces ahead of him, a small bridge led over the canal into which he had just been crumbling his supper. He and Merle had met the three traitors from the City Council as well as the Egyptian spy in a narrow house on the left. That was where they had foiled the councillors' attempt to hand over the Flowing Queen.

The house now looked abandoned and insignificant. No one would have guessed that the Empire's invasion had been planned here, of all places, behind boarded-up windows and a grey, crumbling facade.

A figure in a long dark cloak was standing on the bridge, its face invisible under a capacious hood.

For a moment Serafin felt as if he had stepped through an invisible door and back into the past. He had seen the same man before, in the same place and at the same hour of the night: it was the Egyptian envoy, the spy from whom they had snatched the flask containing the Queen. Merle had burned his hand with the aid of her magic mirror, while Serafin set a pack of angry alley cats on him.

Now the man was here again, hiding under his hooded cloak like a thief once more.

Serafin overcame his surprise quickly enough to stay out of sight. He immediately pressed closer to the front of a building. The moon was shining on the opposite side of the canal and a large part of the narrow piazza, but where Serafin was making his way along all was in deep shadow.

Under cover of darkness, he approached the bridge. The envoy was waiting for something, and Serafin's discovery just now left him in little doubt what it was. Sure enough, he heard a hollow, metallic sound, repeated at regular intervals. Something struck the wall of the canal bank under the bridge.

Something was being made fast.

The envoy strode quickly to the foot of the bridge and looked down into the water. By now Serafin was only ten metres from him. He hid behind a little altar to Our Lady that someone had built on to the wall of a house long ago.

Presumably it was a long time since any votive offerings had been placed here. Most people had prayed to the Flowing Queen over the past thirty years; no one now believed that the Church had any power, although there were still those who persisted in attending church services as a matter of form.

Serafin watched the envoy take several steps back from the edge of the bank. He was making way for six men who climbed up a narrow flight of steps from the water.

Men? Serafin bit his lower lip. Those six figures had once been men, but now they bore very little similarity to their former selves.

Mummies.

Six of the Empire's mummy warriors, with gaunt, dried-up faces, all looking as like each other as identical twins. Any distinguishing marks had disappeared. Their faces were like death's heads covered with grey skin.

All six wore dark armour which flashed metallically in the moonlight from time to time. Each held a sword of a kind that Serafin had never seen before: the long blades were curved, almost crescent-shaped, but the cutting edge, unlike that of a normal scimitar, was on the inner side of the curve, so that the weapon was handled in a completely different way. Egyptian crescent swords, the dreaded blades of the imperial mummy warriors.

There must have been room for two of them in each of the strange vehicles in the water. They would have had to lie one behind another, as if they were in a hollow tree, unable to move. But Serafin supposed, wryly, that mummies didn't itch and have to scratch. They would only have scraped the dry skin off their bones.

So this was what the Egyptians made dead bodies into. Creatures with no will of their own, slaves mercilessly spreading death and destruction. Such scenes were probably going on all over Venice at this moment. The invasion had begun.

There was a difference, however, between being conquered by flesh-and-blood enemies and by . . . by something like this. You could talk to human beings, beg for mercy, hope they might have retained some trace of humanity. But mummies?

Serafin felt he could no longer bear the idea of a Venice from which all life had been dragged away, ruled by an inhuman Pharaoh. He knew it would be best to stay perfectly still, not moving, not even breathing, but that was impossible. At the moment it became clear to him that the Egyptian envoy was in command of the six warriors, he knew he couldn't go on skulking in the darkness. He had to do something, had to act, even if it was madness.

He gave several shrill whistles. For a moment nothing happened. Then the envoy spun round so fast that his dark robe rippled. His hood slipped back briefly, just long enough for Serafin to see what the cats had done to him. The spy's face was criss-crossed with encrusted wounds, not harmless scratches but deep furrows which would leave ugly scars when the scabs came off. And the man knew who was responsible for it. He remembered the sounds that had set the cats on him.

He remembered Serafin.

The envoy shouted something in a language that Serafin didn't understand, and pointed to the altar as if his eyes could see through its solid stone. The mummies moved faster than Serafin would have thought possible, raising their crescent swords. One of them stayed behind with the envoy. The man put his hood up again, but first he cast a malevolent glance at Serafin, a glance promising him pain, misery, long torment.

The mummies were halfway to the altar and Serafin had

just leaped out of hiding when the cats finally came.

Thirty, forty, fifty stray cats scurrying up from all directions, out of every aperture, from the rooftops and the canals. And every moment more arrived, until the piazza was swarming with them.

The envoy screamed and fled backwards up on the bridge, shouting a shrill order to another of the warriors to come back and keep the cats away. The other four hardly seemed to notice the animals attacking them from all sides. Claws dug into the mummies' parchment skin, teeth sank into clothes and armour, snapped at fingers, tore dusty rags of skin from cheeks and arms.

None of it stopped the mummy warriors.

They continued on their purposeful way, stamping through a sea of fur and claws, each hung about with a dozen cats like living Christmas-tree decorations. The crescent swords whistled through the air, striking down their victims in blind fury, some on the ground, some in mid-leap. Mews and screeches echoed back from the buildings. But the animals learned fast. They dug their teeth into the warriors' sword arms with grim determination, until the mummies gave ground under the sheer weight of cats' bodies.

Serafin was paralysed by horror. Not long, just for a couple of seconds, enough to see that the cats were sacrificing their lives for him. Despite the danger threatening him, he couldn't let them do that. Cats were the friends of their allies the master thieves, not their unthinking slaves. He hesitated for just a moment and then uttered another sequence of whistles. Immediately the tide of cats retreated; only those who had their teeth and claws actually dug into the mummies stayed put for a couple of seconds longer. Then they too gave up, dropped to the ground and scurried away.

Serafin's command was meant to send the cats back to where they had come from, but they did not obey it. They withdrew only a few paces from the mummy warriors, stopped at the edge of the piazza and watched their enemies with glowing eyes.

Meanwhile Serafin had run to the far side of the piazza. He now looked back and saw the cats gathering together in front of the buildings like a tide of fur, but he realised too that the mummy warriors were striding after him with undiminished speed.

The cats were waiting for him to summon them to the attack again. He couldn't bring himself to do it. Almost a dozen animals lay dead or dying in the path cleared by the four mummy warriors. The grief that overcame Serafin at the sight paralysed him more than his fear for his life.

Another ten metres and the four warriors would reach him. They were making for him in silence. In the background, the envoy stood on the bridge with his arms folded, protected by his two guards.

'The cats!' a clear voice suddenly called from the shadows behind Serafin. 'Send them further off!'

Serafin spun round. A torch was flaring in a gap between the buildings, but he couldn't make out who was holding it. He whistled again, moving towards the torchlight.

This time the cats obeyed. At lightning speed they climbed up buildings, on to window sills, into gutters, up stairs, wooden rails and balustrades.

'Watch out!' called a second voice, this time from the left.

Serafin turned and ran. The mummy warriors had almost reached him. He glanced back over his shoulder — and saw two bright flames licking their way towards the mummies from both sides of the opening of the alleyway. There was a crackle and a hiss, and then the four mummies were on fire. The blaze darted over their dried-out bodies, leaped from limb to limb, ate its way under the steel of their armour. One warrior fell to his knees, while the other three ran on. Two of those were flailing wildly around them as if they could drive back the flames with their crescent swords. But the third raced on towards Serafin unchecked, his weapon raised ready to strike a deadly blow.

Serafin was unarmed except for the knife that he snatched from his belt. He knew he had no chance with it. However, he stood his ground as if he had taken root. He had been a Master Thief of the Guild, the youngest master of them all, and he had learned that you don't run away from enemies. Not when others were ready to risk their lives for you. And it seemed that those others were not only the cats but also the mysterious helpers who had come to his aid, breathing fire.

Now he saw three figures leap out of the niches on both sides of the alley. Two of them flung their torches to the ground, while the third made for one of the burning warriors with a drawn sabre. The thought flashed briefly through Serafin's mind that he knew that face, indeed all three faces, but he had no time to make sure of it.

The burning mummy warrior went for him like a

demon, a tall pillar of fire striking out at him with the razor-sharp blade of the crescent sword. Serafin avoided the stroke, and at the same time tried to put more distance between himself and his opponent. He might perhaps be able to escape the sword, but if the blazing creature fell on him he would burn to death horribly.

Out of the corner of his eye, he saw the figure armed with the sabre strike his mummy opponent's head from its shoulders with an elegant stroke that spoke of either long practice or enormous natural talent. The other two had also drawn swords and were fighting the rest of the mummies, by no means as skilfully as their leader, but the fire was their ally. It consumed the undead warriors so fast that they literally fell apart before they could be dangerous. Serafin's adversary was growing weaker too, despite his strength of will; his movements became more uncoordinated, until finally his legs gave way under him. Serafin took a couple of steps back and saw the flames devour the mummy like a pile of straw.

'Watch out!' cried a voice.

Serafin quickly looked round. The envoy's two bodyguards had come hurrying up, followed by their master. They attacked his rescuers. Serafin's eyes were streaming from the smoke of all the fires, and he still couldn't clearly see who was standing beside him. Just now, when he had glimpsed their faces . . . but no, that was impossible.

He quickly ran round the first fire, jumped over the second and snatched up a crescent sword lying on the ground. One of the mummies had dropped it before being entirely consumed by the flames. Its hilt was warm, almost hot, but not too hot for him to hold. The weapon seemed to him clumsy, the weight strangely distributed, but he wasn't going to stand by idle while others fought for him. He grasped the weapon with both hands and flung himself into the fray.

The leader of the three was leaping nimbly back and forth, avoiding sword strokes and wounding one of the mummy warriors over and over again. Then his sabre pierced the warrior's defence in a firework display of cut and thrust, and struck his head off. Once again dust spread like a cloud in all directions, but no blood flowed. The torso collapsed. Serafin quickly realised that this was the best way to defeat a mummy: the Egyptians' magic worked on the dead brain, and without a skull the mummies were ordinary corpses again.

And then, when he finally saw who had rescued him, he could hardly believe his eyes. He might have expected it of anyone else, but not *him.*

The two others had their hands full defending themselves against the last mummy. Serafin helped them as best he could with the heavy crescent sword, while the leader of the rescue party pressed forward, avoided a shot from the envoy's revolver, chased him back to the bridge and cut him down there in a flurry of sword strokes.

Finally the last mummy fell too. Gasping for breath, Serafin looked across the piazza. The trail of dead cats was clearly visible in the flickering firelight. He swore to himself that never again, under any circumstances, would he ask the cats for help. He had acted selfishly, without thinking, and bought his life with the lives of the poor creatures lying there.

One of his companions laid a hand on his forearm. 'If what I hear about the friendship between thieves and the cats is right, they made their own decision.'

Serafin turned to him, and looked into Tiziano's face. Arcimboldo's former apprentice smiled wryly, and then bent down to wipe the dust off his sword blade on the clothing of one of the mummy torsos. Boro, the second fighter, came up and did the same.

'Thank you.' Serafin himself thought he should have sounded a little more fervently grateful, but he was still too surprised to find that they, of all people, had come to his aid. Although perhaps Tiziano and Boro hadn't been too bad at heart — or so at least Merle had claimed — their problem was that they were such close friends of Dario. Dario was the eldest of Arcimboldo's apprentices and had been Serafin's arch-enemy from the time when he gave up the thieving profession. They hated each other's guts. Dario had even once pulled a knife on Serafin in Arcimboldo's workshop on the Outcasts' Canal.

And now Dario of all people, whom he loathed like poison and considered sly, deceitful and cowardly, that very same Dario was walking across the piazza towards him, carelessly sheathing the sword with which he had just saved Serafin's life.

Dario planted himself in front of Serafin, scrutinised him and then grinned. It was not a friendly grin, it was superior and absolutely infuriating. Very much the Dario he knew.

'Looks like we got here just in time.'

Tiziano and Boro exchanged awkward glances, but neither of them said anything.

'Thank you very much,' said Serafin, still unable to think of anything better. To deny that he had been in dire need of the three boys' help would have been stupid and obviously untrue — and just the kind of answer that Dario himself would have made in Serafin's situation. Instead, to distance himself even more from his former enemy, he paid him a compliment with his most sincere smile. 'You're good with a sword. I'd never have thought it of you.'

'Sometimes one can be wrong about other people, isn't that so?'

'Very likely.'

Boro and Tiziano picked up their torches and ground them out on the facades of the buildings until there was no spark of fire left. Only now did Serafin notice the bulbous bottles dangling from their belts. They must contain the fluid that had helped them to breathe fire just now. He had heard that Arcimboldo's apprentices had left the magic-mirror workshop two days ago to join the resistance fighters opposing the Empire, but he was surprised to see how quickly they had learned to master fire. On the other hand, it was possible that they'd been able to do it before. He didn't know enough about them.

'I thought you'd run faster,' said Dario. 'Thieves aren't great fighters, are they?'

'Or cowards either.' Serafin hesitated. 'What do you want with me? It can't be just chance that you crossed my path.'

'We were looking for you,' said Boro, earning himself a dark sideways glance from Dario. The sturdy Boro took no notice; he would have reacted quite differently in the past. 'There's someone who wants to see you.'

Serafin raised an eyebrow. 'Oh yes?'

'We're not mirror-makers any more,' said Dario, before one of the others could get in ahead of him again.

'So I've heard.'

'We've joined the rebels.'

'Sounds great.'

'Go on, laugh.'

'Your display was pretty impressive. You simply wiped out six of those . . . animals.'

'And the envoy,' said Dario.

'And the envoy,' repeated Serafin. 'I could never have dealt with them on my own. Which probably means I wouldn't make a particularly good rebel, right?'

They all knew better, for although Serafin was not as skilful a swordfighter as Dario, as a former master thief he had a whole repertory of other talents.

'Our leader wants to talk to you,' said Dario.

'And there was I thinking the leader was you.'

The look that Dario gave him was dark as a mummy warrior's empty eye sockets. 'We don't have to be friends, no one expects that. You just have to listen. I think you owe us that much, right?'

'Yes,' said Serafin. 'I believe I do.'

'Then come with us.'

'Where to?'

The three of them exchanged glances, then Dario lowered his voice to a conspiratorial whisper. 'To the Enclave,' he said.

LILITH'S CHILDREN

Merle saw the statues from a long way off, and they were larger than anything she had ever seen in her life. *Much* larger.

Ten stone figures – each at least 120 metres high, but that was a rough estimate and in reality they might be even taller – stood around a gigantic hole in the landscape. That was exactly what it was: a hole. Not a crater, not a deep valley. The closer they flew to the opening, the clearer it became that you could see no bottom to the hole, as if a blow from a divine fist had simply hammered a piece out of the earth's crust, like a splinter broken out of a glass globe. The hole was irregular in form and must be larger than the whole of Venice's main island.

As Vermithrax flew closer still the edges of the hole blurred, merging with the mist that drifted over the land like very fine rain. Soon Merle could see nothing but the mighty edge of the hole in front of her, as if the lion had carried her to the end of the world. The opposite side of the abyss was no longer visible. Merle was overcome by a sense of great emptiness and loneliness, in spite of the Queen there inside her, in spite of Vermithrax.

For hours now she had noticed a strange smell – not of sulphur, like the smell when the envoy from Hell appeared in the Piazza San Marco, but sweeter and almost as unpleasant, as if something down inside the earth were rotting. Perhaps it was the heart of the world, she thought bitterly. Perhaps the whole world was simply dying from the inside, like a fruit still on the tree but infested by parasites and decay. The parasites were the Egyptians. Or else, she corrected herself, perhaps the parasites were all of them, unable as they were to think of anything better to do than plunge into a war of fabulous dimensions.

But no – *she* hadn't begun this war, and nor had billions of other people. At this moment she first became fully aware of the responsibility she had taken on, with all its far-reaching consequences. She had come seeking help for a whole world in the fight against the Egyptians.

The fight against the Egyptians. There it was again, and she was in the middle of it. She was no better than all the others involved in this war.

'*Don't tell yourself such nonsense*,' said the Queen.

'But it's true.'

'No, it's not. No one wants more war and bloodshed. But the Egyptians won't listen to anyone. So there's no other way. The fruit on the tree is helpless when it decays — but we have a choice. We can make our own decisions. And we can try to defend ourselves.'

'And that means even more war. Even more dead.'

'Yes,' said the Queen sadly, 'so it does.'

Merle looked ahead over Vermithrax's mane again. His obsidian wings were rising and falling to left and right. Their gentle rushing sound swelled and died away again softly, in an almost leisurely manner, but Merle hardly heard it any more. It had long ago passed into her body, her flesh and blood, like the lion's regular heartbeat; she felt him under her as if she were a part of the stone colossus herself and had merged with him, just as the Queen was a part of her now. She wondered whether everything was going that way, whether the three of them, as they had once been, were becoming more and more like one, just as the Egyptians could be counted in millions but obeyed only one mind, one hand, one eye — the Pharaoh's.

Yes, said a cynical voice that was not the Queen's,

and in the end a handsome prince will come along on a white horse, just waiting to carry you off to his rose-petal castle.

Vermithrax brought her back to reality. 'They're so . . . so huge!'

Merle saw what he meant. The closer they came to the statues, the more titanic they appeared, as if they were growing further and further up from the earth itself, until at some point their stone skulls would break through the clouds and their mouths would swallow the stars.

'They're guardians. The Egyptians built them,' said the Queen in Merle's voice, so that Vermithrax could hear her too. 'This is where the Egyptian armies once clashed with the forces of the Tsarist Empire. Look around you. The whole place is devastated, destroyed, uninhabitable. Even the birds and insects have left. It's said that at last the earth itself reared up in pain and misery and swallowed all who stood on it, in a last violent act to end the fighting.'

'It does look as if the ground has fallen in,' said Vermithrax. 'Just collapsed on itself. No earthquake does that.'

'Something comparable has happened only twice in the course of history. There was the earth slide that swallowed up Marrakesh a few years ago – and probably the same forces as here were at work – and then of course there was the wound torn in the earth by the fall of Lucifer, the Morning Star.'

'Morning Star?' asked Vermithrax.

'Even a stone lion must have heard the tale,' said the Queen. 'Infinitely long ago – so human beings tell the story – a bright light is said to have fallen from heaven straight to earth. There are many tales of its origin, but even today most people still believe it was the angel Lucifer, who had rebelled against his Creator and was turned out of heaven by him. Lucifer fell burning to the depths below, tore a great rift in the earth and plunged down into Hell, where he made himself its ruler, and his Creator's most mighty adversary. And the angels became devils – or at least that's what the old legends say.'

'Where did Lucifer fall through the earth's surface?' asked Vermithrax.

'No one knows. Maybe at the bottom of the sea, where no one has yet looked – except, perhaps, the inhabitants of the Sub-Oceanic Realms, who knows . . .'

Merle felt her tongue loosening and at last she

was able to speak for herself. 'I can't stand it when you do that.'

'*Sorry.*'

'You don't mean it.'

'*I have to rely on your voice. We can't shut Vermithrax out.*'

'But you could be civil enough to ask if I mind.'

'*I'll try to remember.*'

'Do you believe the story? I mean, about Lucifer, the Morning Star, and all that?'

'*It's a legend. A myth. No one knows how much of it matches the truth.*'

'Then you haven't seen this place in the sea for yourself?'

'*No.*'

'But you know the Sub-Oceanic Realms?'

'*I don't know anyone who has seen them with their own eyes. Or anyone who knows for certain if they ever existed at all.*'

She wasn't going to get any more out of the Queen this way. But why should she be bothered about the sub-oceanic civilisations either at this moment? A much more urgent problem lay directly ahead of her, and by now it reached from horizon to horizon.

They were still a few dozen metres away from the edge

of the hole above Hell. In front of them towered one of the ten statues, even more impressive than the Basilica of San Marco. It was the figure of a bare-chested, bare-legged man. He wore only a loincloth around his hips, in the ancient Egyptian style. His head was hairless, smooth as a polished ball. It alone must weigh several tons. The figure held both elbows out at an angle and had the palms of its hands placed together in front of its chest, so that the arms between them formed a roughly triangular shape. The stone fingers were intricately intertwined.

Merle suppressed the impulse to imitate the pattern they made with her own hands. If she did that she'd have had to let go of Vermithrax's mane.

'*Ask him to fly past two more statues,*' said the Flowing Queen.

Merle passed this request on to the obsidian lion. Vermithrax immediately looped around and turned east, where the next stone giant stood a few hundred metres away. Each of the monumental figures had its back to the abyss, while its blank and stony eyes were fixed on the distance.

'And the Egyptians built them?' asked Merle.

'*Yes. After the battlefield had sunk into the ground, those of* the Tsarist armies who were left seized their chance to flee. They withdrew many thousands of kilometres to the north-east, where they set up a second border that they hold to this day. The Egyptians marched around the battlefield area and continued advancing, while their priests had these statues erected to watch over the way down into the interior of the earth.'

'Only symbolically, I hope.'

The Queen laughed. '*I don't think the statues will suddenly come alive when we fly past them, if that's what you mean.*'

'I was thinking along those lines, yes.'

'*Well, of course I wasn't here myself at the time, and –*'

Merle interrupted her by clearing her throat.

'*Yes?*'

'Would you please keep your mouth shut?'

'*If I had one I wouldn't have to keep using yours.*'

'Has anyone ever told you you're a clever clogs?'

'*No, never.*'

'Then it's time someone did.'

'*What's a clever clogs?*'

Merle groaned and turned to the lion. 'Was she always like this, Vermithrax?'

'Like what?' asked the obsidian lion, and she had a

feeling that he was smiling even if she couldn't see his face from behind.

'Such a pain.'

'A pain, eh? Yes . . . yes, I think you could say so.'

The Queen laughed inside her again, but refrained from answering back. Merle could hardly believe that for once she was *not* insisting on having the last word.

The second statue was very like the first, with the exception of its fingers, which were linked in a different way. The third figure too was making a different gesture. Otherwise they were as alike as peas in a pod.

'Is that enough?' asked Vermithrax.

'*Yes*,' said the Flowing Queen, and Merle passed the answer on to the lion.

Vermithrax flew around the third statue and it did not come to life.

'*Were you really expecting it to start moving all of a sudden and pluck us out of the air with its hand?*'

Merle shrugged her shoulders. 'I don't think I know what to expect or not expect any more. I'd never have expected to set Vermithrax free from his prison either. Or fly around this place on him. Apart from all the other things that have happened in the last few days.'

She tried to catch a glimpse of whatever was beyond the edge of the abyss, but she could see only rock and fine mists bathed in a reddish glow. She wasn't sure if it came from the sun high above this desolate country or if the source of that diffused glow was in the interior of the earth.

'Do you think it's really Hell down there? I mean, like in the Bible or the pictures over church altars?' She was surprised by her own sceptical tone. Hadn't she just said that nothing else could seem strange to her after all she'd been through?

Vermithrax did not answer; perhaps he was still thinking, or perhaps he had no clear opinion on the matter.

The Queen, however, threw the question back to her. *'What do you think yourself?'*

'I don't know.' Merle's eyes passed over the expressionless face of the next statue, and she wondered whether the sculptors had made those features so utterly without emotion because the most appalling dangers lurked below. 'At least, Professor Burbridge didn't mention any huge bonfires with damned souls roasting in them. Or boiling cauldrons and torture chambers. I think we ought to believe him. Apart from the fact that . . .' She stopped.

'The fact that what?'

After a moment's hesitation, Merle returned to what she had been going to say. 'Apart from the fact that a Hell like in the Bible doesn't make sense. Hurting someone forever and ever is so . . . well, unreasonable, don't you think? I mean, you punish people to stop them doing any more bad things. And of course to scare everyone else off doing them too. But if the blessed spirits who go to heaven are incapable of sinning anyway, while the sinners can't do any good because they're imprisoned in Hell forever . . . I mean, what's the point of it?'

The Queen did not reply, but Merle had a feeling that she quietly agreed and was even a little proud of her. Encouraged, she went on, 'If God is really infinitely good, as the Bible says, how can he condemn so many people to eternal damnation? How do being good and punishing people fit together?'

To her surprise, Vermithrax spoke up. 'You're right. Why punish a guilty person if the punishment can't help him to change?'

'It sounds wasteful, if you ask me.'

'*We may call the place down there Hell*,' said the Queen, '*but I don't think it has anything to do with what your priests preach.*

Or with God or the Devil.'

'What's it to do with, then?'

'Only ourselves. We survive or we die. It all depends on us.'

'Can a being like you die?'

'Oh yes,' said the Queen. *'I live and die with you, Merle. Whether I want to or not.'*

Her words made Merle feel quite dizzy – and to her surprise she felt something like pride yet again. But at the same time the invisible burden on her shoulders seemed to weigh a little heavier.

'What do you two think?' Vermithrax called back. 'Do we venture down?'

'That's what we came here for.'

Merle nodded. 'Let's try it!'

Between her knees, she felt the lion take a deep breath, briefly tensing all his muscles. Then he tilted his body, flew in a narrow arc and shot over the edge of the great hole.

The sweetish smell grew stronger once they were above the abyss, but there was still nothing to be seen but the steep rock face and a sea of vapour. The red glow of the swathes of mist was more intense now, as if there were a sea of lava hidden down below and it might make them evaporate into hot air in the twinkling of an eye.

Vermithrax was obviously troubled by similar alarming ideas. 'What's under those clouds?'

'*May I?*' the Queen asked. Merle thought she sounded a little too ironic and sure of herself.

'Carry on.' And before she knew it the Queen was speaking through her mouth again.

'It's just ordinary mist, that's all. Something to do with the way different air densities meet. You two will probably have to get used to it before you can breathe properly down there.'

'What are air densities?' asked the lion.

'Just trust me.' And with that she withdrew again.

'She's always saying things like that,' Merle told the lion.

'How do you stand it?'

Merle had a dozen cutting remarks on the tip of her tongue, but she bit them all back. Secretly — as she admitted to herself only reluctantly — she was actually a little glad to have the Queen in her. It was sometimes good to have a person who knew everything about you, shared everything and could often answer questions.

Although it was sometimes a nuisance too.

Vermithrax began his descent. He did not drop in a straight line, but flew down in wide curves, tilting dangerously to one side, so that Merle soon felt her stomach rebelling yet again. She'd never get used to this flying business.

The obsidian lion kept close to the southerly rock wall. The stone there was dark and looked brittle. Once Merle thought she saw a kind of groove reaching down from the top of the abyss; it looked like a makeshift staircase, or a path carved by someone out of the rock. But when Vermithrax turned into his next curve she lost sight of the narrow ribbon cut into the rock again. Anyway it was as much as she could do to hold on and keep her eyes more or less fixed on the back of Vermithrax's head, hoping that that would help her to control her nausea and dizziness.

The mist was a few metres below them now, smooth as a frozen sea. Further down inside it, however, there was constant movement, with swathes of mist lazily turning around themselves like solitary dancers made of water vapour. The red glow was brighter in some places than others. Whatever awaited them down there in the depths, it wouldn't be long before they came face to face with it.

High in the air above it had been chilly, but the further down they went the warmer it felt. Not hot, not sultry in spite of the damp air, but pleasantly warm. However, Merle's mind was in far too much turmoil to be glad of that. Only a few minutes ago, when Vermithrax was circling the statues, the wind had cut through her clothes like a blade going through parchment, but even there she hadn't really noticed the cold. Other ideas were clamouring for her attention: worries, speculations, forebodings and a great deal of confusion.

Then they plunged through the mist.

It was only a brief moment, certainly not sixty seconds, before Vermithrax's downward flight had carried them through the layer of vapour, and they emerged below it in a star-shaped eruption of steam and grey swathes of mist. Merle had instinctively been holding her breath and now, when she tried to take a deep breath again, she panicked. It didn't work! She couldn't breathe! Her throat constricted, her thorax burned like fire and then she felt nothing but fear: pure, instinctive fear.

But no, there *was* air, and now her lungs were filling with it, but it somehow seemed different, perhaps thinner, perhaps heavier, different anyway. Gradually Merle calmed down again and only now did she realise that Vermithrax himself had been staggering in his flight, gripped by the same fear of suffocation, by the certainty that it had all been a great and deadly mistake. But now his wing beats grew calmer, were gentler and more regular again, and the spiral tumbling of their descent stabilised.

Merle leaned slightly forward. Not too far, because she already guessed what she would see – *an abyss, a bottomless abyss* – but the reality far outstripped her fears.

If a concept like depth had ever matched anything – pure, terrifying *depth* beyond all reason – it was this shaft going down into the entrails of the earth. The mist had entirely dispersed now, and was replaced by a clarity that seemed to Merle somehow wrong, unreal. She had last had that feeling as she swam beside the mermaids through the canals of Venice, her head protected by a glass globe that gave her a wonderfully sharp view of the underwater world. All the same, it was a sight for which the human eye was not intended, for everything she saw should really have been blurred, clouded, a veil flickering on her retina.

Down here inside the abyss she felt very much the same. This was no place for human beings, and it amazed her that nonetheless she could perceive it with all her senses, even if she couldn't grasp its nature.

The rock face continued to drop straight to the depths, but it seemed to Merle as if she saw every indentation and projection in the stone a little more clearly than above the layer of mist. And she could make out the opposite side of the shaft better too, although there was no impression that the walls were any closer together. Everything was bathed in a bright, red-gold light that seemed to shine out of the stone itself, out of a fine network of glowing veins, clustered together in some places, almost invisible in others.

'*Impressive*,' said the Queen, and Merle felt it was a wholly inadequate description: a dry and empty term in view of such marvels.

Suddenly she realised that this must be a part of the real, genuine country of Hell. Something that no other human being had ever seen except for Professor Burbridge and a small number of privileged persons.

Then she caught sight of the tents.

'Do you see that?' roared Vermithrax.

'Yes,' Merle whispered. 'Oh yes. I see them.'

A little way below them, and about eighty metres to one side, a ledge projected from the rock face like the tip of a giant's upturned nose. Its upper surface was smooth and, at a rough guess, twenty by twenty paces across. Three tents stood on it. One was torn to rags, although its tent poles still rose in the air like the branches of a dead tree. Something had slit the tarpaulin of the tent. A knife, perhaps. Or claws.

The other two tents seemed to be intact. The flap over the entrance of one was turned back. As Vermithrax approached this camp, Merle saw that the rocky ledge was deserted.

'What do we do now?' she asked.

'You're curious, aren't you?'

'Well, aren't you?'

'The mind can take in only a limited amount of information, and mine makes no distinction.'

Show-off, thought Merle. 'Then aren't you interested in what happened to the people who were here?'

'You're interested. That will do.'

Vermithrax circled in the air in front of the ledge several times. Merle noticed how carefully he was inspecting the tents and the other remnants of the camp. There were the remains of a camp-fire; a number of crates stacked at the back of the ledge up by the rock face; a bowl beside the charred wood of the fire; and three guns propped against the wall, as if their owners had simply disappeared behind the rocks for a moment. Whatever had happened to these people, they hadn't even had time to reach for their weapons. A cold shudder ran down Merle's back.

Finally the obsidian lion had seen enough. He turned abruptly and landed on the ledge, only a little way from the ragged tent. Now Merle realised that the path she had seen further up led to this plateau, and went on down into the depths to their right.

She jumped off Vermithrax's back, landed on both feet – and immediately sat down with a thump. Her knees were weak and her muscles stiff. By now she was familiar with the feeling, but it had never been as bad before – it was probably another result of the changed air conditions, like the weariness she now felt more strongly than over the last few days. Yet it was less than six or seven hours since they had left the plateau where they spent the night.

Unless, she suddenly thought, they had lost track of time in some way as they entered this other world, coming down through the mist or even earlier, when they flew past the stone guardians. Had they really spent not just a couple of seconds but several hours passing through the layer of vapour?

Nonsense, she told herself, and in her mind the Flowing Queen agreed, *'Nonsense!'* But somehow it didn't seem entirely convincing to Merle either time.

Once her legs had loosened up and her knees could carry the slight weight of her body again, she began searching the tents. Vermithrax told her to be careful, while he himself sniffed the guns and explored the crates with his nose and paws. Even the Queen warned her to be cautious, which was something entirely new.

In the end they found little that was of any use to them. Merle discovered a thin leather thong in one of the intact tents. It had a dried chicken's foot dangling from it like a pendant, and several sinews stuck up from the severed foot like the wires of a puppet. When Vermithrax told her to pull the sinews, the chicken's claw closed on itself, as if it had come back to life all of a sudden. Merle was so startled that she almost dropped the nasty thing.

'That's disgusting.' She let go of the foot and held it only by the leather thong.

'It's a lucky charm,' the Queen explained.

'Oh yes?'

'*The people of the Tsarist Empire wear them. I expect you know they're under the protection of Baba Yaga?*'

Merle nodded, although she realised that the Queen couldn't see her and, at the most, could only feel her assent.

On the other side of the plateau, Vermithrax was pulling another crate out with his forepaws and investigating its contents with his nose.

'*What do you know about Baba Yaga?*'

'Not much. She's a witch or something.'

The Queen was perceptibly smiling. '*A witch. A goddess. People have seen her in many different ways. But it's certain that she protects the Tsarist Empire just as I –*' she stopped short, as feelings of pain and guilt welled up in her and in a curious way rubbed off on Merle too – '*just as I protected Venice.*'

'Do you know her? Personally, I mean.'

'*No. She is not like me. At least, I suspect not. But what I was going to say is that since time immemorial Baba Yaga has taken a certain shape, and human beings identify her by it. She appears as an old woman living in a little house, but the house stands on two chicken legs as tall as trees, and it can run about like a living creature.*'

Merle swung the pendant. 'Then this is a kind of symbol?'

'Yes. Just as Christians wear a cross to protect them from evil, the people of the Tsarist Empire wear a chicken's foot like this – or those of them who believe in the power of Baba Yaga anyway.'

'But that means –'

'That this is all that's left of an expedition sent here by the Tsar, yes.'

Merle thought about what that might suggest. The Egyptian armies had overrun the whole world within a few decades – with the exception of Venice and the Tsarist Empire. Yet there had never been any contact between the two, or at least none known to the general public. All the same, the sight of the wrecked camp filled her with a strange sense of loss, as if some important opportunity had been missed. What was it like in the Tsarist Empire? How did they defend themselves from the attacking Egyptians there? And not least, what form did Baba Yaga's protection take? They might have found answers to all those questions in this camp, if someone else hadn't been here first.

'Do you think they're dead?' Merle deliberately put this question to both the Queen and Vermithrax.

The lion ponderously moved over to her. 'Well, that tent wasn't slit with a knife. The edges of the fabric are too frayed and roughened for that.'

'Claws?' asked Merle, and guessed the answer already. Goose pimples stood out on her forearms.

Vermithrax nodded. 'And they left marks on the ground too.'

'They left scratch marks on the *rock*?' Merle's voice sounded as if she had swallowed something too big to go down.

'I'm afraid so, yes,' said the lion. 'Quite deep marks, in fact.'

Merle's eyes went to the obsidian lion's paws and inspected the ground. His own claws left no trace on the stone. What must the claws of the creatures encountered by the Tsarist expedition be like?

Then she knew. The answer surfaced from her memory, like the mind of a sleeper suddenly woken. 'Lilim,' she said immediately.

'*Lilim?*'

'When Professor Burbridge discovered Hell sixty years ago and first met its inhabitants, he called them Lilim. The teacher in the orphanage told us about it. Burbridge named them after the children of Lilith, Adam's first wife.'

Vermithrax put his head on one side. 'A human legend?'

Merle nodded. 'Perhaps the oldest of all. I'm surprised you two don't know it.'

'Every nation and every race has its own myths and legends about the creation of life,' said the obsidian lion, sounding almost insulted. 'I don't suppose you know any of the old lion legends.'

'*I know who Adam was,*' said the Queen, '*but I've never heard of Lilith.*'

'Adam and Lilith were the first two human beings created by God.'

'*I thought the woman was called Eve.*'

'Eve came later. First God created Adam and Lilith as man and wife. They were alone in Paradise, and they were supposed to have children together and populate the world with their descendants. In fact they were the first living creatures of all.'

Vermithrax growled something, and Merle looked enquiringly at him.

'That's typical of you humans,' he said crossly. 'You always think you're first and best. But the first stone lions had been in existence for ages.'

'So *your* legends say,' retorted Merle with a grin.

'That's right.'

'Then we'll never find out which is true, will we? Not now, not here, probably never.'

Vermithrax had to agree.

'*All creation myths tell the truth*,' said the Queen mysteriously. '*Each in its own way.*'

Merle went on. 'Well, anyway, Lilith and Adam were chosen to have children together. But whenever Lilith tried to approach Adam he shrank away from her in fear and disgust.'

'Huh!' growled Vermithrax. 'That never happened to the first lion with his lioness!'

'Anyway, Adam was afraid of Lilith, and in the end God lost patience and banished her from the Garden of Eden. In fury and disappointment she wandered through the desert regions outside Paradise, and there she met creatures that were nothing like Adam. Beings stranger, more dreadful and terrible than anything we can imagine.'

'I can imagine them, or something like them,' said the lion, with a sideways glance at the claw marks on the rock.

'Lilith mated with these creatures, and she's said to have borne them children even more fearsome than their fathers. Those children were the Lilim. In legends, they are the demons and monsters that wander by night in forests and deserts and over the bare rocky mountains.'

'*And Professor Burbridge knew this story*,' said the Queen.

'Of course. When he needed a name for the inhabitants of Hell, to put in his notes and scientific studies, he called them after the Lilim.'

'Yes, very well,' said Vermithrax, 'so our Tsarist friends met some of these creatures. Don't you both think it would be a good idea for us to avoid them?'

'*Vermithrax is right*,' replied the Queen. '*We'd better take off again. We'll be safer in the air.*' But there was something in the way she emphasised that last remark that made Merle even more uneasy. Who was to say that the Lilim didn't have wings?

'Wait a moment.'

She went over to the crates that the lion had already searched. Just now she had seen out of the corner of her eye a few objects that Vermithrax might discard as worthless but could come in useful to her. She found a small knife in a leather sheath no longer than her hand and put it in the pocket of her dress where she kept the magic mirror. In addition she found several cans of iron rations, strips of dried meat as hard as stone, sailors' tack, several bottles of water and even a few biscuits. She packed all these things in a small leather rucksack that she had found in one of the tents and strapped it on her back. As she did so she chewed on a piece of the dried meat. It was as hard as the bark of a tree and as tough as the soles of her shoes, but somehow she managed to get the fibres down. She had eaten nothing but roots and berries for the last few days, so the rations left by the Tsarist expedition were more than welcome.

'Hurry up,' called Vermithrax as she fastened the buckles of her new rucksack.

'Just coming,' she said — and suddenly felt they were being watched.

Her fingers let go of the leather straps and a shudder ran down her back, despite the heat all around them. The ends of her hair felt electrified. Her heart missed a beat, and then began racing again so suddenly that it almost hurt.

Fearfully, she looked at the rock face at the back of the plateau, then at the tents and the path, both where it ended on its way down here from above and where it continued leading further on. Nothing moved, there was no one there. Only Vermithrax, standing on the brink of the ledge and tapping the rock impatiently with a claw.

'*What's the matter?*' asked the Queen.

'Don't you feel anything?'

'*Your fear drowns out everything else.*'

'Come on,' called Vermithrax. He hadn't noticed anything yet.

Merle ran for it. She didn't know what she was running away from, or even if there was any good reason for her fear. She had almost reached Vermithrax when a shrill screech, long drawn out and painful to the ears, made her spin round.

She didn't see it at first glance. Not really. There was *something*, maybe a movement, some change close to the place where she had stood strapping the rucksack on.

'Merle!'

The rock shook under her feet as Vermithrax raced towards her, much faster and more nimbly than she would have thought possible, a flash of black obsidian lightning that was suddenly behind her, picking her up from the ground with one of his wings and slipping her on to his back as if she were passing over a ramp of stone feathers.

'*Lilim*,' she heard a voice in her head, and it was a moment before she realised that it wasn't her own thought but a cry from the Flowing Queen.

Vermithrax prepared to take off, and a moment later

they were racing over the edge of the rock, still leaping rather than flying, and dropped a good metre down into the void before the lion's wings caught up his mighty weight, stabilised them in the air and carried them away from the rock face, the Tsarist expedition's abandoned camp and the aura of death around the empty tents.

Merle was going to look back, but the Queen said sharply, *'Don't do that!'*

Of course she did it all the same.

The rock face was coming alive. Then Merle realised that it wasn't the stone itself moving, but something that might have been there all the time, lying in wait, lurking under cover, or only now crawling out of invisible cracks and crevices like the Empire's swarms of scarabs.

Whole areas of what she had taken for rock now shook free of it, streaming from all sides on to the ledge, in a dense, crowded conglomeration so strange and bizarre that it suggested no comparison with any kind of human or animal movement. It was not like the crawling of insects, although that perhaps came closest; instead, dark scales and shells surged over the plateau in grotesque zigzag movements, apparently in disorder and total chaos, yet so purposefully that within seconds the whole ledge was surrounded.

Under the moving surface made of countless man-sized bodies, angular and sinewy structures kept coming into view. They might be limbs, complex and bent at odd angles, spider-like and yet very different from spider's legs. And they left a trail of deep grooves in the rock where their invisible claws had clung, churning up the stone into a confusion of tracks like a relief created by some deranged sculptor.

The dark torrent flowed over the edges of the plateau from all directions, coming up from below the overhang too, crawling over the tents and crates and burying them beneath it. The creatures hid under their stone shells, or what looked like shells to Merle, yet every brief flash of fangs and claws was enough to make her feel sheer horror.

Vermithrax was flying faster and faster into the void, away from all the activity behind them, but nonetheless Merle saw the plateau collapse completely under the assault of the Lilim, swallowed up like a stone falling inexorably into a swirling quicksand.

As if of itself, Merle's hand went to the pocket where she kept her mirror. Lost in thought, she dipped her fingers through the surface of the water, then deeper into the warmth of the magic place behind it. Very briefly she thought she heard a whisper, a voice — *the voice of the phantom caught in the mirror?* — and then she put her arm right in up to the elbow, and at last she felt it again: the hand reaching for hers on the other side, caressing her fingers, very gently giving her a sense of safety.

THE ENCLAVE

The sky hung heavy and grey over Venice, heralding the rain that would soon be beating down on the city's palaces and canals. A sharp wind blew from the north, far too cold for this time of the year, whistling down crooked alleys, across empty piazzas and over the promenades on the banks of the islands. It caught up pamphlets and whirled them through the air. Tireless folk had distributed them a few days ago, after the appearance of the envoy from Hell offering to protect the Venetians from the henchmen of the Empire. The pamphlets had been written by resistance fighters and contained slogans denouncing the councillors, the Pharaoh and everyone else they blamed for their desperate situation. Slogans that at any other time would have brought them to prison or at least the pillory. But today no one bothered about them, for all Venice was in the grip of fear, so finally and inescapably under its spell that even the soldiers of the City Guard forgot to arrest troublemakers and rioters.

Serafin sat at the heart of this uproar, in the rebels' secret hiding place – the Enclave, as Dario had called the building – eating breakfast.

He was not, of course, eating breakfast at his leisure, but not at top speed either, for he knew there was nothing he could do but wait. They would come for him sooner or later, and take him to their leader, the lord of the Enclave. Neither Dario nor any of the others had told Serafin the name of the rebels' commander, which in itself was a sensible precaution. Yet their secrecy made Serafin uneasier than he liked to admit.

The palazzo lay in the centre of Venice, not a stone's throw from half a dozen famous buildings and other sights. Yet it was surrounded by a sense of seclusion which seemed to Serafin a little too strong not to be of magical origin.

On the way here last night, he and his three companions had met with signs of the forthcoming invasion all over Venice. On the banks of several canals, they had found more of the empty metal pods in which the mummy warriors had made their way along the labyrinth of waterways. They found no trace of the warriors themselves beside these capsules, but it was clear to them all that there was no going back now. Mummies were patrolling the streets, alone or in small troops, spreading fear and terror and ensuring that the city would be conquered from within. Here and there Serafin and the others had caught the sound of loud voices and screams in the distance, and once they heard the clash of steel from the other side of a block of houses, but when they ran to the place they found only corpses. Serafin identified the dead as members of the Guild of Thieves.

No one really understood what purpose the Pharaoh's method of attack served. His war galleys and Barques of the Sun lay within view of the lagoon's quays, and it would have been easy to send warriors ashore all round the main island.

Serafin suspected that the Pharaoh's sole intention was to make the Venetians feel insecure. Yet the lagoon dwellers' sense of security could hardly be in a worse state than it was already, after more than three decades of the siege. Suppose it was sheer cruelty? A macabre pleasure in beginning the invasion on a small scale, only to bring the assault to its culmination in a storm of fire and steel?

Serafin didn't understand any of it, and he hoped the lord of the Enclave would be able to answer some of his questions.

The room into which Tiziano had led him was on the first floor of the palazzo. As in most of the old palaces, the ground floor was empty. Once, when all these buildings still belonged to the rich merchant families of the city, wares and goods had been stored there in plain, undecorated halls that were flooded every few years by the *acqua alta*, the notorious high tide of Venice.

Today, however, after so many years of isolation, there was hardly any trade in Venice, and the little that still went on made no one rich. Most of the prosperous families had fled to the mainland long ago, at the very beginning of the war, never guessing that once there they would be easy prey for the armies of mummies and swarms of scarabs. No one could have foreseen that the power of the Flowing Queen would protect the city, and it was a savage irony of fate that those who had enough money to flee had been the first to fall victim to the Egyptians.

The windows and doors of the empty ground floor had been walled up with large blocks of stone, obviously at a time before anyone yet dreamed that the Pharaoh might be brought back to life. So the rebels had not taken up residence in an empty building. Instead, Serafin assumed, the leader of the rebellion had been living here himself for a long time already. A nobleman, perhaps. Or a merchant, one of the few left.

Serafin was putting his last piece of bread in his mouth as the door of the unassuming room was opened. Tiziano indicated that he was to go with him.

He followed the former mirror-maker's apprentice along corridors and past many suites of rooms, up a flight of steps, under arches. They met not a soul on their way. It seemed as if everyone was strictly forbidden to enter the apartments of the lord of the Enclave. At the same time, however, Serafin had a feeling that the atmosphere of the corridors and high-ceilinged halls was changing. There was an almost imperceptible shift from reality to something else, something confusing. It wasn't the light that changed, or the smell — everything here smelled of mould and damp stone — no, it was the *feel* of Serafin's surroundings, as if he were perceiving them with some sixth sense that had just been waiting to be activated.

At Tiziano's command, he stopped outside a double door almost three times as tall as himself.

'Wait here,' Tiziano told him. 'You'll be called in.' He turned to go.

Serafin held him back by his shoulder. 'Where are you off to?'

'Back to the others.'

'You're not staying here?'

'No.'

Serafin looked suspiciously from Tiziano to the door and then back to the boy again. 'This isn't some kind of trap?' He felt a little silly voicing his suspicion, but he couldn't forget his old quarrel with Dario. He could believe anything of his arch-enemy – or did he mean his *former* arch-enemy?

'What would the point of that be?' asked Tiziano. 'We could just have left you to the mummies, right? That would have dealt with everything straight off.'

Serafin was still hesitant, but he nodded slowly. 'Sorry. That was ungrateful of me.'

Tiziano grinned at him. 'Dario can be insufferable, can't he?'

Serafin himself couldn't suppress a smile at that. 'Oh, so you and Boro noticed?'

'Even Dario has his good points. One or two of them. Or he wouldn't be here.'

'I suppose that applies to all of us.'

Tiziano jerked his head encouragingly at the door. 'Just wait.' And with that he finally turned and walked away fast, but not in too much of a hurry, retracing the way they had come together. An alarming thought shot into Serafin's head: he'd never find the way back on his own. The interior of the Enclave was a positive maze.

The right half of the door swung back, as if opened by a ghostly hand, and suddenly he was surrounded by something bright and soft playing around his body like a hundred gentle fingers, light as a feather, almost incorporeal. He took a step back in surprise. Only a diaphanous silk curtain wafted to him by the air.

'Come in,' said a voice.

A woman's voice.

Serafin did as he was told and pushed the curtain aside, very cautiously, feeling that the delicate fabric might tear in his fingers like a cobweb. Beyond it billowed a whole wall of curtains, all made of the same material and in the same pale, bright yellow that reminded him of the colour of a sandy beach. Before he moved forward, he remembered to close the door behind him. Only then did he venture further into this silken labyrinth.

He passed curtain after curtain until he began to lose his

sense of direction, although he was simply going straight ahead all the time. How far behind him was the door? A hundred metres, or only ten or fifteen?

Gradually he could make out shapes beyond the silk, rectangular outlines, presumably pieces of furniture. At the same time the damp, mouldering smell of Venice was overlaid by a far more exotic scent, a whole firework display of aromas. It reminded him of the rare spices he had once stolen years ago from a merchant's warehouse.

Beyond the curtains lay a different world.

The floor was covered with such a deep layer of sand that the soles of his boots sank into it without meeting firm ground. Around him more curtains floated, all the same yellow as the sand on the floor. The ceiling was draped with lengths of dark blue fabric in sharp contrast to the surrounding brightness, like an evening sky above the desert. And then he realised that all this was meant to give exactly that impression: the illusion of a desert landscape, entirely artificial, yet very different from anything else to be found in Venice. There were no painted dunes, no statues of camels or Bedouins; nothing here was real, yet it felt as convincing as a genuine visit to the desert — or so at least Serafin, who had never left the lagoon in his life, imagined a desert would look like.

At the centre of this wonderful place were several heaps of soft cushions, like islands. The spicy aroma came from bowls with delicate columns of smoke rising from them. Among the cushions was a rough sandstone rostrum and on it, heavy and bulky, stood a round basin made of the same stone and containing water. The water was a metre or more across and rippled slightly. Behind the basin stood a woman, with only the upper part of her body in view. She had plunged her right arm into the water up to the elbow. At first Serafin thought she was stirring it, but then he saw that she kept her arm perfectly still.

She looked up and smiled. 'Serafin,' she said, and he was amazed to hear how musical his name could sound when spoken by such a being.

She was beautiful, perhaps the most beautiful woman he had ever seen – and as errand boy to Umberto, who wove magical fabric for the dresses worn by Venetian noblewomen, he had met many beauties. She had smooth hair, as black as a raven's wing and so long that its ends flowed down beneath the rim of the sandstone basin. Her slender body was clothed in some close-fitting material ruffled like fine fur and the same yellow as the curtains. Large nut-brown eyes scrutinised him. Her lips were full and dark red, although he was sure that she wasn't wearing cosmetics. The skin of her face and her left hand resting on the rim of the basin was dark; not black like the skin of the Moors – there were still a few Moors left in Venice – but deeply browned by the sun.

Then, all of a sudden, he knew.

She was Egyptian.

He knew it with absolute certainty before she could say another word to him or introduce herself. The leader of the rebellion against the Egyptians *was* an Egyptian.

'Don't be afraid,' she said when she saw him take a step back. 'You're safe. No one here means you any harm.' A touch of regret showed in her eyes as she withdrew her right hand from the water and placed it on the stone rim before her. The hand was not wet, nor was her arm. Not a trace of water trickled from her skin or the strange material of her dress.

'Who are you?' He felt he was stammering badly, and for very good reasons.

'Lalapeya,' said the woman. 'I don't think you know the language from which that name comes.'

'Egyptian?' He felt bold, positively daring as he uttered the word.

She laughed with a clear, almost melodious sound. 'Egyptian? Oh no, definitely not. My name was old long before the first Pharaohs ascended their golden thrones thousands of years ago.'

And with those words she came round to the front of the basin with a curious, flowing movement that confused and unsettled Serafin – until he saw her legs.

She had four of them.

The legs of a lioness. The *lower body* of a lioness.

Serafin flinched so instinctively that he got caught up in one of the silken veils, lost his balance, fell over backwards and brought down a tide of yellow silk with him.

When he had finally freed himself she was right in front of him. He had only to reach out his arm to touch one of her paws, the delicate yellow fur that covered her and that he had taken for a close-fitting dress.

'You're . . . you are . . .'

'Not a mermaid, certainly.'

'A sphinx!' he exclaimed. 'One of the Pharaoh's sphinxes!'

'That last part's not true. I don't even know the Pharaoh, and I am deeply sorry that some of my own people serve him.'

Serafin tried to get to his feet again, but he was not entirely successful, and when he retreated from her once more he dragged the curtain that he had brought down with him two or three steps further back.

The sphinx followed him on her lion's paws, moving elegantly. 'Please, Serafin. I showed you that so you would know who you are dealing with, but it was not absolutely necessary.'

'How . . . how do you mean?'

She smiled, looking so pretty that it almost hurt him to see both her smiling face and the animal part of her body at once. 'How do I mean? Oh, Serafin – like *this*, of course.'

As she spoke, her image blurred before his eyes. At first Serafin thought sand was swirling up from the floor, but then he realised it was more than that.

She did not just blur within his field of vision; her whole body seemed to dissolve for a split second and then reassemble itself, not in a smooth transition but in a flurry like an explosion, as if she were coming apart as a cloud of tiny particles which then, in the same instant, came back together to form something new. Something different.

Her face and her slender figure from the waist up were the same, but no longer rose from a lion's body. Instead, they merged naturally with narrow hips and long, suntanned thighs. A woman's thighs.

Her fur had gone and nothing had taken its place.

'May I?' Naked, she bent forward, picked up the silken curtain from the ground at Serafin's feet and with a swift movement wrapped it around her body. The yellow veil clung to her figure like a dress; no one would have suspected that only just now it had been a curtain hanging from the ceiling. It looked as natural on her and fitted as perfectly as the most expensive fabric woven in Umberto's workshop.

Serafin had tried to look away, but she gave him no time, so he still had the image of her perfect body before his eyes, as if burnt into his retina. Like those spots of light you see when you have been looking into the sun too long.

'Serafin?'

'Y . . . yes?'

'Is that better?'

He looked at her, down at her narrow feet standing half buried in the soft sand. 'But it doesn't change anything,' he said, and he had to force himself to utter every word. 'You're still a sphinx, whatever form you take.'

'Of course I am. But now you needn't fear my claws.' There was pure mischief in her eyes.

He tried hard to ignore her mocking undertone. 'What are you doing here?'

'Leading the counter-attack.'

'Against the Pharaoh?' He laughed, and hoped it sounded as mirthless as he had intended. 'With just a few children?'

She rubbed her right foot over her left; he almost fell for the embarrassment she was trying to persuade him she felt. But only almost. 'Are *you* a child, Serafin?' The innocent look she gave him was a little too flirtatious to be just chance.

'You know what I mean.'

'And I believe you know what *I* mean.' Her tone of voice was suddenly sharper, more emphatic. 'Dario and the others may be only fifteen, sixteen, seventeen,' she said, indirectly confirming what he had already suspected, that there were no adults among the rebels, 'but they are clever and they move fast. And the Pharaoh will underestimate them. That may be our strongest weapon: the vanity of Amenophis.'

'You said you didn't know him.'

'Not in his present shape. But I know what he was like before, in his first life.'

'How long ago was that?'

'Well over three thousand years.'

'You're *three thousand* years old?'

She laughed again, but only briefly. 'Give or take a few thousand.'

Serafin tightened his lips and said no more.

Lalapeya went on. 'The vanity and arrogance of Amenophis are the reason why I have chosen only boys like you. Do you think I couldn't have found men larger and stronger than anyone now in this house? But it would have been pointless. The Egyptians will be arresting all grown men and gradually deporting them. Whereas a handful of children . . . Well, I think the Pharaoh will put his mind to more important matters first, like the colour of the furnishings for his apartments here in Venice. Or that's what the old Amenophis would have done.'

'You're really going to fight the Egyptians with Dario

and the others?' Some of what she said might be true, but he still thought she made it sound too simple.

'I am not a fighter.'

Yes, well, anyone can see that, he thought. But then he remembered those lion's claws, sharp as knives, and he shuddered.

'However,' she went on, 'we have no choice. We must fight. That's the only language Amenophis understands.'

'If only a fraction of what they say about the Empire is true, the Pharaoh can wipe out Venice within a few minutes, so why would a few rebels bother him?'

'You shouldn't believe all you hear about the power of the Egyptians. Some of it is true – and much of that's bad enough, certainly – but some of it is based only on rumour cleverly spread and the power of illusion. The priests of Horus are masters of deception.'

'It's hopeless, all the same. I've seen the mummy warriors. I saw how they fight.'

The sphinx nodded. 'And you saw how they die.'

'That was sheer luck.'

Lalapeya sighed deeply. 'No one here is planning to go into battle against the mummy warriors. Or at least not the way you imagine it.'

'How, then?'

'First I have to know if you will help us.' She took another step towards him on the delicate feet of a dancer. It was impossible to withstand her charm.

'Why me?'

'Why you?' She smiled once more, and now her voice sounded gentler again. 'I think you underestimate your own reputation. A master in the Guild of Thieves by the age of thirteen, the youngest ever seen in Venice. No one climbs buildings faster or more skilfully. No one slips past every guard more quickly. And no one is braver in carrying out a task when all who tried before him failed.'

Lalapeya's words made him uncomfortable. She didn't have to flatter him, which meant she was appealing to his sense of honour. In addition, what she said was very near the truth. Yet all that was an eternity ago, in another life.

'I was thirteen then,' he said. 'And today,' he continued, 'I'm not what you just said about me. I've left the guild. I don't steal any more. I'm an apprentice to Umberto the master weaver, that's all.'

'Yet you stole the Flowing Queen from the Egyptians.'

He stared at her in surprise. 'You know about that?'

'Of course.' But she didn't explain how she knew, which aroused his suspicions again. When she noticed, she added quickly, 'You and the girl. Merle.'

'What do you know about Merle?'

Lalapeya hesitated. 'She's left Venice.'

'On a stone lion, yes, I know,' he said impatiently. 'But where is she now? Is she all right?'

'Nothing has happened to her,' said the sphinx. 'That's all I know.'

He had a strong notion that she was lying, and did his best to let her feel it. At the same time, he guessed that she had made a decision to tell him no more and would stand by it. For now, anyway. But if he stayed here a little longer he might manage to get more out of her. More about Merle, and the Queen, and –

He was startled to realise that he had fallen for her ruse. He'd swallowed the bait.

'I'll help you,' he said, 'if you tell me more about Merle.'

Lalapeya seemed to be considering the offer. 'I would rather you did it because you understood that it's necessary.'

He shook his head. 'Only for Merle.'

The sphinx's deep brown eyes moved over his face,

testing him to see if he was telling the truth. He felt nervous, although he knew she would find out nothing else: he meant every word he had said. For Merle, he'd even go to Egypt if he must and defy the Pharaoh. And no doubt have his skull split open by the first mummy warrior he met. But somehow it seemed as if making the attempt was what mattered.

'Are you in love with Merle?' asked Lalapeya after a while.

'That's none of your business.' As soon as the words were out he realised that he had answered her question. 'Or anything to do with what's going on here either,' he quickly added.

'It's nothing to be ashamed of.'

He was going to answer back, but swallowed what he had been about to say and asked instead, 'Do you know Merle?'

'Perhaps.'

'Oh, come on, what kind of an answer is *that*?'

'The truth. I'm not sure whether I know her.' Her eyes flashed, startled, as she realised that by saying so she might have given too much away. Perceptibly in better control of herself now, she added, 'And I'm not used to being interrogated either.' But her smile showed that she was not angry with him.

Serafin looked away from her and took a few paces up and down, as if wondering whether or not to stay here any longer. However, he had made his decision by now. Where else could he go? Umberto's workshop was empty, his master had fled God knew where. Serafin had turned his back on his former friends from the Guild of Thieves long ago. Should he go back to Arcimboldo, Eft and Junipa? Something told him that might be the right thing to do. But perhaps he could protect Junipa from Lord Light better by joining the sphinx and her strange company.

Finally he stopped pacing. 'You'll have to tell me what you're planning to do.'

'We don't intend to wage war against the Egyptians. That would indeed be foolish and suicidal. Our war will be against Amenophis himself.'

'Against the Pharaoh?'

When she nodded, the strange desert light of their surroundings flickered like tiny flames over her black hair.

'You want to kill *him*?' asked Serafin, baffled. 'An assassination?'

'That would be one way. But it wouldn't be enough. Amenophis is not an independent ruler. He himself is ruled by those who brought him back to life. For now, anyway.'

'The priests?'

'The priests of Horus, yes. They lost their importance for many centuries, and the worship of Horus had shrunk to a secret cult long forgotten by most people. Until they woke the Pharaoh to life in the pyramid of Amun-Ka-Re. When they did that, they gave new power to an enfeebled nation eking out a miserable existence. A new leader. A new identity. That and their magic were the means they used to create the Empire. They, not Amenophis, pull the strings.'

'Then that just makes everything even more hopeless.'

'Where the Pharaoh is, the leaders of the priesthood are too, headed by Seth, his vizier and Grand Master of the cult of Horus.'

'You seriously want us to go to Heliopolis, the city of the Pharaoh, find not just the Pharaoh himself but his vizier and probably a lot of priests too and – and *eliminate* them?' He emphasised that last phrase, as if it were an idea worthy only of a small child, because that was just how sensible he thought this whole crazy notion was.

'Not Heliopolis,' said the sphinx, her voice very calm. 'Amenophis and Seth will soon be here in Venice. And unless I am very much mistaken, they'll take up residence in the Doge's Palace.'

It took Serafin's breath away. 'The Pharaoh is coming here?'

'Oh, certainly. He won't want to miss the moment of his greatest triumph. This isn't just victory over a single city, it means victory over the Flowing Queen and all she stands for. His triumph over the past and over his own death. Then there'll be no one left in the world, outside the Tsarist Empire, who could possibly withstand him.'

Serafin rubbed his forehead with one hand and tried hard to keep up with what the sphinx was saying. 'Even if that's true and the Pharaoh does come to Venice – and moves into the Doge's Palace for all I care – what would that change? He'll be protected by an army of bodyguards. By his mummy warriors, and by the magic of Seth and the other priests, let's not forget that.'

Lalapeya nodded slowly, and her smile was as kind as if she were talking to a young kitten. 'That's why I want you to help us.'

'You want me to break into the Doge's Palace?' Serafin rolled his eyes. 'While the *Pharaoh* is there?'

The sphinx didn't have to answer. He knew that was exactly what she was planning. But she said something else, something that moved him more deeply than any rousing call to arms or any promise.

'Yes. For Merle.'

IN THE HERALD'S EAR

There was no day in Hell. And no night either.

After their long descent, Vermithrax had come down on a rock shaped like a hatbox. No human being could have scaled its high, vertical walls without special climbing equipment. Of course they all knew – the obsidian lion as well as Merle and the Flowing Queen – that it made little difference where they stopped to rest if they must face adversaries like the Lilim at the expeditionary camp.

'Perhaps there aren't any more of those down here,' said Merle, without much conviction.

The Queen's voice in her mind was firm, her enthusiasm undimmed. All the same Merle felt she was just trying to encourage her and did not herself fully believe what she said. *'It's possible that a few of the most dangerous live up there, just to guard the entrance, so to speak.'*

At least they agreed in thinking that there must be a wide variety of different Lilim, for the envoy sent to the Venetians by Lord Light had had nothing in common with the creatures of the rock face.

'Which doesn't mean that the others aren't just as terrible and don't move just as fast.' The obsidian lion preened his wings with his stony tongue. 'Far from it: we may have met only the most harmless specimens so far.'

'Thanks very much, Vermithrax,' said Merle bitterly, feeling that the Queen had just been thinking exactly the same. 'Having a cheerful soul like you around is amazingly helpful just now.'

The lion didn't even look up. 'I'm only saying what I think.'

Merle had been sitting cross-legged on the rock next to Vermithrax. Now she sighed and lay back until she could feel the smooth stone under her. She linked her hands behind her head, and looked up to where the sky would have been in their own world.

A great expanse of mottled red met her gaze. It looked more like a layer of cloud in a sunset glow than anything else: a roof of rock a few thousand metres above them and extending further than the eye could see in every direction. The glowing network of red veins that had run through the walls of the rocky shaft bathed the interior of Hell in dull orange light too.

And anyway, *Hell* . . . the word seemed to Merle less and less suitable for what they had found at the bottom of the shaft. The ground of this realm below the earth — or at least the part of it where they now were — was a desolate, rocky landscape, and like the roof was covered in many places with fiery veins, some as thin as hairs, others as wide as Vermithrax's legs. The stone felt warm, but was not really hot anywhere, and the winds that blew down here smelled of pitch and the strange sweetness that Merle had already noticed on the edge of the abyss.

The roof she was looking up at was also made of rock, but its great height blurred its structure, so that to the human eye it looked like patches of light and dark, all bathed in the flickering red of the veins of fire.

Merle wasn't sure what to think of the place. On the one hand, their surroundings were impressive and frightening because of their vast size; on the other, she told herself that this was only a gigantic cavern inside the earth, perhaps a whole system of caverns. It was nothing like Hell as described in the Bible. However, and here came the snag, that impression might quickly change as soon as they actually met more of the Lilim — which they could expect to do at any time. Even now, as he rested, Vermithrax was on the alert, his body tensed.

Yet Merle realised that Professor Burbridge had called this place Hell simply for lack of a better name, just as he had christened the creatures who lived here Lilim. He had covered the truth with a mask of myth to make it easier for the general public to take in his discovery.

'Vermithrax?'

The obsidian lion stopped preening his wings and looked at her. 'Hmm?'

'Those creatures up on the ledge in the shaft – they looked as if they were made of stone.'

The lion growled agreement. 'As if the rock itself had come to life.'

'Isn't that a strange coincidence?'

'You mean because *I* am made of stone?'

She rolled over on her front and propped her chin in both hands so that she could look Vermithrax in the eye. 'In a kind of way. Well, I know you don't have anything to do with them. But it's odd, though, isn't it?'

The lion sat up so that he could look at Merle while still keeping an eye on the rocks around them. 'I've been thinking about that myself.'

'So?'

'We just don't know enough about the Lilim.'

'How much do you lions know about yourselves? For instance, how come your mane is stone but still feels soft? And how can your tongue move although it's made of obsidian?'

'It's animated stone,' he said, as if that were sufficient answer. When he saw that it wasn't good enough for Merle, he went on, 'It's stone, but it's flesh or fur too. It has the structure and the strength and the toughness of stone, but there's life in it, and life changes everything. That's the only explanation I can give you. There were never any lion scientists to study such subjects. We're not like you human beings. We can accept things without taking them apart and seeking to know their last secrets.'

Merle thought about this as she waited for the Queen to say something. But the voice inside her remained silent.

'And what about the Lilim?' asked Merle at last. 'Do you think they're made of animated stone too?'

'Those creatures didn't look to me as if they had souls. But there are people who say the same about us lions. So who am I to judge the Lilim?'

'That sounds quite wise.'

Vermithrax laughed. 'It's not so difficult to make ignorance sound like wisdom. Your scholars and philosophers and priests have been doing it all through human history.' After a brief pause, he added, 'And so have the leaders of the lions too.'

It was the first time Merle had ever heard him say anything derogatory about other lions and she felt that it had cost him a great effort. In fact the lions differed from humans much more than she had known before. Perhaps, she continued her train of thought, they were more closely related to the Lilim than to mankind. She wondered whether that ought to frighten her, but she felt only curiosity.

In addition, of course, she found *everything* down here frightening in some way, even the rock on which she was lying and the mysterious warmth rising from inside it. She felt as if it might explode at any moment, like the volcanoes she had heard about. But she suppressed this uncomfortable thought, as she did with so many others.

'What are we going to do when we've found Lord Light?'

She put the question to no one in particular. The aim of their mission had been occupying her mind on their long flight down into the abyss. Her glance travelled slowly over the desolate rocky wilderness all around them. The landscape didn't look as if anyone would live here by choice, certainly not a prince or ruler like the mysterious Lord Light.

'The Queen should know,' said Vermithrax. He had mastered the art of making his voice sound perfectly indifferent even if he was, presumably, as churned up inside as Merle herself.

'*We shall ask him for help,*' said the Flowing Queen.

'I know that much.' Merle got to her feet, went over to the edge of the rocky plateau and let the warm, sultry, tar-scented wind blow around her nostrils. Vermithrax called to her to be careful, but she felt she must let her own body sense the dangers of their surroundings to make sure she wasn't dreaming it all.

The rock wall fell fifty or sixty metres at her feet, and Merle felt dizzy. Strangely enough, it was an almost pleasant feeling. A genuine, real sensation.

'I mean, I know we've done all this to ask him for help,' she said again. 'For Venice and all the others. But *how* are we going to do it? I mean, what's he going to think when a girl turns up in front of his throne on a flying lion and –'

'*Who says he has a throne?*'

'I thought he was a king.'

'*He rules Hell,*' said the Queen patiently. '*But down here things aren't the same as in the world above.*'

Merle couldn't take her eyes off the rugged, rocky landscape. It didn't seem to her so very different from other wildernesses she had seen in drawings and engravings. A desert people like the Egyptians would probably have felt at home down there.

Then a thought struck her like a blow. 'You *know* him!'

'*No,*' said the Queen tonelessly.

'Then how can you be sure he doesn't have a throne? How do you know he's not the same as other rulers?'

'*Just a suspicion.*' The Queen was not usually so disinclined to talk.

'A suspicion, is it?' Merle's voice was reproachful and angry, making even Vermithrax look at her in surprise. 'That's how you knew so well just where to find the entrance,' she cried. 'And how you knew that everything's different down here . . . but for once you were wrong. It's not that different at all. Personally I think it looks like an ordinary grotto.' Not that she had ever seen a grotto, but never mind that. She had no better arguments.

'The surface area of this grotto, Merle, is probably as big as half the planet. Perhaps much bigger. And how would you describe the Lilim if not as "different"?'

'But that's not what you meant just now,' said Merle with certainty. She was tired of giving in meekly in all their discussions. It was an odd feeling to be arguing with someone you couldn't see and who didn't have a real voice. 'I don't understand why you won't be honest with me . . . with us.'

Vermithrax was brushing his whiskers with one paw, but not a word escaped him. He could guess what they were talking about from Merle's half of the conversation.

Once again, she thought it was most unfair that only she could hear the Queen and argue with her.

'I've heard various rumours about Lord Light, things the mermaids have picked up, that's all.'

'What sort of rumours?'

'They say he's not the usual kind of ruler. Power doesn't matter to him.'

'What does he want, then?'

'I can't tell you. I don't know.'

'But you have an idea.'

The Queen was silent for a moment, and then said,

'*What can matter to the ruler of a whole realm if not power? And how great, if he doesn't have power, can his influence over his subjects be? The Lilim in the rock face didn't look as if they'd take orders from anyone out of sheer personal humility.*'

'So what does matter to him?' Merle insisted.

'*Knowledge, I think. He may rule this world, but most of all I think he studies it.*'

'Studies it? But —'

A loud cry from the lion interrupted her. 'Merle! Over there!'

She spun round, almost losing her balance. For a split second the edge of the precipice was dangerously close and the rocks below leaped to meet her. Then she recovered herself, retreated hastily from the edge of the abyss and followed the direction of the lion's gaze.

At first she could see nothing at all, only a red void above the expanse of the wilderness. Then she realised that Vermithrax, with the keen eyes of a beast of prey, could see much better than she could. Whatever he had spotted must still be outside her field of vision.

But before long she saw it too. And whatever it was, it was coming closer.

'What is it?' she exclaimed breathlessly, suddenly

overwhelmed by a torrent of horrible images. Fantasies of winged Lilim, thousands of them, danced in her mind.

But there were not a thousand, only three. And although they were hovering high above the rocks, they had no wings.

'Are they . . .?'

'Heads,' said Vermithrax. 'Gigantic heads.' And after a moment he added, 'Made of stone.'

She shook her head, not because she doubted his words but because it seemed the only appropriate reaction. Heads made of stone. Flying high in the air. Of course.

But after a while she could see the heads for herself. She saw them coming closer, moving rather fast, even faster, she felt sure, than Vermithrax could fly.

'Come on, climb up!' roared the lion, and before she could think of any good reason not to she was leaping on to his back, burying her hands in his mane and pressing her upper body close to his obsidian coat.

'*What's he doing?*'

'What are you doing?'

'Look at them. They're not alive.' Vermithrax's paws pushed off from the ground and seconds later they were hovering several metres above the hatbox plateau.

'They're not alive,' Merle repeated to herself and then added, rather louder, 'So what does that mean?'

'It means they're not Lilim. Or at least not dangerous Lilim.'

'Oh no?'

'*Wait and see*,' said the Flowing Queen, sensing Merle's doubts. '*He may be right.*'

'And suppose he isn't?'

She received no answer. She probably wouldn't have heard one anyway, for now the three heads were close enough for her to make out details.

They were shaped like human skulls, no doubt of that, and they were carved from stone. High as they were in the air, Merle had no clue to help her judge their size, but she suspected that each was at least fifty metres tall. Their faces were fixed and grey, their eyes open but blank, without pupils. Their stone hair lay close around the heads like a helmet, leaving the ears uncovered. The mighty lips were open just a crack, but what Merle had thought from a distance was a way into each head proved, as they came closer, to be an illusion. It was meant to suggest that the heads were speaking.

And now she heard voices too.

Words streamed through the air above the plain like flocks of birds, fluttering and restless, spoken in a language that Merle had never heard in her life.

The skulls were still about 800 metres away, approaching in an arrow formation, one head leading, the other two to right and left behind it.

'Those voices . . . are *they* talking?'

'I don't know if the voices are theirs, but they're coming from inside the heads,' said Vermithrax.

Merle noticed that he had pricked up his ears. He could not only see better than she could, he could also hear much more and was able to distinguish between the sounds and pinpoint their source.

'How do you mean, not their voices?'

'Someone else is speaking out of them. They're not alive. The stone they're made of isn't . . .'

'Animated?'

'Exactly.'

Vermithrax fell silent and concentrated entirely on his flight. Merle had expected them to fly away from the heads, but the lion had been hovering motionless in the air at a point straight in the flight path of the leading stone skull, and to her boundless horror she now realised that

Vermithrax was turning – not away from the heads but towards them. He intended to go and meet them.

'Vermithrax! What are you doing?'

The obsidian lion did not reply. Instead, he beat his wings up and down faster still, manoeuvring himself a little further to the left – and waited.

'What are you –'

'*He's planning something.*'

'Oh yes?' Merle would probably have gone red with fury if fear had not drained all the blood from her face. 'They're making straight for us!'

The eerie voices were ringing out louder and louder above the wilderness, caught and thrown back by rocky walls and towers of stone. It seemed to Merle as if they were hovering in the middle of a firework display of strange sounds and words, with many different noises exploding round them like bright fountains of flame. Even if she had known the strange language she probably wouldn't have been able to make anything out, the sounds were so loud and shrill at such close quarters. By the time the skulls reached them there was already a high piping in Merle's ears.

Vermithrax shook his head, as if he could rid his own

sensitive ears of the noise that way. He tensed his muscles. Abruptly, he shot forward, towards the leading skull, and at the last minute tilted sideways, roaring something at Merle that she couldn't make out – probably a warning to hold on tight – and dived under the rocky edge of the right cheekbone. Merle saw the vast face rush past like a granite wall, too large for her to take it in at a glance, too fast for her to get more than an impression of its weight, its size, the sheer power of its speed.

She called Vermithrax's name, but the wind blowing towards them tore the syllables from her lips, and the voices of the flying skulls drowned out every other sound.

Then, so suddenly that her fingers gave way and her whole body was jerked back, Vermithrax dug his claws into the head's stone ear and hauled himself up on it. At the same time his wings stopped beating, folded inwards and caught Merle before she could fall to the depths below. The tips of their feathers pressed her down on his back again with the force of gigantic fists, while Vermithrax did his best to counter the brutal jolt that had passed through them both as he first made contact with the skull.

Somehow he did it. Somehow he got a grip. And then they were sitting inside the ear of the giant head, racing across the rocky land at crazy speed.

It took Merle some time to calm her breathing enough to speak again. Even then thoughts were whirling in her head like midges around a candle flame, wild and nervous, and she had difficulty in thinking clearly at all, or realising what had just happened. Finally she clenched her fist and hit Vermithrax. He didn't even seem to notice.

'Why?' she shouted at him. 'Why did you do that?'

Vermithrax clambered over a stony swelling and deeper into the ear. It opened out around them like a cave, rocky, dark, a deep funnel. Surprisingly, the noise was muted in here, partly because they were now hearing only a single voice and were shielded from the noise the other two skulls were making, partly because the voice of the head was shouting at the world outside it.

Vermithrax let Merle slide off his back and then lay down, exhausted, between two stone curves. He was panting, with his long tongue resting on his mighty paws.

'The chances are fifty-fifty,' he managed to say between two deep breaths.

'What chances?' Merle was still furious, but gradually

her anger was giving way to relief that they were alive after all.

'Either the head will take us to Lord Light or it's carrying us in the opposite direction.'

Vermithrax drew his tongue in and laid his head on his forepaws. Only now did Merle realise how he had exhausted his strength in that leap for the flying skull, and how close they had been to slipping and falling to their death.

'This head,' said Vermithrax wearily, 'is announcing something. I don't understand the words it speaks, but they're the same over and over again, as if it were giving a message. Perhaps it's some kind of herald.'

'A message from Lord Light to his people?'

'*Possibly*,' said the Flowing Queen. '*Vermithrax may be right*.'

'What else?' asked the lion.

Merle rolled her eyes. 'How am I supposed to know? Down here it's all different. These things could be goodness knows what!' As she spoke, she looked around the stony cave. Incredible as it might seem, they really were sitting inside a gigantic ear.

'These heads aren't living creatures,' said Vermithrax.

'That's the difference between them and the Lilim. Someone made them. And made them for a certain purpose. As Lord Light is ruler of this place, it must have been him.'

'And why are the chances fifty-fifty?'

'The head may be on the way back to its master because its mission is accomplished – or it has only just set out on its journey and is going away from Lord Light. One or the other.'

'That means we can only wait and see, right?'

The lion nodded in a strangely clumsy way, for his muzzle was still resting on his paws. 'That's what it looks like.'

'What do you think?' Merle asked the Queen.

'*I think he's right. We could probably wander around Hell for months without finding any trace of Lord Light. This way at least we have a chance.*'

Merle sighed, and then moved closer to the lion and patted his nose. 'But next time tell me first, will you? When you nearly kill us all I'd quite like to know *why*.'

The lion growled something – was it a yes? – and pushed his fist-sized nose further into Merle's hand. Then he purred comfortably, waved his tail a few times and closed his eyes.

Merle sat with him a moment longer, then hauled herself up, still weak at the knees, and climbed to the outer stone swelling of the giant ear.

She looked down at the depths, awe-struck. The dreary landscape was passing by a few hundred metres below them, so monotonous that there was nothing, absolutely nothing at all, for her eyes to fix on. They were probably going too fast anyway. She doubted whether Vermithrax could have kept up with them for very long at even half this speed.

'What a miserable spot!' she groaned quietly. 'I wonder if Lord Light ever tried planting anything here? I mean, to bring a little colour into the place. Just for a change.'

'*Why should he? Nothing lives here. At least nothing that would appreciate such efforts. Do you think the Lilim at the camp up there would like to see a few pretty flowers?*'

'You don't have to make fun of the idea straight off.'

'*I didn't mean to. Only you have to apply different standards in this world. It has different concepts. Different ideas.*'

Merle said nothing and leaned back. But then a thought came into her mind and she expressed it at once.

'If these heads are flying machines of some kind, like the Empire's Barques of the Sun, then oughtn't there to be someone in them? Someone steering them?'

'*We are alone.*'

'Are you sure?'

'*I'd feel it. And I think Vermithrax would too.*'

Merle stretched out on the hard stone, watched the sleeping obsidian lion for a while, and then looked out again over the landscape of Hell. What a strange place! She tried to remember details of Professor Burbridge's travels, but couldn't. And she hadn't really read any of his books; the teacher in the orphanage had read them a few passages, but most of what she had heard about him was from second-hand accounts. A few descriptions, that was about all. Now she was sorry that she hadn't taken more interest in them at the time.

On the other hand, she remembered all about the dangers of Hell mentioned in Burbridge's books. Fearsome creatures lying in wait for unsuspecting victims behind every rock and every . . . yes, every tree. She was sure trees had been mentioned. Iron trees with leaves like razor blades. But here anyway, in this part of Hell, there seemed to be no plants at all, whether made of iron or wood.

And she also remembered stories of barbaric beings moving in great tribes over the plains, landscapes enveloped in eternal fire, mountains that unfolded wings and flew away, ships made of human bones sailing the lava oceans of Hell. All these images had impressed Merle so much that they had stuck in her memory.

None of that was anywhere in sight.

She was both disappointed and relieved. The Lilim in the rock face were murderous enough for her, and she felt she could happily do without cannibal tribes and gigantic monsters. Yet she felt a little cheated, as if all those infernal images had turned out, years later, to be pure fantasy.

However, Hell was gigantic, and there might be all kinds of different landscapes and cultures down here, just as there were in the world above. If a traveller from another world was put down somewhere in the Sahara, no doubt he too would be disappointed if he'd been told in advance about the magnificent palaces of Venice and its many branching canals. He might not even be able to believe in them at all.

Merle climbed up on the outer stone swelling again and looked at the rocky ground racing past far below them. No change there, no sign of life. Curiously, she couldn't feel any wind. Surely they ought to have been generating a slipstream at this speed.

Slightly bored, even after all she'd been through, she looked back at the second stone skull following them at a little distance. She couldn't see the third from here; it was on their other side.

Then she gave a start of surprise and her boredom was instantly gone.

'But that's not . . .' she began, and never finished her sentence. After a moment she asked, 'Can you see it too?'

'I see through your eyes, Merle. Of course I can see it.'

There was a man crouching between the lips of the second head.

He was huddled behind the lower lip, lying with his torso and outstretched arms hanging over the stone, apparently lifeless, as if the mighty head had half eaten him and then forgotten to swallow the rest. His arms were dangling, swaying back and forth, his head was on one side with his face turned away from them. He had very long snow-white hair, and Merle would have taken him for a woman if he hadn't suddenly turned his head and glanced her way. He was looking at her through the white strands that covered his features like newly fallen snow. Even at this distance she could see how thin and emaciated his face was. There was hardly any more colour in his skin than his hair; it was as pale as the skin of a corpse.

'*He's dying*,' said the Flowing Queen.

'Are we just going to sit here and watch?'

'*There's no way we can get to him.*'

Merle thought about it and then came to a decision. 'Maybe there is, though.'

She slid back into the ear, shook Vermithrax awake and hauled the lion, who was tired and not pleased to be woken up, over to the outer rim of the stone ear with her. The white-skinned man had turned his face away again and was slumped over the lip of the huge head like a dead body.

'Can we get there?' Her tone of voice made it clear that she wasn't going to take no for an answer.

'Hmm,' said Vermithrax darkly.

'What do you mean, hmm?' In a state of agitation, Merle was gasping for breath, waving her arms about and gesticulating wildly. 'We can't just leave him there to die. Anyone can see he needs our help.'

Vermithrax growled something that Merle couldn't make out, and when she gesticulated even more angrily, appealed eloquently to his conscience and finally even said

'Please', he murmured, 'He could be dangerous.'

'But he's a human being!'

'Or something that looks like a human being,' said the Queen with Merle's voice.

Merle was far too upset to mention this new infringement of their agreement. 'Anyway, we can't just stay here and watch.' She repeated, with even greater emphasis, 'Well, we can't, can we?'

The Queen retreated into silence, which in a way was an answer, but Vermithrax replied, 'No, I suppose not.'

Merle breathed a sigh of relief. 'So you'll try?'

'*Try what?*' asked the Queen, but this time Merle just ignored her.

From the rim of the ear, Vermithrax looked thoughtfully across the abyss to the second stone skull. 'That head isn't flying exactly behind us. It's at an angle, which makes things more difficult. But perhaps . . . hm, if I push off hard enough, get a good way ahead and then simply let myself fall back, I could probably get my claws into it and –'

'Simply! Did you say "simply"?' the Queen asked through Merle's mouth.

Oh, stop it! thought Merle.

'But that's madness. We don't know who or what he is, and why he's in such dire straits.'

'And if we sit around here we never will.'

'That might be better.' But the Queen's tone showed that she had already accepted defeat. She played fair and was a good loser – though perhaps her feelings were hurt too, because she fell silent again.

'It will be difficult,' said Vermithrax.

'Well, yes.' As if Merle didn't know.

'I can't just hover in the air until the head's face collides with me – that would kill me. All I can do is try the sideways approach again and hope to land in its ear or somewhere on its hair. And then I'd have to climb down and round the head to reach the man.'

Merle took a deep breath. 'I can do that bit.'

'You?'

'Of course.'

'But you don't have any claws.'

'I weigh less than you, though. And I'm quicker on my feet and I can get a hold on any little irregularities in the stone.' She didn't really believe that herself, but she somehow felt it sounded plausible.

'Not a good idea,' said Vermithrax, unimpressed.

'Look, just take me over and I'll do the rest. I'm tired of sitting on your back the whole time.' She gave him a fleeting smile. 'I mean, I've nothing against sitting on your back, but I can't just do – do nothing. I was never much good at doing nothing.'

The lion twisted his mouth into what Merle recognised only after a moment as a grin. 'You're rather a brave girl. And totally crazy.'

She beamed at him. 'Then we're going to try it?'

Vermithrax licked his finger-length fangs with the tip of his tongue. 'Yes,' he said, after another glance at the abyss, 'I think we'll simply have a shot at it.'

'*Simply*,' groaned the Queen. '*There you go again*.'

JUNIPA'S FATE

'What do you mean, you have to go out for a while?' shouted Dario.

Serafin held his gaze with ease. Being shouted at had never particularly impressed him. Blustering was usually just a sign of weakness. 'I mean exactly what I said. Before the attack I have to go out. And don't worry, General Dario, I'm not planning to desert from your army of heroes.'

Dario was seething with rage, and looked as if he were sorry he didn't have more than two fists to clench. 'We don't do things that way here,' he said in cutting tones, his voice rather quieter than before but just as angry. 'You can't simply go off for a few hours while the rest of us are making preparations for getting into the Doge's Palace and –'

Serafin interrupted him. '*You* may have to make preparations. *I* don't. You *asked* me,' he said, emphasising the words with particular relish, 'you *asked* me to help you because you know I'm the only one who has even the ghost of a chance of breaking into that palace. You see, the rules are perfectly simple, Dario: I try to get into the palace and anyone who wants to follow me does exactly as I say. If not, then either he stays here or he'll probably be dead within the first few minutes.' He chose these dramatic words intentionally, because he felt it was his best way of holding Dario's attention. Moreover, he was tired of this discussion before it had even really begun.

'With all due respect to your instincts,' said Dario, controlling himself with difficulty, 'I still –'

'Let me remind you that my instincts are all you have.' Serafin pointed to the little troop of rebels assembled in the dining hall of the Enclave: a dozen boys of his own age, some younger, most of them street children. They were used to fending for themselves, stealing for a living and outwitting the City Guard. Some still wore their old ragged clothing, and those who had found new clothes from the stocks in the sphinx's house looked dandified and almost ridiculous in their brightly coloured shirts and trousers. Most of these garments looked like costumes for a fancy-dress ball; only after a while did Serafin realise that the clothes must in fact date from many different centuries and had survived all that time in the sphinx's chests and trunks. Once again he wondered just how long Lalapeya had been living in Venice. She herself hadn't told him.

Dario had shown enough sense to pick a new shirt and trousers in purple velvet, a colour dark enough to merge with the night. The others, who had been less careful in their choice of clothing, would stay here. They didn't know it yet, but Serafin would make sure of that. He couldn't afford to set out with companions whose minds were not entirely on the job.

'Your mind's not on the job,' said Dario, as if he had read Serafin's thoughts and could now turn his own argument against him. 'We can't rely on you if you have something else in your head all the time.'

'That's exactly why I want to go out again.' Serafin ignored the silent faces of the boys listening attentively to every word that he and Dario exchanged. 'There's something I have to settle before I can clear my head for what we're going to do. I can't let it distract me.'

'And what matter of world-shaking importance might that be?'

Serafin hesitated. Was that what Dario wanted? Not, as he had assumed at first, to make him look a fool in front of everyone else. Not to deny that he had leadership qualities either (and Serafin would have been the first to agree with him there: he had never been good at leading a group, he'd always been a loner). No, it looked as if Dario was just curious. Perhaps he even guessed what Serafin planned to do and was ashamed.

Lalapeya, thought Serafin. She's told him. And now he's trying to make me look bad in front of the others because he's feeling bad himself. In fact it's himself he's angry with, not me.

'I want to go to the Outcasts' Canal,' he said, watching every movement of Dario's face, every suggestion of any emotion other than anger. And suddenly Dario's features betrayed his admission of guilt.

'What would you want to do there?' asked Dario quietly. His tone of voice was very different from what it had been only moments before. A murmur went through the ranks of the rebels.

'I want to go to Arcimboldo's workshop,' said Serafin. 'I have to make sure he and Eft are all right. And most of all Junipa.' He lowered his voice so that only Dario could hear him. 'I have to get her away from there. Take her somewhere she'll be safe. If I don't, she won't survive the next few days, and Arcimboldo probably won't either.'

Dario stared at him with narrowed eyes, as if he could see right through into his innermost heart. 'Someone wants to kill Arcimboldo?'

Serafin nodded. 'I'm afraid that's what it looks like. I can't imagine him really giving up Junipa. And if he refuses, they'll kill him.'

'Giving her up? Who to? The Egyptians?'

Serafin took Dario's upper arm and led him away from the others, through a door into the next room where they could talk undisturbed. 'Not the Egyptians,' he said.

'Who, then?'

Serafin looked thoughtfully out of the window. Darkness had fallen. They were planning to break into the palace that very night. According to the reports brought back by their scouts, the Pharaoh had entered it only a few hours ago. By the time they made their move, Serafin must have found somewhere for Junipa, Arcimboldo and Eft to go. Compared to that everything else, even the struggle against the Egyptians, was unimportant.

Serafin shook himself and looked Dario in the face. He knew one thing for certain: he just didn't have time to explain things to Dario now.

'Why not come too?'

'Do you mean it?'

Serafin nodded. 'You're good with a sword. Much better than I am.'

Dario's expression still showed reluctance to ally himself with his old arch-enemy. But there was something else in his eyes too: a trace of relief and – yes, gratitude. Serafin was making it easy for him to go too without having to ask if he might. That was what surprised Serafin most: Dario had *wanted* to go with him from the first. He just couldn't bring himself to say it, not to Serafin.

'What about the others?' asked Dario.

'They'll have to wait.'

'Lalapeya?'

'So will she.'

Dario nodded. 'Then let's go.'

Back in the dining hall, Dario told the surprised Tiziano to take command until they were back. Tiziano and Boro exchanged intrigued glances, but then smiled, and Tiziano nodded proudly. The other boys wanted to know what Dario and Serafin were planning, but when Boro promised them all a second helping of supper their interest faded and they turned to the steaming dishes. Serafin smiled when he saw them. At heart, they would be street children all their lives, eager to make the most of every meal.

Serafin and Dario left the Enclave through the main entrance, after cautiously inspecting the street outside. The sphinx's palazzo was in the Castello quarter, in the middle of Venice, but tonight none of the inhabitants would venture out on the street even here.

The arbitrary attacks by mummy warriors had become organised patrols over the past day – and Venice had fallen into enemy hands without a fight. The City Guard had put up no resistance. The treacherous councillors had made sure at an early stage that the city would capitulate as soon as the Queen had gone and the enemy army moved closer. The attacks on civilians by mummy troops the night before had done yet more to destroy the citizens' will to fight. Most had simply given the city and themselves up for lost. Now the moment when the first would be dragged from their houses and taken away by boat was only a question of time.

The two boys slipped past the facade of the sphinx's palazzo. In a whisper, Serafin asked about the walled-up windows on the ground floor, but Dario didn't know what was behind them. No one ever entered that bottom floor of the building; it was an iron rule. There weren't even any doors to it.

It wasn't far to the Outcasts' Canal; if they had run it would have taken less than fifteen minutes. But they had to make a detour several times when they heard the clash of steel round a bend or the sound of marching footsteps, although never voices. They once saw a mummy patrol only a few paces away as they stood well back in a niche, hoping that the Pharaoh's slaves would not get wind of them. A cloud of dust rose to Serafin's nostrils as the bony figures marched by.

Some minutes later, they reached a small junction where the Outcasts' Canal branched off from a wider waterway. Serafin's heart leaped when he saw the abandoned bridge and the deserted footpaths by the water. Here, at a lantern-lit party not so long ago, it had all begun for him and Merle. The memory filled him with grief and fear. Where was Merle now?

The Outcasts' Canal itself was the same as ever. Almost all the buildings in the blind alley were long uninhabited, their doors and windows destroyed. Only the two workshops with grey facades, like old men's faces staring at each other over the water, had been in use until recently.

But now Umberto's weavers had left their house, and the windows of the mirror-making workshop were dark too.

'Are you sure they're still here?' asked Dario as they approached the workshop. They kept checking that no one was following them, and Serafin watched the sky for flying lions, although he could make out hardly anything in the darkness. If something dark and massive was racing past the stars up there, it moved too fast for his tired eyes.

'You ought to know Arcimboldo better than I do,' he said. 'I didn't get the impression he was a man to leave his house and crawl into some hole in the ground.'

Dario responded with an angry flash of his eyes, but then realised that Serafin's words were not hostile. He slowly nodded. 'Perhaps we ought not to have left him and Eft behind.' He hadn't forgotten all he owed to Arcimboldo.

Serafin placed a hand on his shoulder. 'He knew you'd be going. He told me so. And I think he even rather wanted you to go.'

'He talked to you about it?' Dario looked at him. 'When?'

'A few days ago. I was out on the lagoon with him when you and the others had loaded the mirrors into the gondola.'

'That last consignment . . .' Dario's voice sounded suddenly thoughtful as his eyes wandered to the entrance of the mirror-making workshop. 'He never said where he was taking all those mirrors. Or who was buying them from him.' He started suddenly and looked at Serafin. 'Are they the people we're to protect him from? Is that why we're here?'

Serafin was on the point of telling him the whole story: how he had watched as Arcimboldo handed over his magic mirrors to the emissary from Hell, Talamar; how the creature Talamar, speaking on behalf of its master, Lord Light, had demanded the girl Junipa. The girl with the mirror-glass eyes.

But he said nothing after all, just nodded briefly.

'What are they like, those people?' asked Dario.

Serafin sighed. 'If our luck is out, we'll meet one of them tonight.' He was about to walk on, but Dario held him back by the shoulder.

'Come on, out with it.'

Serafin looked from Dario to the dark workshop and then back to the boy. It was not easy to tell the truth. Dario wasn't going to believe him.

'They're from Hell,' he said at last. 'Arcimboldo has

been selling his magic mirrors to Lord Light for years. To one of his envoys.'

'Lord Light?' Dario's voice was level, as if this news didn't really surprise him. Then he nodded slowly. 'The Devil, then.'

'That has yet to be proved,' said Serafin. 'No one's ever met Lord Light.' But he knew he was only trying to look on the bright side.

'And Arcimboldo obeyed him?' asked Dario.

A sudden gust of wind blew on Serafin's face, making him shiver. He looked up at the night sky once more. 'He wasn't just making mirrors for him. He took Merle and Junipa into his house on Lord Light's orders too.'

'But . . .' began Dario, and then shook his head. He had never liked the two girls, but he wouldn't go so far as to blame them. 'Tell me the rest of the story,' he asked.

'There's no more to tell. Junipa was blind, as you know, and it was at Lord Light's wish that Arcimboldo gave her mirror-glass eyes.'

'Those terrifying eyes,' whispered Dario. 'They're eerie. Like ice. As if a cold wind blew out of them.' He stopped and after a moment added, 'But why? What good does it do Hell or Lord Light for Junipa to see again?'

'I've no idea.' Serafin saw the doubt in Dario's eyes. 'No, honestly, I really don't know. And I think Arcimboldo himself wasn't sure. He just did as he was told. To save the workshop, and you apprentices too. He was afraid he'd have to send you all back to an orphanage if he refused to do what Lord Light wanted. His only thought was for you.' Serafin hesitated for a moment and then said, 'And he was glad he could help Junipa. He said she was so happy to be able to see at last.'

'So why are we here now?'

'Lord Light's messenger, Talamar, told Arcimboldo to deliver Junipa up to him. But I think it knew quite well that Arcimboldo would refuse. It gave him a deadline. That's why we have to get your master, Junipa and Eft to safety before . . .'

'Before this Talamar fetches the girl,' Dario ended his sentence. 'And punishes Arcimboldo for his disobedience.'

'Then are you still with me?' Serafin had not forgotten that time in the past when Dario went for him with a knife in the mirror-making workshop. Dario had used Junipa as a shield. On the other hand, Serafin felt he was dealing with a different Dario today. A more honest Dario than the old one – more honest with himself too.

'Of course.' Dario drew his sword, a determined if slightly empty gesture. 'Never mind who we have to fight. And if the Pharaoh and Lord Light are drinking each other's health in there, the two of us will show them what we can do.'

Serafin grinned and set off. Together they went the last few metres to the workshop. The lettering over the doorway, *Arcimboldo's Divine Glass*, seemed more unreal than ever. The gods had never been further from Venice than they were tonight.

There was a soft thud as the mirror-maker's empty rowing boat bumped against the wall of the canal beside them. Serafin and Dario jumped. Something had disturbed the calm water. Perhaps it was just the wind.

Still no lions in the sky.

The entrance was open. Dario cast Serafin a glance of surprise, but Serafin merely shrugged. Only when they had cautiously gone in did they see that the lock of the door had been broken off – or rather smashed to pieces, like the wood of the oak door itself, which had slammed back against the wall so heavily that plaster had flaked away in several places.

Dario peered intently into the dark.

Serafin whispered a single word. 'Talamar.'

He didn't know what made him so sure. It might just as well have been mummy warriors who had invaded the house. But he sensed the breath of Lord Light's slaves like a bad smell infesting the air here. Like something that singed the little hairs on the nape of his neck and made the roots of all his teeth ache at once. The presence of something entirely evil, perhaps even worse than the power that had sent it here.

'Talamar,' he said again, louder, more grimly.

Then he ran on, ignoring both Dario's warning and the darkness that was seething in the entrance hall like black broth in a witch's cauldron. He raced upstairs, reached the first floor and was alarmed to see frantic movement to right and left of him: shapes flitting swiftly over the walls. But they were only his own reflection thrown back by countless framed mirrors all over the walls.

Dario was directly behind him when a deafening screech was heard. Dario quickened his pace and was now almost passing Serafin.

Who had uttered that cry? Man, woman or girl? Or perhaps something quite different crying aloud not in torment but in shrill, exultant triumph.

A whispering drifted down the corridors from all directions at once: 'The wish is granted, the spell cast, the pact fulfilled.'

The boys turned a corner and went straight into the corridor leading to the tall double door of the workshop. The large room where Arcimboldo worked had always been more like an alchemist's laboratory than the workshop of an ordinary craftsman. His mirrors were made of silvered glass, magic and the essence of the Flowing Queen.

But the acrid vapours that wafted towards them now had nothing to do with magic or alchemical substances. They were the breath of damnation, the black pestilence of Talamar. Serafin knew it, felt it with every nerve and fibre. His senses were raising the alarm. His mind screamed at him to turn back.

However, he ran on, raising his sword, opened his mouth in a great cry of helpless rage – and raced through the open door into the laboratory, plunged through dense clouds of pungent smoke and acid vapours, stumbled, stopped, could hardly breathe. And *saw*.

Eft was lying motionless in a corner, perhaps dead, perhaps just unconscious. In the livid mists that filled the room it was impossible to see if she was breathing. She was not wearing her mask, but had turned her face aside. Serafin wasn't sure whether Dario had ever seen the former mermaid unmasked; if not, it was better for her not to look at them just now. Her shark-like mouth, all that remained of her oceanic origins, might have given Dario a shock.

Something like a large four-legged spider was moving in the mists. It had angular joints, as if someone had put a puppet together the wrong way. A body with its stomach upwards and a face on top of the head, pointed chin above, malicious eyes below. Like a human being building a bridge with its body, yet far removed from anything human.

The envoy from Hell was pulling something along behind it, a motionless bundle. A body.

Junipa.

Serafin hesitated only for a moment, assured himself that Dario too was seeing what he saw, and then raced through the acrid vapours towards Talamar so fast that even the reflexes of the envoy from Hell could hardly react. Instead of avoiding him, the creature let go of Junipa, raised an arm in a weird movement like nothing earthly and fended off the sword stroke with its bare skin, which was hard as stone and impervious as an insect's horny shell.

The blade was deflected with a horrible, hollow sound, and the force of his own stroke almost knocked Serafin to the ground. He recovered his balance at the last moment, was driven back two paces, then stood there with his legs apart, ready for the next exchange of blows.

Shrill laughter came from the creature's distorted mouth. Its eyes seemed to search the place, probed it for the second adversary and discovered him.

Dario had learned from Serafin's mistake. Instead of attacking Talamar head on, he took a step towards the creature, spun round, jumped to the right and then to the left, and finally took an acrobatic leap right over his opponent, turning in the air and bringing his sword down with both hands on the body of the envoy of Hell.

The creature groaned as the point of the sword scratched its skin. It shook itself, as you might when bitten by an insect, uttered a series of staccato sounds and then simply brushed the sword blade aside. The point had gone only a finger's breadth in, not enough to weaken or seriously injure the strange being. Dario snatched the sword back before Talamar could grasp the blade, rose to stand on both feet, swayed briefly, then got his balance and called something to Serafin that was drowned out by the creature's angry bellowing.

Serafin understood all the same.

Dario was now on Talamar's right side, while Serafin was still on the creature's left. They could corner the envoy from Hell between them if they managed it cleverly. If they moved quickly enough.

Talamar could speak the language of the Venetians – as Serafin had heard for himself – but the sounds the creature uttered now were so strange that they hurt Serafin's ears. It was as if they were living things, sent out to weaken Talamar's enemies and disturb their concentration.

Serafin forced himself to keep calm. He looked for the motionless body of Junipa, half hidden by Talamar's body, and he thought he saw a metallic flash, a reflection in her eyes. They were open. They were watching him. Yet Junipa couldn't move, as if Talamar had cast a spell on her. Her joints were rigid, her muscles frozen. She was breathing, however, he saw that now quite clearly. She was alive, and that was what mattered.

Dario whistled. Serafin looked up and nodded to his companion. Then they both attacked at once, whirling their swords through the air and bringing them down on Talamar's hard shell.

Steel struck horn and left no wound.

The creature called Talamar screamed again, not in pain but in rage. Then it counter-attacked.

It had recognised Dario as the more dangerous opponent and went for him first. The claws on Talamar's fingers, as long and sharp as daggers, shot forward and back, darting, whirling shapes, and then Dario screamed, staggered and collided with a workbench. With great presence of mind he flung himself back, losing his grip on his sword, slid over the surface of the bench and dropped into cover behind it. Just in time, for Talamar's claws bored into the wood as they made for him, driving five deep grooves into the surface.

Serafin used the moment when the creature's attention was distracted. He didn't know how he could get through Talamar's horny skin, but instinct told him to attack the creature's head. His sword cut through the grey mist, sweeping the vapours away from Talamar's features and uncovering the whole face. For a brief moment, as if frozen in time, Serafin saw the wreath of iron thorns running like a bandage over Talamar's eyes, and the single thorny spray that had come loose from the others and ran across the creature's mouth.

Then his sword blade came down on Talamar's features – and bounced off again.

The scream that emerged from the being's throat now sounded tormented and out of control, and for the first time Serafin felt that in spite of everything he could be a threat to Talamar, could even kill the creature.

Instead of retreating to gather his strength for another attack he pursued his enemy at once, thrust with his sword, felt it meet resistance – and saw the blade burst into a thousand splinters.

Talamar drew back one limb and gave him a blow that would have killed him if it had been better aimed. As it was, the claws just touched Serafin, leaving deep scratches in his right cheek and then meeting air. Serafin swayed and crashed to the ground. He landed so hard on the base of his spine that he was knocked breathless. When his vision cleared again, Talamar was gone.

And so was Junipa.

'Serafin?'

He looked up and saw Dario getting to his feet behind the workbench, retrieving his sword from the floor and then looking incredulously at the five deep grooves in the surface of the bench. It didn't take much imagination to work out what would have been left of him if the blow had hit its target.

'Here!' called Serafin, but it sounded like an inarticulate cry of pain, not a word.

'Where is it?' Dario staggered towards him, leaning on his sword as if it were a crutch. His own face was twisted with pain, and a dark bruise around his left eye was flowering like some exotic plant.

'Gone.'

'Gone where?'

Serafin struggled up before Dario reached him, still holding the hilt of his broken sword. He stared at it incredulously and then tossed it carelessly aside. The metal hilt crashed to the wooden floor, slid a little further, and was caught by a hand that darted suddenly out of the swathes of vapour like a hungry animal.

'Eft!' Serafin parted the mists, leaned forward and helped the woman to her feet. 'I thought –'

She gave him no time to finish. 'Where's Arcimboldo?'

Serafin looked round, saw only Dario, who shrugged, and then shook his head. 'I don't know.'

Eft freed herself from his hands and made her way forward with difficulty, bending double, dragging herself on through the acid fog that burned in Serafin's lungs like liquid fire.

'He must . . . be here . . . somewhere.'

Serafin and Dario exchanged another glance, then moved off in different directions to search the interior of the workshop.

A little later they were sure that neither Talamar and Junipa nor Arcimboldo were still here. Instead, they came upon an opening in the floor with charred edges, a jagged shape like a star clumsily painted on the floorboards by a child.

At first Serafin thought for a moment that the hole led straight down to Hell. But once his eyes were used to the darkness, he saw the floor of the lower storey at the bottom of the opening. He was on the point of jumping down into it, but Eft took his arm and held him back.

'Don't,' she said. 'It's gone.'

'What about Junipa?'

'It took her too.'

'We must stop them!'

She shook her head. 'It moves fast. By now they could be anywhere.'

'But . . .' Serafin fell silent. Whatever he had been going

to say, it had gone out of his mind. They had failed. Talamar would take Junipa to Lord Light. The girl was lost.

'*Master!*' Dario's voice came through the vapours, muted, probably from another room, but even at a distance the despair in his cry lost none of its intensity.

Serafin ran, but Eft was even faster. She had a cut on her head and blood was trickling down beside her ears to the corners of her mouth. That broad mermaid mouth was open just a crack, and Serafin saw the rows of sharp teeth inside it flashing.

He followed her into the vapours and through an open door.

Arcimboldo used to keep his magic mirrors in his storeroom. Most were gone now; he had delivered them to Talamar in his last consignment. Only a few still hung on the walls or were propped against them, mirrors made on commission for his occasional Venetian customers.

The old man was lying face down on the floor. His left arm was stretched close to his body at an unnatural angle, as if it had been broken behind his back or dislocated from its socket. His right hand was clutching a hammer. Very close to him lay the remains of a mirror, jagged shards of glass that he had obviously smashed out of the frame himself.

An idea went through Serafin's mind even before he felt the full weight of horror and grief: had Talamar reached the workshop through one of the magic mirrors? And had Arcimboldo destroyed that way of access with the hammer?

Dario was kneeling beside his master but dared not touch him, whether out of respect or in fear of what he might see.

Eft pushed the boys aside and rolled Arcimboldo over on his back. Then they all looked at his dead eyes, half covered by strands of the tangled white hair that lay around his skull like wet thread.

With a gentle gesture, Eft closed the old man's eyes. Her fingers were trembling. She raised Arcimboldo's upper body, hugged it tight and laid the back of his head carefully in her lap. Her hands shaking, she pushed back the hair and stroked his cheeks.

Dario looked up for the first time. And saw Eft's face.

He let out a gasp and for a split second it looked as if he would flinch away from her. But he soon had himself under control again, glanced briefly at Eft's legs — no fish-tail;

Serafin could read his thoughts — and then took his old master's hand and pressed it tightly.

Serafin felt out of place. He hadn't known the mirror-maker well, but he had liked him. He wanted to pay his respects to the dead, but he feared that any gesture of his own might seem false and empty. These two owed Arcimboldo so much, their grief must be infinitely deeper. He just bowed briefly, turned and went back to the workshop.

He didn't have to wait long before Dario joined him.

'Eft wants to be alone with him.'

Serafin nodded. 'Yes, of course.'

'She says we're to wait for her.'

Dario perched on the edge of the workbench. His glance was turned inward. It surprised Serafin that in spite of everything Dario was not in more of a hurry to get back to the Enclave; the attack on the Pharaoh was to take place today, and it wasn't in Dario's power to change that plan.

'What will she do?' asked Serafin.

'I think she'll come with us.'

'To the Enclave?'

Dario nodded.

Perhaps that wasn't a bad idea. Eft was old, over 100, he

thought, perhaps even older, but to all outward appearance she was a woman in her thirties. She was slender and agile, and he wouldn't have been surprised to hear that she knew how to use a sword.

'You didn't know, did you?' asked Serafin.

'That she's a mermaid?' Dario shook his head. 'No. We wondered why she always wore that mask, of course. She never let anyone see her whole face, only the upper part above her nose. We thought it was because of some disease or an accident.' He shrugged his shoulders. 'Well, perhaps we did have some slight idea, who knows? Tiziano once made a joke — what if Eft was really . . . But no, I didn't know. Not really.'

They left the workshop and sat down on the floor of the corridor outside, Serafin on one side of it, Dario on the other, leaning against the wall. They had both drawn up their knees and were looking at each other across the corridor. Dario's sword lay at his feet.

The silence was broken by the click of the lock as Eft closed the workshop door from inside. The last thing Serafin saw through the crack of the doorway was Arcimboldo's body, which Eft had laid out on a workbench, half hidden behind the drifting banks of mist.

'What's she doing?'

Dario looked at the door as if he could see through the wood of its two wings. 'No idea. We'll have to wait.'

Serafin nodded.

And so they waited.

They waited for an hour. Perhaps two or three hours.

They didn't talk much, but when they did there was none of the old enmity between them left, only respect and something that might perhaps turn to friendship one day.

But they had paid a high price for it. Arcimboldo was dead, Junipa abducted.

Far too high a price.

The idea of breaking into the Doge's Palace after all this and trying to assassinate the Pharaoh suddenly seemed so improbable, so totally crazy, that Serafin quickly put it out of his mind.

The acrid vapours had long ago dispersed by the time they heard the sound of the lock again. But now another smell replaced them.

The smell of burning. Fire in the workshop!

Roused from their rigidity, Serafin and Dario leaped up. Eft came out to meet them, with something shining in her hand. At first Serafin thought it was a blade, but then he saw a mask of silvery mirror-glass. Eft was pressing it to her breast like something unspeakably precious, more than just a memento that she was taking with her.

Behind her, the workbench was burning. A column of black, greasy smoke rose, was caught under the ceiling and crawled along it towards the door like the vanguard of a column of ants.

'Let's go,' said Eft.

The two boys exchanged uncertain glances. Then Serafin looked back at the inside of the workshop again. The flames dancing above Arcimboldo's body hid the work of destruction that they were doing. Something about the corpse's outline seemed to him strange, as if the old man's face were now smooth as a ball.

His glance returned to the silver mask in Eft's hand. Its features were thin and gaunt. The face of an old man.

'Let's go,' said the mermaid again, pulling a scarf over her mouth with her free hand, so that she looked like a burglar preparing for his last great robbery.

Dario nodded, and Serafin joined the two of them as they hurried down the corridor. He looked back once over his shoulder, but now all he could see were fire and smoke billowing out into the corridor.

Moments later the three of them were running along beside the Outcasts' Canal, away from Arcimboldo's funeral pyre.

Flames were shooting out of several windows now, and a wall of thick smoke formed above the water.

THE PHARAOH

A falcon appeared in the air behind the gilded domes of the Basilica of St Mark, a falcon larger than any creature on earth, taller than the tallest tower, mightier than the statues of the Pharaoh at home in Egypt.

It rose to its full height, taller than 100 men standing one above the other, with round, black eyes and a beak the size of a ship's hull. Its plumage was pure gold and stood out against the night sky as if it were burning.

Horus, the falcon god.

He unfurled his wings like golden sails and folded them around the facades of the basilica from both sides, clasping their rich Byzantine ornamentation, their pediments and windows and reliefs. The tips of the wings met in front of the porch and folded over each other until the whole cathedral was caught in his embrace, hidden behind a curtain of glowing, sparkling lava.

The falcon god was claiming his own.

He was letting everyone see who held power in Venice

now, showing that it was a part of Egypt, part of the Empire, a fief of the old gods.

Seth, high priest of Horus and vizier to the Pharaoh, stood on a roof opposite. His head was slightly bowed and his arms crossed over his chest. Sweat stood out in shining beads on his forehead, and his golden robe was drenched with it. At this moment he *was* the falcon, the absolute master of this illusion.

Seth held the magic in place for a minute longer, then flung his arms wide with a rapid movement and let out the air sharply through his nose and mouth.

The towering falcon dissolved into a fountain of sparkling sequins that settled in the Piazza San Marco around the basilica as if the stars themselves were falling from the sky.

Applause rang out from the ranks of the priesthood gathered down there in the piazza. Only the mummy warriors, several dozen of them stationed in various places, stared indifferently ahead from dead, sunken eyes, some from empty eye sockets.

But Seth needed no acclamation or applause to know the extent of his skill. He was well aware of his power and every aspect, however small, of his god-like talents. The golden falcon god was nothing but a clever trick, one of those symbols of the victory of the Empire that always threw the Pharaoh into naive ecstasies. A toy for a child.

What a waste, thought Seth scornfully. What a waste of power, respect, credibility. He himself, high priest and the second most important man in the Empire, the revered figure of Seth, was wasting his energies on the ridiculous wishful dreams of Amenophis. And everyone within the priesthood, even his closest and most intimate colleagues, knew that he had no choice in the matter. Not at times like these, when the sphinx commanders were winning more and more influence and power, supplanting the priests in the ruler's favour. He had to keep the Pharaoh happy – long enough for the power of the priests of Horus to be rid of the threat of the accursed sphinxes.

Seth snorted angrily at the thought. The Empire was celebrating one of its greatest victories, the conquest of Venice after three decades of siege, and that victory was first and foremost Seth's, his personal triumph over the Flowing Queen – yet he could not enjoy it to the full. His contentment was all on the outside, only for show.

The sphinxes were to blame. And of course the Pharaoh himself.

Amenophis was a fool — a stupid, vain jackanapes on a throne made of gold and human lives. The priests of Horus had chosen him and made him the imperial figurehead because they had considered him weak, malleable and easily influenced. Only a child, they had said to themselves, rejoicing when they succeeded in waking him to new life in the stepped pyramid of Amun-Ka-Re.

He was their work, their puppet, so they had believed. And in a certain way that was still the truth.

But only in a *certain* way.

Wordlessly, Seth let a long cloak be draped around his shoulders and took a cloth that one of his subordinate priests handed him. He used it to mop the sweat from his bald head and the spaces between the golden network that had been let into his scalp partly as an adornment, partly to emphasise his spiritual power. The network had been tattooed on the skin of the other priests' heads with paint, but his own was pure gold, worked by the goldsmiths of Punt in the far south of Africa.

With measured tread, Seth entered the stairwell, followed by his priests. A large number of mummy warriors had been assigned to his protection. A strikingly large number. Seth wondered who had given the order. Not he himself, anyway.

As he stepped into the piazza at the bottom of the stairs, a novice priest approached him, bowed three times, kissed his hands and feet and asked permission to deliver a message from the Pharaoh: Amenophis wished to see Seth immediately in his new apartments in the Doge's Palace.

Inwardly Seth was seething with rage as he left the novice and his subordinates behind, crossed the piazza and entered the palace. Amenophis was summoning him like one of his slaves. Seth, the high priest of Horus, spiritual head of the Empire! And in front of the assembled priesthood too. Through the mouth of a lowly novice!

Seth entered the palace through the richly adorned Porta della Carta, a masterpiece of Gothic architecture. On the far side of the great inner courtyard he climbed a magnificent flight of steps in the shadow of two mighty statues of gods. Mars and Neptune looked coldly down at him. Seth would have them removed as soon as possible and replaced by Horus and Re.

Passing down wide corridors and through several rooms between them, he finally reached the door beyond which several halls had been furnished as the personal residence of the Pharaoh. These apartments were on the top floor of the palace, as befitted the status of a ruler, just below the *piombi* in the loft. Up there, under the leaden roofs, prisoners had once been locked in tiny cells. But today, as Seth knew, the dreaded leaden chambers were empty. He would look at them later and decide whether they might be a good place to detain any troublemakers among the city councillors.

Not all the councillors had been in the plot to hand over the Flowing Queen. Amenophis had had the three ringleaders, including Councillor de Angeliis, publicly executed in the Piazza San Marco on the evening of the conquest. He was grateful to them for their help, but would have no men around him whose word could not be trusted. Since then the other councillors had been held somewhere in the palace, separated from their bodyguards. Most of the Venetian soldiers had been imprisoned too. An attempt would be made later to win them over to the side of the Empire; Amenophis was fascinated by the powerful link between the soldiers and their stone lions. The winged lions in particular, available only to the city councillors' bodyguards, had attracted the Pharaoh's interest.

In Seth's own opinion it would be better to kill all the lions, however difficult such a task might be – even if a few dozen mummy warriors had to be sacrificed in destroying each lion. It was a mistake to leave them alive. Amenophis might see the lions only as beasts to be trained for the Egyptians' own purposes. Seth thought otherwise. The winged lions were not dumb animals to be made to do mankind's will. He could sense the divine spark in them, their intelligence and their ancient knowledge. And he wondered whether the sphinx commanders were not in fact behind the Pharaoh's decision to keep them alive. The sphinxes were half lion themselves, and it seemed likely that they knew more about the stone lions of Venice than they said.

Was there even some relationship between the sphinxes and the stone lions? And if so, what significance did it have in the intrigues of the commanders?

Seth had no time to pursue this thought further. A servant of the Pharaoh had already announced his arrival and now asked him to come in.

The Pharaoh was reclining on a divan covered with jaguar skins. He wore a flowing robe of human hair shot with gold thread. It had taken 100 slave girls almost ten years to make it. Amenophis had several dozen such robes and he would rip up one that had only just been made if the fall of a drape or a detail of the pattern displeased him.

The Pharaoh smiled as Seth approached. Amenophis was receiving him alone, which was more than unusual. Normally the Pharaoh was surrounded at all times by his tall warriors from the Nubian desert, whose crescent swords had dealt efficiently with so many would-be assassins.

It was strange, too, that the Pharaoh wore brighter make-up than usual. But even that could not hide the fact that he had the face of a child not yet thirteen years old. That was the age at which the young Pharaoh had been poisoned and died over 3000 years ago. Once the priests of Horus had brought him back to life, he never aged any more. Amenophis had reigned for over thirty years now and he still looked like a spoilt, snotty child.

Yet that impression did not cover even a fraction of all his bad qualities. Seth had often wondered whether that poison of the past had not been mixed by his own predecessors, priests of Horus who could no longer endure the tempers of the cruel, dwarfish boy.

Secretly, he guessed that Amenophis might be asking himself the same question — which could be one of the reasons why the Pharaoh had recently shaken off the influence of the priesthood more and more aggressively, and was turning to the sphinxes.

'Seth,' said Amenophis, casually waving his right hand by way of greeting.

The high priest bowed low and waited for the Pharaoh to indicate that he should rise again. Amenophis took a particularly long time over it on this occasion, but Seth allowed the insult to pass without showing annoyance. Some day circumstances would change, and then it would be he, Seth, who made the Pharaoh crawl. A very edifying thought which drew a smile of satisfaction from him.

Amenophis asked him to come closer.

'You wanted to see me, Re?' The Pharaoh liked to be addressed by the name of the sun god.

'To be precise, we want *you* to see something, Seth.'

The priest raised an eyebrow. 'What might that be?'

Amenophis stretched on his jaguar-skin divan and smiled. The gold make-up under his left eye had run, but he did not look as if he had any reason to shed tears of grief. So what, as it seemed, had recently made Amenophis laugh until he cried?

Seth was feeling increasingly uneasy.

'Re?' he asked again.

'Go to the window,' said the Pharaoh.

Seth went over to one of the tall windows, where he could look out over the nocturnal Piazza San Marco. Countless torches and braziers were still burning, but the scene illuminated by the flames had changed.

Mummy warriors were herding together the priests of Horus, several dozen men in long robes standing not far from the place where the envoy of Hell had risen through the paving stones a few days earlier. A mighty sphinx was supervising their arrest, which was going ahead in eerie calm. Among the prisoners Seth recognised his closest companions, men with whom he had planned and carried out the resurrection of the Pharaoh. Men who had warned him, and had trusted him when he dismissed their fears. What a fool he had been!

For his priests were now to pay for his folly with their lives, there could be little doubt of that.

Very slowly, and with all the dignity he could muster, Seth turned to the Pharaoh.

Amenophis was no longer alone. Without a sound, two sphinxes had come to stand at his side, moving on velvety soft lion paws. Their torsos were human, their lower bodies those of gigantic beasts of prey. Both held crescent swords that an ordinary man could hardly even have lifted.

'Why, Re?' asked Seth quietly, and with a self-control that surprised himself. 'Why my priests?'

'The priesthood of Horus has served its purpose,' said Amenophis nonchalantly, still smiling. 'We thank you and your followers, Seth. You were very helpful to us, and we will not forget it.'

The Pharaoh liked to speak of himself in the first-person plural, but at the moment it seemed to Seth almost as though Amenophis really did mean several people — himself and his new advisers, the sphinx commander.

'This is treachery!' he managed to say.

'To whom?' Amenophis's eyes widened in pretended surprise. 'Not to the Pharaoh. Nor the gods either.'

'We made you what you are.' Seth no longer used the ceremonial title of Re. 'But for us you'd be just one more body in the old tombs, a mummy in its sarcophagus, hated so much by those who poisoned you that they didn't even place any gold in your tomb as grave goods. And everyone knew it. Why else, do you think, did tomb robbers never try breaking into your vault over thousands of years?' He laughed scornfully. 'They knew what they'd find there.

Only the body of a spoilt child whose demands for games and entertainment even his closest confidants couldn't stand any more. Only the body of a silly boy who –'

One of the sphinxes took a smooth step towards Seth, but Amenophis held him back. 'Seth,' he said calmly, although the priest could see from his eyes how much his words had angered the Pharaoh. 'Be silent. Please.'

'I am telling the truth. And your new . . . *lap-cats* will soon understand that too.'

He had hoped to annoy the sphinxes, but saw that they were not falling for his ploy. One grinned wearily, the other remained impassive. It had been a silly attempt to ruffle their composure, as Seth himself realised.

'We don't want to kill you,' said the Pharaoh. His lips twisted into an unpleasant smile. 'Not *you*.'

'What do you want, then?' Seth looked out of the window again and saw his priests huddled together. The sword of the warriors guarding them glowed in the torchlight.

Amenophis smiled. 'First, their death. And then your attention.'

Seth spun round, and again one of the sphinxes took a menacing step forward. This time Amenophis did not hold him back.

'It's not necessary for them to die,' said Seth. He was seeking for a magic spell, an illusion that would take the Pharaoh by surprise, but he knew it was pointless. The magic of the sphinxes was equal to his own and they would fend off any attack. If not these two, then some of the others who were certainly in hiding behind these walls, watching him.

'Not necessary?' repeated Amenophis in his childish voice. He ran his forefinger over the gold make-up on his face and looked at his fingertip with interest. It was glittering like some exotic beetle. 'We will make you an offer, Seth. You would be well advised not to refuse it. We know very well that we owe this victory to you and your priests alone. It was you who found a way to drive the Flowing Queen from these waters – wherever she may be hiding now. So do not think that we feel no gratitude.'

'No,' said Seth with difficulty. 'I understand that.'

Amenophis put out his gold-stained finger to one of the sphinxes. The creature came closer at once, and stood there expressionless as he allowed the Pharaoh to mark his cheeks with two gold stripes. Warpaint.

'We are ruler of the Empire, we are the One, the Greatest, the Most Powerful,' said Amenophis. 'Is that not so?'

'It is so, Re,' replied the sphinx obediently.

The Pharaoh dismissed him with a gesture, and the creature took up his position by the divan again.

'You mentioned an offer,' said Seth.

'Ah, yes, we knew that would interest you.' Amenophis stroked the jaguar skins with the palm of his hand. 'We want more of these.'

Seth swallowed, at a loss. 'You – you want me to go hunting jaguars for you?'

The childlike Pharaoh burst into shrill laughter. 'Oh, Seth, you fool! No, of course not. We think we will find someone else to bring us a few of these exquisite animals, do we not?' He was still laughing, but now he gradually calmed down. 'It is like this, Seth. In their boundless wisdom our new advisers . . . our friends . . . had a vision.'

Everyone knew that sphinxes could indeed draw on ancient wisdom. Seth would have given his right hand to discover what game they were playing. It infuriated him to be unable to read their minds.

'A vision of our death,' Amenophis continued.

'The priesthood of Horus would never have allowed you to die.'

'Well answered. But we both know that you are lying.

Some day you would have grown tired of us. And who would have taken our place on the throne then? You yourself, Seth? Yes, we are inclined to think that possible.'

Seth had to control himself not to spit on the floor before him. 'So what do you want?'

'It is the opinion of the sphinxes that the power which could endanger us is not of this world. Or at least not of the earth's surface.'

'Hell?'

'Indeed. The sphinxes, looking ahead, predict that something will come from Hell and destroy us. Isn't that delightful?' He laughed again, but it did not sound so supercilious this time. 'And who rules Hell?'

'Lord Light.'

'That outcast! That filth! But yes – Lord Light. He has already tried to stir up the Venetians against us. Our honoured advisers prevented that by giving orders to kill the envoy from Hell. But Lord Light will not rest, we know, and the prophecy of the sphinxes will come true.' His eyes narrowed. 'On the other hand, we will *not* die, Seth. Whatever weapons Lord Light uses against us, he will not defeat us. Because we will pluck out the evil by its root.'

It was Seth's turn to laugh now. He laughed so loud and heartily that Amenophis looked at him as if he doubted the high priest's sanity.

'You intend to kill Lord Light?' exclaimed Seth. His voice sounded too shrill, and he had to take a deep breath. 'Do you seriously mean it?'

'Yes – and no. Because not we but *you* will kill him, Seth.'

'That amounts to suicide!'

'It's up to you.'

Seth shook his head. He didn't know what he had expected, but not this.

His gaze wandered to the two sphinxes. They must know what madness any such plan was. If their sole concern was to get him, Seth, out of the way, why not put an end to this farce with their swords?

He gave himself the answer, and it was deeply disturbing: because they believed what the Pharaoh said. Amenophis had not been lying. Their vision was not an invention. The sphinxes *feared* Lord Light.

Seth recovered his self-control and asked, 'What exactly did the sphinxes see?'

'Nothing,' said one of the two, speaking for the first time, unasked.

Amenophis did not reprove the sphinx.

'Nothing?'

'Our visions do not come to us in the form of images,' said the sphinx very gravely. 'They are feelings. Impressions. Too densely coded to provide concrete details.'

Seth laughed again, a little too shrilly. 'So one of you has a . . . an uneasy feeling, and you plan to kill Lord Light for that? Risking a war with Hell?' He took several paces up and down in agitation, and then stopped again. 'It's total madness!'

The sphinx ignored these last remarks. 'Something will come from Hell and kill the Pharaoh. That's the prophecy. And you will prevent it from coming true.'

The Pharaoh gestured. Behind an opening in the panels on the wall something rustled, someone scurried past. A moment later a brief trumpet signal sounded.

Seth spun round to look out of the window, and saw the mummy warriors advance on the huddled priests with their crescent swords raised.

'Stop that!' Seth's voice was toneless.

Another signal, a second trumpet call. The warriors froze in mid-stride.

All was deathly quiet for some moments. Even down in the piazza all seemed to fall silent.

'I'll do as you ask,' said Seth.

'That we know.' The Pharaoh gave him a gracious smile. 'We never doubted it. Those priests are like your own children to you.'

'A high priest stands by his responsibilities. A Pharaoh should do the same.'

Amenophis made a dismissive gesture. 'Idle talk! You will set off today.'

'Why do you pick me?'

'Because you are truly devoted to us, of course. Why else?' Amenophis looked genuinely surprised. 'Because we can rely on you. No one else would stand by his word in such a situation. But you, Seth, will do so. That we know. And you will settle the matter quickly.'

Seth's hatred threatened to overcome him, but outwardly he remained calm. 'How am I to get from here to Axis Mundi?'

'A friend will take you to Lord Light's city,' said the Pharaoh. 'And to his throne.'

The door swung open and in walked the largest sphinx that Seth had ever seen. He had long hair the colour of bronze, hanging far down his back and tied into a ponytail as thick as a man's arm. The muscles of his torso were no less impressive than those of his lion's legs, and were far more powerful than Seth had ever seen in a human being. And his face was strange. It was covered with pale brown hair, like the remnants of a mane — something unknown among the sphinxes, who were beardless. His eyes had slits for pupils. The eyes of a big cat.

The creature smiled at Seth, baring yellow fangs. As if nonchalantly, he twitched his flanks and unfolded gigantic wings, leathery but covered with a furry down.

This is impossible, thought Seth. Sphinxes have no wings and their eyes and teeth are human.

But this being was something else. Power and cruelty emanated from it like a terrible stench.

'Iskander,' said Amenophis, and — incredibly — bowed to the beast. Turning to Seth, he said softly, 'Your companion.'

WINTER

Vermithrax took off from the rim of the gigantic ear.

Merle immediately lost any sense of direction. Right, left, above, below – it was all the same, a headlong whirl of red light and rock. The stone skull raced past them, they were caught in its slipstream, tumbled, almost somersaulted – and then, briefly, hovered stable in the air.

Only for a few seconds.

Then Vermithrax let out a roar, flung himself to one side, turned a somersault and came up flying level again before Merle could lose her grip and fall.

Her heart was thudding so noisily that it seemed to fill all her senses. There was a great booming inside her head, actually painful now. No room for clear thought.

Then the second stone head was coming up and the world sank into chaos. The obsidian lion roared again, and then a jolt passed through his body, continuing on its way through Merle's like a hammer hitting her bones, her muscles, her joints. She might just as well have been picked up and slammed against a wall, her head striking stone.

When she returned to consciousness she was lying beside Vermithrax behind the outer swelling of a stone earlobe, on a bed of something that she took at first for ashes. Then she saw that it was black down. Bird's feathers, she would have said in the world above. Here they might come from heaven knew what creatures.

With her luck, probably carnivores who had chosen to hibernate in this spot.

There was a remarkably large number of feathers. And they smelled of pitch, like the wind blowing over the deserts of Hell.

'*There's no one here*,' said the Flowing Queen inside her head. '*Not inside the ear.*'

'Are we where . . . where we wanted to go?'

'*Not us – we're where* you *wanted to go.*'

Splitting hairs, thought Merle. 'This is the second skull?'

'Yes,' said Vermithrax, answering instead of the Queen. 'It worked. Just as planned.'

Merle struggled up. Her head was still echoing as if she had been shut up all Christmas Eve right underneath a church bell. She swayed, and Vermithrax moved to support her with his tail. But she shook her head. It was only another moment before she could keep on her feet by herself.

This was something she had decided to do, and she'd go through with it.

'*How heroic.*'

Merle ignored this comment. She had to clamber along the side of the gigantic stone jaw from ear to mouth. And all this perhaps to find a dying man who was already past help.

She was going to try it, all the same.

Vermithrax was breathing heavily. He looked exhausted, his eyes were glazed. Nonetheless, he realised what Merle was planning.

'Rest a moment longer.'

'And then perhaps I'll come to my senses and see reason?' Merle's voice was shaking slightly, but she immediately got a grip on herself again.

The lion put his head on one side and looked at her intently. 'When you've taken something into your head you don't give up easily, do you?'

Merle wasn't sure whether she ought to feel flattered. She sensed the obsidian lion's goodwill. He was trying to give her courage, and to be honest she could do with plenty of that.

'Better now than later,' she said, and began clambering over the barrier formed by the front swelling of the earlobe.

'*Are you sure you really want to do this?*' asked the Queen.

'Not trying to make me change my mind, are you?'

'*It's all your own decision.*'

'You bet it is.' She guessed that the Queen could in fact force her to stay put by taking control of her whole body instead of just her tongue. But she didn't. She respected Merle's intentions even if she didn't approve of them.

Without any words of farewell — for she refused even to think of the word farewell — she clambered on to the outside of the ear. The stone had coarse pores and was full of rifts and crevices. Some might be a natural part of the structure of the stone, others were clearly the result of collisions with . . . well, yes, with what? Flying rocks? Lilim claws? Birds' beaks as hard as steel?

You don't want to know about that. Not really. Don't let anything distract you.

The quickest way to the corner of the stone head's mouth led across its hollow cheek, a deep cavity beneath the prominent cheekbone. She wondered whether the face might be the portrait of a real man. If so, he was either old or undernourished. No one she knew had such hollow cheeks, not even the hungry children in the orphanage.

'*Don't look down*,' said the Flowing Queen.

'I'm trying hard not to.'

Her hands and feet sought support and found it surprisingly quickly. It wasn't really half as difficult as she'd expected. She took the Queen's advice as far as she could and kept her eyes on the stony wall ahead. Sometimes, when she had to look down in order to be sure she was placing her feet on firm projections, she couldn't help seeing a tiny part of the ground racing by infinitely far below. Her heart beat crazily, and her stomach contracted to a knot lying like a stone on her guts.

One of her fingernails broke as she put her right hand into the next crevice. She might perhaps have gone more than half the way, but she couldn't be sure. As long as she stared at nothing but the stone ahead she had no standards of measurement. Suppose she'd gone only a few metres? Much less than she thought?

Go on. Keep going on.

Not much further now.

Very slowly, she turned her head and looked along the

wall of rock. The corner of the mouth wasn't far away now. If she could only manage to haul herself over the stony lower lip she'd be safe for the time being.

Provided the man in the mouth was as well disposed to her as she was to him.

And suppose he wasn't as weak as he looked?

Suppose he attacked her?

She dismissed the thought and concentrated entirely on her hands and feet again.

But however much she tried to suppress it, she couldn't help picturing her present situation: she was clinging to the side of a stone skull fifty metres tall, far above the rocky desert, and the skull was moving forward at such crazy speed that the landscape beneath her eddied and blurred.

And all this for a stranger she knew nothing about. He might be dangerous, he might even be a murderer, perhaps a faithful slave of Lord Light. She was risking her life for him all the same. Not just her life either. Because, if the Queen was to be believed, the fate of Venice depended on her.

She wasn't prepared for that realisation when it hit her, and for a split second she lost her balance. Her left hand slipped; only her right hand was still clutching a stone ledge so narrow that there wasn't even room to stand a flowerpot on it. She panicked and began to kick and struggle. Her feet slipped on the edge of a crevice, and for a moment she was hanging in the air above the abyss.

'*Here we go*,' said the Flowing Queen drily.

Merle tensed her muscles and pulled herself a little way up. Her left hand got a grip on a projecting rock again, she found footholds and made her way on.

'*Not bad.*'

'Thanks very much for your support,' said Merle between her teeth.

Another few metres and she had reached the corner of the mouth.

'*You've nearly done it.*'

'Sounds as if you didn't expect me to.'

'*Do you really think I'd have let you fall?*'

She was indirectly confirming Merle's fears: the Queen could take Merle's body into her power if she wanted to. It was not a pleasant thought, but not worth worrying about just now either.

She managed to catch hold of a notch in the lower lip and pulled herself up by it. Summoning all her strength, she found handholds, and hauled herself over the lip and into the mouth of the stone head.

Gasping, she rolled over the curve of the lip, slipped, fell . . . and came down on a hard surface.

At least there weren't any teeth to impale her. Not even a tongue. Just a hollow space, like a cave. The back of it was in total darkness. No way of seeing what was in there. A tunnel going deeper into the head? Or just a wall at the back of the cavern?

Merle got to her feet and looked along the inside of the lip.

The man had changed position. And not, she thought, by his own efforts. He had slipped, and like herself had fallen to the floor of the mouth cavity. He was lying there among his flowing white hair, as if in a puddle of milk.

But he was breathing. He was even groaning quietly.

On hands and knees, Merle crawled closer to him. Her heartbeat echoed in her ears. She wondered whether to wait a moment, get her breath back, have a rest. Her arms had been under such strain that she could hardly feel them. If the man did attack her she wouldn't be in good shape to defend herself.

What was she doing here anyway?

'Hello?' she said cautiously.

The back of his head was turned to her, and he was lying on his side. His white hair was spread out around him like a star, in long strands that must reach almost to his hips when he was standing upright. His left hand was out of sight under his body, but he had stretched out his right arm. The fingers were long and bony. Merle could clearly see the veins under his pale skin, threads of blue like ink running on a sheet of white paper.

'Hello?'

The fingers of the right hand moved, curled into claws, clenched a fist. Then they relaxed again.

Merle took a deep breath, summoned up all her courage and walked slowly round the man. As she did so, she had to decide whether she would rather turn her back to him or to the darkness in the mouth cavity. She decided on the darkness and kept her eye on the stranger.

She was grateful that the Flowing Queen was keeping quiet. Merle didn't need any cutting remarks to tell her how absurd her behaviour was. How ridiculous.

'Are you hurt?'

As she moved forward she could see more and more of his face. His eyes were open and staring at her. His gaze was following her footsteps.

Merle felt her flesh creep. 'So you're awake,' she commented. 'Why don't you say something?'

His lips were shaking uncontrollably, giving the lie to the clear gaze of his eyes. Or was he just pretending? Waiting for her to bend over him?

Did all the Lilim have claws?

His face and body began to move. The skin rippled slightly, as if something were crawling along underneath it. His brow furrowed and suddenly he looked rather miserable.

A trick?

'He can't hurt you.'

The Flowing Queen's words surprised her. Merle had not expected any reassurances from her.

'Are you sure?'

'He's weakened. Dying of thirst, by the look of it.'

Merle remembered her rucksack and the food she had packed in it at the Tsarist expedition's camp. The bundle was strapped to her back so firmly that she had almost forgotten it. Now she took it off, unscrewed the top of one of the water bottles, sniffed it – who knew when it had last been refilled? – and held it out to the man's face.

'Shall I?'

'*That's what you came here for.*'

Merle nodded in silence and then put her left hand under the man's head, raised it and trickled water over his chapped lips. His white hair felt strange, curiously light in weight, although it was thick and looked abundant. The eyes that were so unsettlingly alert and clear were watching Merle with such intensity that they might have belonged to a different man, as if they were quite separate from the rest of his weakened body. That profound, fierce gaze unnerved her and scared her slightly.

Merle pressed the top of the bottle closer to his lips, withdrew it again, waited until he had swallowed some water, then put the bottle to his mouth once more. She did the same four or five times, letting him drink a little more each time.

Finally he faintly shook his head. He had had enough.

She wiped the mouth of the bottle on her dress and carefully screwed the top on. They might have to make their water supplies last for some time longer. Merle had already finished the first bottle, this was the second – and it was almost empty. They had just the third and last left.

She put the bottle back with the other things in her rucksack.

A sound came from the man's mouth. 'Thank you.' She hadn't seen him utter the words, it was as if he hadn't moved either his tongue or his jaw, but she could hear him distinctly.

'I . . . I thank you.' He was speaking her own language with a very slight accent.

Merle helped him to sit up, leaning his back against the inside of the stone lip. Yet again she noticed how light in weight his hair seemed, almost as if it wasn't there at all. It felt like flower petals.

'What's your name?' she asked him.

'Winter.'

Flower petals — or snowflakes.

'Winter? And what else?'

'Just Winter.'

She looked at him, slightly annoyed, and then grinned. 'And I'm Merle. Just Merle.'

He was enfeebled and his hands were trembling slightly, but Merle had only to look into his eyes to realise that his mind was bright and active. He could see and hear her perfectly well, and he was thinking. Thinking hard.

'What are you doing here?' he asked.

That didn't sound particularly polite, and he must have

noticed Merle frowning. But he didn't apologise. Instead, he repeated his question.

'*We should never have bothered with him,*' said the Flowing Queen drily. For the first time, it crossed Merle's mind that she could be right. But she wasn't about to admit it. The Queen had probably read it in her thoughts anyway.

'We're just passing through,' she said hastily. In the circumstances, it sounded rather silly, but she couldn't think of anything else in a hurry.

Winter smiled. His eyes flashed, but he did not question her statement.

'Like me,' he said.

'Where are you going?'

'There's only one place to go down here.'

Down here, he'd said. That might indicate that he too came from up above. From her own world.

'And where's that?' she asked innocently.

'Axis Mundi.'

'Axis what?'

'*Axis Mundi,*' said the Flowing Queen. '*The axis of the world.*'

'The city of Lord Light,' said Winter. 'I suppose you three are on the way there too.'

So he knew that Merle was not alone. She remembered the way he had looked at her when she was still in the leading skull.

As if to confirm her thoughts, he said, 'That was a brave thing you did just now, you and your lion.'

'He's not *my* lion.'

'No?'

'Just my friend.'

'*Your* friend?'

He was smiling again and this time the corners of his mouth twitched too. 'You humans are strange creatures. Exactly the same word, yet you take offence. My lion, my friend . . . Odd, don't you think?'

'Then aren't you human yourself?'

'I am Winter.'

'*Here it comes*,' whispered the Queen.

But Winter fell silent, offering no further explanation.

'Do you come from the world above?' asked Merle.

'Yes.'

'Why are you here?'

'I'm searching.'

'What for?'

'For someone.'

'How long have you been down here, then?'

'A long time.'

'Longer than a year?'

'I don't know how long a year is.'

'But you said you came from the world above.'

'There are no years for me. Only winter.'

'*He's crazy*,' said the Flowing Queen.

'When you say winter, do you mean the season?'

'*I* am Winter.'

'Yes, I got that bit. Are you saying that you're –'

He leaned forward with such a rapid, sudden movement that she instinctively flinched back slightly, startled. He took no notice, but just leaned even closer to her.

'I am ice. And snow. And frost.'

Merle managed to stop herself smiling. 'You're winter *itself*?'

He nodded, obviously satisfied, and leaned back again.

'Like summer? And autumn?'

He nodded once more.

Wonderful, she thought. Great. Someone like this was exactly what we needed.

'*You see?*' said the Queen.

'I hate it when you say that,' growled Merle.

'*I know.*'

Winter's eyebrows drew together. 'What did you say?'

'I was talking to myself.'

'Do you do that often?'

'Don't go saying it's a sign of . . . well, confusion. I don't think you for one are qualified to talk.'

Winter's face twitched again and he suddenly burst out laughing.

Merle frowned. 'What's so funny?'

'You.'

'Thank you very much.'

'You don't believe me.'

'Anything you say.' She was beginning to lose her fear of him. She hoped that wasn't just an indication of increasing indifference. If she made the mistake of thinking everything was all the same to her she might as well fling herself straight into the depths below.

She guessed that Winter would stick to his claim. A living season. Of course.

Ultimately it made no difference.

'This thing here, this head,' she said. 'Do you know what it is?'

'A herald. It makes the wisdom of Lord Light known

throughout the wide expanses of Hell.'

'Can you understand what it's saying?'

'I never stopped to think about it.'

'You're travelling about in it and you never stopped to wonder whether you could understand it?'

He shrugged his shoulders. 'No.'

Merle noticed something. From far away she had been able to hear the voices of the stone heads distinctly. Then, inside the ear of the first head, they had sounded muted and blurred. And now, right in the mouth of this one, she could scarcely hear more than a distant murmur. Here, of all places, surely the words should have been deafening? So the source of the voice must be somewhere else, probably under the head, in the stump of its neck. The fact that it couldn't be heard more clearly here must mean that there was no connection between the throat and the mouth cavity. She felt that was reassuring.

'Who got you into such a bad way?' she asked.

'I did. And others.'

'*Well, well,*' said the Flowing Queen.

'What sort of others?'

'Lord Light's subjects. I have met many of them. I have travelled far and wide in this land, I have been everywhere

– except to Axis Mundi.' He sighed quietly. 'I should have gone there straight away.'

'Why didn't you?'

'There were . . . indications that the one I am looking for isn't there. But Axis Mundi is the last possibility.'

'Just who are you looking for?'

Winter hesitated, then smiled. 'Summer.'

'*Who else?*'

'Summer?' Merle blinked.

A dreamy look veiled Winter's eyes. 'My beloved Summer.'

Merle could think of absolutely nothing to say in reply. She had saved a raving lunatic from dying of thirst.

'Is this head . . . this herald on its way to Axis Mundi?'

'By the direct route.'

'Are you sure?'

He nodded. 'I know this country, I have travelled here. And I have seen many things. The heralds group together only on the way back to their master.'

So Vermithrax had been right. She was sorry he wasn't here. All alone in the ear of the stone head, he must be feeling anxious about her.

'When will we reach the city?'

'Soon. The heralds are flying faster and faster. Not long now before they fall silent. Then there isn't far to go.'

Well, at least that was something.

Merle searched her rucksack. 'Are you hungry?'

'Winter does not eat.'

'Winter drinks, though,' she said drily. 'Or that was what it looked like.'

'What would Winter be without water? There would be no –'

'No ice, no snow – yes, I get the idea.' She heaved a sigh and began chewing a piece of dried meat; it felt terribly tough between her teeth.

Winter watched her eating for a while and then leaned forward again. 'May I have some more water?'

'Help yourself.'

'Getting to be bosom friends, aren't you?' said the Flowing Queen sarcastically.

Merle handed Winter the opened bottle. They would find water in Axis Mundi, or at least she hoped so. And in an emergency they still had the third bottle.

'Winter?'

He put the bottle down. 'Yes?'

'This Summer. Is he . . .'

'She,' he said with emphasis. 'Summer is female.'

'All right. Summer . . . is she, er, a person like you?'

He smiled. 'You mean does she look human?'

Merle nodded.

'Yes, she does,' he said. 'If she wants to. Just like me.'

'How did you get to know her?'

'There are only the four of us. We might be expected to cross each other's path now and then, don't you think?'

Spring, Summer, Autumn, Winter. It struck Merle that a few days ago she herself had been thinking how long it was since there'd been any real summer and winter, how spring and autumn kept merging imperceptibly with each other.

No wonder, she thought cynically, if the other two are hanging around down here.

'So now you're looking for her? Did she go away?'

'She disappeared. Overnight.'

'You're in love with her.' It was a statement, not a question. Once she had decided to go along with his strange story she found it easier and easier to discuss it seriously with him. It was like an absurd kind of play in which she had come on stage a little late.

'Love?' He let the word drift between them like an ice

crystal. 'There was never a greater love. Never a more wonderful day than the one when Winter first put his arms around Summer.'

'*He* is *a human being after all*,' said the Queen.

'That sounds kind of . . . romantic.'

With a melancholy expression, Winter looked through the open stone jaws and up to the roof of Hell. 'Up there, in the world above, I can't touch anything without turning it to ice.' His hand darted forward like a snake and grasped Merle's leg. She jumped. 'If I touched you like that, you wouldn't even have time to feel afraid. You'd freeze to solid ice on the spot.'

She coolly removed his hand. 'I would?'

'It's my curse. My eternal misery.'

He's acting a part, thought Merle, but he doesn't know how to appeal to his audience. 'What about down here?' she asked politely.

'Nothing happens.' He shook his head as if he could hardly believe it himself. 'No ice, not even a chilly breath. I am nothing here, almost like a human being.'

'Thanks very much.'

'I didn't mean it that way.'

'Of course not.'

Winter heaved a sigh and twisted a strand of white hair in his thin fingers. 'I don't often talk to humans. I only notice I've offended one of you when it's too late.'

'What about Summer?'

His eyes took on that dreamy light again. It brightened and at the same time saddened them. 'Summer is like me. But quite different.'

'People often say that about lovers,' she said with an air of wisdom.

'*You're thinking of Serafin*,' said the Queen, putting her oar in.

'I'm not!'

'*Yes, you are!*'

Winter's eyes narrowed. 'Is *that* the way you talk to yourself?'

Merle shook her head vigorously, in the faint hope that it would make the Queen feel sick – but she knew that was nonsense. 'All right.'

'There's someone else here.' Winter kept his eyes fixed on her. 'Inside you. I can feel it.'

Merle was startled. Could he really feel the Flowing Queen's presence in her thoughts? His gaze was as grave as if he had just accused her of a serious betrayal.

'*He knows*,' whispered the Queen.

Merle instinctively moved away from him. He made no attempt to follow her. Perhaps he was still too weak. Only his eyes remained firmly fixed on her, holding her gaze like pincers.

'There's no one else here,' she said without much conviction. 'Tell me more about Summer.'

He didn't believe her. At last, however, he looked away from her eyes. It felt as if two splinters of ice had been plucked from her forehead.

'Summer can't touch human beings any more than I can.'

'What would happen?' She knew the answer before he gave it, and thought with satisfaction that perhaps she was beginning to see through him a little. His madness followed certain rules.

'Everything that Summer touches must burn,' he said.

Merle nodded. She could imagine the rest of the story. 'So only you two can touch each other without one of you freezing or setting fire to the other, is that right? You cancel out the effects.'

Winter put his head on one side. 'How do you know?'

'I guessed.' She had almost said *I can imagine*.

He sighed again. He was beginning to overdo the suffering expression. 'She was the first creature I could ever touch without fear. And it was the same for her, only the other way round. We are made for each other.'

'*Yes*,' said the Queen, sounding cross, '*that's what they all say.*'

'And you think she's here? In Hell?'

'She was abducted.'

Who'd abduct a creature that sent everyone who touched it up in flames? But Merle wasn't about to argue with him.

Instead, she rose to her feet, clambered up on the stony protuberance of the giant lip and looked over the edge. She had really just wanted to stop him staring at her with his dark, unfathomable eyes again.

She caught her breath.

'Winter?'

She heard a rustling sound as he rose with difficulty and joined her at the edge of the lip.

'Is that it?' she asked tonelessly.

Out of the corner of her eye, she saw him nod.

'Axis Mundi,' he said.

Many kilometres ahead of them, a rock face rose from

the ground to the roof of Hell. It could have been the end of this underground world but for a wide cleft in it. She couldn't see what lay beyond.

But she clearly saw the two gigantic stone statues flanking the cleft. Statues of human beings. Each figure must be at least 500 metres high, probably much more. They stood in front of the cleft, one each side of it, with their faces turned to one another. Both stood in a curiously crooked position, with their torsos leaning forward. Their arms were intertwined as if they were about to fight each other.

'The Eternal Wrestlers,' said Winter quietly.

'That's what they're called?'

He nodded. 'Tales of them are told everywhere. Lord Light had them made. Do you see the way they're standing? It's said that at Lord Light's command they would come to life and go on fighting. Crushing everything in the cleft.'

Only now did Merle realise that the two figures formed a gateway. The city must lie just beyond it, on the other side of the rock face.

'Is that the only way in?'

'The only way known.'

'Then there might be others?'

'None that anyone knows about.'

Merle rolled her eyes, but said nothing. Instead, she looked down on the wilderness lying at the Wrestlers' feet. Dark, teeming lines were moving through the rocky desert like columns of ants on the march. Thousands and thousands of Lilim!

There was much coming and going between the feet of the Wrestlers as endless caravans approached Axis Mundi or came away from the city.

'They all have to pass between the legs of those figures,' she said, shivering.

'That's the point. It makes them feel respect.'

'It'll certainly make *me* feel respect if we fly through there.'

One of the corners of Winter's mouth twisted, perhaps in a thin smile. 'As long as they don't come to life, nothing can happen to us.'

'Have they ever done that? Come to life?'

He shrugged. 'Often, if you believe the legends told in the outer regions. But the closer you come to the city the fewer such stories there are. Apparently no one's ever seen it happen with their own eyes.'

'Well, I suppose that's a good sign.'

'*Or alternatively*,' said the Queen, '*it could mean that everyone who saw it happen is dead*.'

The skulls were racing towards the centre of Hell in silence. The closer they came to them, the more breathtaking the two stone giants were: nothing short of two mountains in human form.

Why human, though? Why hadn't Lord Light made them in the likeness of Lilim?

Or were there Lilim who looked like human beings?

Once again she moved a little way further from Winter, she hoped unobtrusively. He noticed, all the same. She could see in his eyes that he knew what she was thinking. He knew her fears, but he did not defend himself. He said not a word, turned his head and looked back at the Wrestlers.

As he changed position, he and his shadow seemed to move in different directions. Only for a moment. Perhaps it was an illusion.

Merle looked at the gateway to the city of Hell again.

THE AXIS OF THE WORLD

They were not the only ones approaching the cleft in the rock from the air. Now Merle could make out creatures swirling around the mighty stone statues like gnats, a vast number of dark dots. They were too far away for her to see any details.

Merle and Winter took cover behind the stone lip. Merle just hoped that Vermithrax was retreating further into the earlobe too. She was worried about him. He was on his own, with no one to explain what was going on out there.

'He's *all right*,' the Queen reassured her.

The leading skull, which was flying at an oblique angle in front of them, plunged into the shadow of those gigantic legs. From above, Merle could see the huge feet on the ground, mighty ovals of rock with the marching columns of Lilim winding their way around them. She still wasn't close enough to see what the creatures looked like in detail: the teeming mass was packed too close together, her distance from them too great.

The heralds rose in the air until they were hovering above the stone knees of the colossal figures. Merle lost sight of the columns far below her, and instead looked up at the gigantic bodies of the Wrestlers. At close quarters, they might just as well have been bizarre rock formations; their true proportions were revealed only from a distance. The stone thighs between which the heralds flew became grey walls, too large for their part in the whole to be estimated.

The sight took Merle's breath away. The idea that these vast statues were works of artifice, made with blood and sweat and endless patience, was almost beyond her power to imagine.

What had the workers who carved these figures from the rock looked like? Human? Or more like the guards further up in the mouth of the abyss, creatures with body parts like scrapers who had eaten the rock away from around the statues instead of using chisels?

In spite of the speed the heralds were making, it was some time before they left the Wrestlers behind. The cleft in the rock itself was rather deeper than Merle had thought, and ran in a slight curve which made it impossible to see the end of it. The walls of rock passed to the left and right of them, and sometimes Merle saw flying Lilim either coming towards them or following their own route. They all seemed to give the heralds a wide berth, as if they feared the gigantic stone heads.

No one specimen of the Lilim seemed to resemble any other. Many were like the image that human beings had entertained for centuries of the inhabitants of Hell: horned, scaly creatures soaring on curved pinions. Others were like outsize insects, clicking and buzzing in black, horny shell cases. The majority, however, were like nothing that Merle had ever seen before. Most of them had limbs of some kind, and sometimes what might be a face with eyes and jaws and teeth.

'They all look completely different,' she said, fascinated.

Winter smiled. 'After a while you'll see recurrent patterns. They're just not so easy to spot as in human beings or animals. But once you're used to the sight of these creatures you can see them at once.'

At long last the cleft came to an end, and an imposing panorama opened out before them.

Axis Mundi. Lord Light's city, the centre of Hell.

Merle had been given a foretaste of truly large scale when she saw the guardian Lilim in the abyss and then the two Wrestlers flanking the cleft in the rock. But this was sheer madness, a sight that you could take in only if you switched off your reason and just *looked* – merely observed instead of trying to understand. For there was really no understanding this place at all.

The city looked like a sea of turtle shells stacked above and below each other, some tilting, others broken. Domes of rock rose among towers, minarets and pyramids, beneath bridges and paths and gratings. The place was entirely built up, all of it was inhabited. The walls of rock between which Axis Mundi stretched like a coral reef were covered with houses and huts; towers had been taken over by whole tribes of insectoid Lilim; the reefs rearing up among the buildings like bones in an elephants' cemetery teemed with life; and dark, fluttering creatures nested even in the pillars of smoke that were lost from view beneath the roof of the city.

The centre of this hotchpotch of bewildering variety was dominated by a dome broader and taller than any of the others. The heralds were making for it, and Merle guessed that they were approaching the holy of holies, the triumphal temple of Lord Light, the place where the centres of Axis Mundi, Hell, perhaps even the entire world were merged in a single mighty building.

It would be some time yet before they reached it, for it was a long way from the end of the cleft in the rock, and they had to fly above many rooftops, spires and pediments. Merle took her chance to look more closely at the chaos below. Once, a couple of years before, she had seen a beggar in the alleys of Venice whose whole face was covered by a great growth like a cauliflower. Axis Mundi, seen from above, reminded her of that sight, a grotesque structure of tumours intricately twisted and intertwined like converging muscle tissue.

And then there was the smell.

A spice merchant might have been able to distinguish components in this appalling mixture of aromas of every kind. To Merle's nose, the stench was like poison corroding its mucous membrane.

The sight of this city, and her vague idea of the creatures that might live down there, were enough to plunge her into deep despair. What had induced them to come here? Had they thought that Lord Light lived in a golden tower and would welcome them with open arms? How were they ever going to get help for their city and their friends in this place?

So this was Hell. In part at least, the horrors conjured up by Professor Burbridge in his travel writings corresponded to the truth. And she had no doubt at all that there were many worse things here too.

'*Don't let it scare you*,' said the Flowing Queen. '*Our business isn't with what's down there. We're interested in Lord Light, not that scum.*'

But he's one of them, thought Merle.

'*Possibly.*'

He won't help us.

'*He offered his help once, and he will repeat the offer.*'

Merle shook her head silently before noticing that Winter was looking at her curiously again. But after all, she missed no opportunity to observe him in secret herself.

'Is that his palace?' she asked.

Winter's hair had been swirled up like a snowdrift by the head wind. 'I've never been here before. I don't know.'

The stone skulls were still on course for the vast dome, and now Merle noticed that the entire building seemed to be shining from the inside. Unlike the underground lava veins that illuminated the whole landscape of Hell, the dome glowed with a light that had no touch of yellow or red in it, but was both bright and soft.

'*Before you ask, no, I don't know what kind of light that is,*' said the Queen.

Winter's gloomy face had brightened. 'It could be her.'

Merle looked at him, wide-eyed. 'Who? Summer?'

He nodded.

Merle had a suspicion of her own about the light and what it might be. So far she hadn't stopped to wonder why Lord Light was called by that name. Suppose it was more of a description?

'*Sorry to have to disappoint you,*' the Queen said immediately. '*Even in the early records, the lord of Hell was called Lucifer, which in your language means simply Bringer of Light. Lord Light is a name that human beings have given him. Quite a recent one too.*'

Bringer of Light, she thought. Someone who brings light – and maybe imprisons it under a dome?

Winter's behaviour was changing. He wasn't brooding in gloomy silence any more, or confusing Merle with dark allusions. Instead, he was pacing up and down behind the rampart of the great stone lip, constantly glancing excitedly at the dome and gnawing his lower lip like a nervous boy. Merle grinned to herself. And he said he wasn't human?

A few hundred metres in front of the gigantic dome the heralds changed course. Instead of flying straight towards the curve of it as before, they were now approaching an interlocking structure of stone slabs and towers built out from its side. It struck Merle that all the buildings here, including the vast vault of the dome itself, were made of solid stone with no joints or mortar. Everything above ground in the city looked as if it had grown there, and the rock had been worked and stretched just as the glassblowers on the island of Murano worked their clumps of hot glass. As if someone had the power to impose a stranger's will on the rock.

The heralds flew through an opening that reminded Merle of the jaws of a giant fish. By comparison with that gateway, the stone skulls themselves were mere pebbles. Beyond the opening was a great hall with about a dozen other stone heralds on the floor in several rows; they looked like the remains of ancient statues in an archaeologist's storeroom.

The leading head came down in an empty place in the hall, and then their own landed. Its base met the ground with a murderous jolt that knocked Merle and Winter off their feet. The noise was deafening. The shock was so violent that the stone went on quivering for some time.

Merle struggled up, still dizzy and deafened after the impact. She looked down fearfully. She had almost expected to see Lilim hurrying towards the stone skull from all directions, like dockers coming to unload a ship that has just put in to port. But the floor of the hall around the herald remained empty. For the moment.

A mighty shadow appeared in front of the mouth cavity, and then Vermithrax was soaring over them, far too fast and beating his wings so hard that they raised a stormy wind. He managed to slow down just in time to avoid crashing against the stone gums of the mouth. Snorting, he landed and turned smoothly, very much the beast of prey, a warrior from head to paw.

He approached them anxiously, keeping his eye on Winter. Without looking at Merle, he asked her, 'Are you all right?'

'We're all alive and well.'

There was a silent duel of looks between Vermithrax and Winter. Merle was glad she wasn't standing between them for fear that lightning might strike her, so great was the suspicion and tension in the air.

'Vermithrax,' she said reassuringly, 'Winter is on our

side.' Even as she spoke she wasn't so sure of that any more. Perhaps he just felt sorry for them. Or perhaps he didn't care.

'Your name is Winter?' asked Vermithrax.

The white-skinned, white-haired man nodded. 'And yours is Vermithrax.' He spoke the lion's strange name unhesitatingly and without stumbling over it, as if he had known it for a long time. And indeed, he added, 'I've heard of you.'

The obsidian lion looked enquiringly at Merle, but she raised her hands in denial. 'Not from me.'

'Your story is an old one, and well known,' said Winter to the lion. 'Well known all over the world. I have heard it in many places.'

Vermithrax raised an eyebrow. 'Yes?'

Winter nodded. 'The mightiest of the stone lions of Venice. You are a legend, Vermithrax.'

In that case, Merle couldn't help asking herself, why hadn't she herself ever heard the whole story of Vermithrax and his revolt against the Venetians before? Not until the Flowing Queen told her about it.

'You come from the world above?' asked the lion.

Winter nodded again.

Hoping to cut this menacing interrogation short, Merle interrupted them to tell Vermithrax what Winter had told her. His story sounded even more outrageously unlikely when she repeated it. Vermithrax was still hostile, and she could hardly blame him. Perhaps it had been a mistake to mention Winter's unhappy love for Summer, which was straining credibility to its limits – and beyond.

'*Merle*,' said the Flowing Queen suddenly, '*we must get away from here. Fast.*'

Vermithrax was about to take another threatening step towards Winter, but Merle came between them. 'Stop it! Stop it at once, both of you!'

Vermithrax stayed where he was, then took his eyes off Winter at last and looked at Merle. All of a sudden the expression in them was gentler. 'He could be dangerous.'

'The really dangerous beings are the Lilim, and they're approaching from all sides,' said Merle – or rather the Flowing Queen speaking through her mouth.

Are you sure? she thought.

'*Yes. They'll be here any minute.*'

Vermithrax leaped forward and landed on the rim of the stone lower lip. 'You're right.'

Winter too clambered up on the stony protuberance,

nimbly followed by Merle. A gasp of alarm emerged from her throat, and she quickly told herself it must have been the Queen, although she knew better.

Vast numbers of Lilim were approaching the herald, absurd travesties of figures with far too many limbs, sharp-edged horny shells and eyeless heads. Most of them scurried over the ground flat on their fronts, others walked upright, although bent slightly forward by the weight of their shells. Some stalked on long, thin, stilt-like legs, and their arms were held at angles like a daddy-long-leg's limbs. These were the ones that terrified Merle most, for they moved fast and with agility, and she couldn't help thinking of gigantic spiders, even if that simplified and glossed over the impression they gave.

'They haven't seen us yet,' said Winter, retreating behind the rampart.

Vermithrax and Merle followed him.

Pawing on the stone, the lion told Merle to join him. 'Climb on!'

She glanced back at Winter and hesitated. 'What about him? There's room for two on your back.'

Vermithrax seemed far from happy. 'Must we?'

Merle looked at Winter again and then nodded.

'Oh, very well. Come on,' he told Winter.

Merle clambered up on the black obsidian of the lion's back and, after a little hesitation, Winter followed. She felt him getting up behind her and, for a moment, trying to find the best position. He was only just in time to get a firm grip, for Vermithrax unfolded his wings, and with a powerful movement carried them into the air.

They shot through the herald's lips just as one of the Lilim thrust the first angular leg over the rampart.

Vermithrax raced out into the hall. Down below the Lilim turned their heads, some of them slow as tortoises, but others quick, with malice in their eyes. Some uttered shrill, animal sounds, while others articulated words in a strange language. Over her shoulder Merle saw a whole torrent of creatures climbing up the herald's chin and streaming into the mouth cavity. But the long-limbed ones stayed below, staring up at Vermithrax. One uttered a series of high, sharp sounds, and immediately the torrent of Lilim changed direction. They were swarming in all directions like angry ants.

While Vermithrax climbed as high in the air as possible, until they were just under the roof of the hall, Merle clung to his mane. Her fingers felt something in it that didn't belong there. When she removed her right hand she saw that something had been caught in the lion's fur, one of the black feathers from the herald's ear. Only it wasn't a feather at all; it was a tiny black crab with such delicate claws that she had taken them for a bird's down. It wasn't moving and was obviously dead. So she hadn't been lying on the remains of Lilim in the stone ear, but on Lilim themselves. The idea nauseated her so much that for a moment her disgust was even stronger than her fear. She felt she wanted to scratch herself all over. Shuddering, she gave the dead crab-like creature a last glance and then flung it into the depths.

At first Winter had tried to cling to the lion's flanks, but now that his hold wasn't strong enough he put one arm round Merle's waist from behind. She felt as if he shrank from the contact, perhaps for fear she might turn to ice after all.

'*They were expecting us,*' said the Queen.

'But how did they know we were here?' It no longer bothered Merle that Winter was listening in on the conversation.

'*Perhaps they can scent one of you two.*'

'Or you.'

The Queen didn't answer that question. Maybe she was actually considering the possibility.

The obsidian lion flew over the rows of gigantic heads and made for the gate through which they had entered the Hall of the Heralds. It must have been a good 500 metres away. From up here the hall looked even larger.

'Vermithrax!'

Merle started when she heard Winter's cry. Her mysterious companion's long fingers were pointing upwards. 'They're up there!'

The obsidian lion flew faster. 'Yes, I can see them.'

Alarmed, Merle looked the way that Winter was pointing. She had been expecting flying Lilim, winged beasts like those they had seen in the cleft in the rock and above the city. But what she saw now was something else.

The Lilim who had taken up the pursuit were not flying but climbing along under the roof.

She had seen the same creatures before, down on the ground, long-legged, spidery, yet far stranger than anything she knew in the world above.

And they were unimaginably fast.

Vermithrax dropped a little lower so that the long legs of the creatures couldn't reach him from above. But they seemed to be coming from everywhere now, as if they had been lying in wait all the time, invisibly merged with the rocky ceiling. And indeed Merle now saw that several that had really been there the whole time seemed to be appearing out of nothing, coming away from the flat stone surface, stretching their long legs and instantly beginning to scurry rapidly about.

'Look ahead!' she yelled, trying to make herself heard above the noise of the air current and the screeching of the Lilim. 'They're at the gate!'

The entire ceiling above the gate of the hall had come to life. A carpet of dry bodies was twitching and pushing and swaying up there, moving under and over each other like a whole daddy-long-legs army, none of them smaller than a human being, most of them almost twice human size. Many were reaching single limbs down, limbs that quivered and shook as they tried groping through the air for Vermithrax.

The lion kept calm. 'If we fly low enough they won't get us.'

Merle was going to say something, and she felt the Queen begin to speak in her mind too, but then they both thought better of it and left it to Vermithrax to take them to safety.

Winter was the only one who objected. 'It won't work.'

Merle looked over her shoulder. 'What do you mean?'

She saw his eyes widen. His grip on her waist became tighter, almost painful.

'Too late!'

She looked forward again.

The ceiling of the entire hall was in movement now, a seething mass of bodies, eyes and dry, spindly legs.

Ahead of them, one of the Lilim fell to the depths below in a whirling tangle of limbs, too far away to endanger them. Merle's eyes followed its fall, 100, 150 metres down, and she was sure that the creature would be shattered to pieces on impact. It hit the floor, lay rolled up like a ball for a moment – then its legs shot out and it ran frantically to and fro as if nothing had happened, back and forth and in a circle, until finally it came to rest in a crouching position and stared up at them.

'*No,*' whispered the Queen, and Merle realised what Winter had meant by 'too late'.

All around them, Lilim began falling from the ceiling like ripe fruit. A spidery leg with a sharp hook on the end of it brushed Vermithrax's left wing and struck a handful of his black feathers out of it. The obsidian lion staggered briefly in the air but then flew on, faster and faster, towards the mighty gate.

The Lilim dive-bombed. More and more of them took off from the ceiling and plunged down. Vermithrax had to perform daring manoeuvres in flight to evade them. Merle leaned forward until her face was almost touching his mane. She couldn't see what Winter was doing behind her, but she suspected that he had ducked his own head too.

It was as if they had been caught in a weird shower of rain, with the difference that it was raining living beings, gigantic spidery creatures, a single one of which would have been enough to put an army to flight. Here they fell in their dozens, finally in their hundreds.

Vermithrax had no chance.

The body of one of the Lilim crashed down on the lower part of the lion's back, slid off and would have carried Winter down with it into the depths, caught in its swirling limbs, if he had not swiftly moved closer to Merle for cover. So the hook on the creature's leg caught only Winter's long hair and tore out a strand of it. Winter didn't even seem to notice.

Another of the Lilim landed on Vermithrax's right wing, and this time they were almost all of them brought down. At the last moment Vermithrax got control of his massive body again — until the next of the Lilim fell in front of him and its hook raked his nose. Vermithrax roared with pain, shaking his head so violently that Merle nearly fell off, opened his eyes again and saw another creature flailing its legs at him as it fell, a whirling black star made up of horn and teeth and hooked claws as sharp as knives.

The next one fell on Merle.

She was torn from Winter's clasp, slipped to one side and fell into the abyss. Above her, she heard Vermithrax roar, then Winter, then both of them, and even as she fell she thought, quite coolly, that she was about to die and there was no hope of escape. This was it.

She felt something clutching her; she felt limbs like dry twigs pressing against her legs, her upper body, even her face. It was as if she had run into branches hanging low in the dark. Her back was pressed against something soft and cool, a body, hairy and moist as a peach cut open.

The moment of impact was bad. Much worse, however, was her realisation of *what* had saved her.

The Lilim creature had wound itself around her in a protective ball, much as spiders curl up just before they die. It had turned in the air and come down on its back.

Through the latticework of its limbs Merle could make out the roof of the hall, an inferno of falling bodies in which she couldn't see any sign of the obsidian lion. But her vision was blurred and her mind was in no condition to make sense of what she saw.

She had fallen over 100 metres into the depths and she had survived. The shock went deep, though not deep enough to paralyse her entirely. Her mind was clearing with every breath she took, forming the beginning of distinct thoughts out of the confusion in her head.

The first thought to enter her mind was whether she ought to be grateful to be alive. She felt the moist, sticky underside of the Lilim creature against her back, its bristly hairs sticking through her clothes like blunt nails. She saw the hairy limbs above her, all skin and bone, convulsed together, motionless.

'*It's dead,*' said the Flowing Queen.

It took Merle a moment to understand the sense of the words.

'*If it had landed on its feet like the others it would have survived. But it fell on its back to protect you.*'

'To . . . protect me?'

'*Never mind why it did it — you'd better try to get yourself out of its clutches before rigor mortis sets in.'*

Merle pushed at the intertwined limbs with all the strength she had. They creaked and cracked, but she finally managed to shift them. She had to fight against not only her nausea but also the shaking of her arms and legs. Her head might understand that she was still alive, but the rest of her body seemed to be lagging some way behind. Her muscles quivered and twitched under her like fish in a net.

'Hurry up!'

'It's all very well for you to talk.' At least her voice was back to normal. A little shrill, perhaps, a little breathless. But she could speak.

And swear too. At the top of her voice.

'That was quite something,' said the Flowing Queen, impressed, once the torrent of curses that issued from Merle's mouth had died down.

'Years of practice,' gasped Merle, pushing the last Lilim leg aside. She did her best not to look down as she placed both hands on the soft, moist thing behind her and hauled herself up. Somehow she managed to free herself from the corpse's embrace and jump down to the ground, past two branching limbs.

Her feet gave way and she fell. Not from exhaustion this time.

Hundreds of Lilim were standing around her, staring at her, swaying back and forth on their long legs and whetting their hooked claws on the rocky ground. They had encircled their dead comrade and Merle, but they didn't come any closer, as if something held them back. Perhaps the same command that had made the dead Lilim sacrifice itself for her.

The Queen was the first to sum up what she herself was thinking. *'They won't hurt you. Someone has plans for you.'*

For us, Merle wanted to say, but now her voice finally gave out. She looked up, and saw that no more Lilim were plunging to the ground. The ceiling of the great hall was still in motion, but the teeming swarms were gradually calming down and the creatures were merging back into the rock, becoming invisible.

Vermithrax, she thought.

'He's alive.'

Merle looked round the hall, but her vision wouldn't reach further than the second or third ranks of the army of Lilim. 'Are you sure?'

'I can feel him.'

'You're only saying that to make me feel better.'

'*No. Vermithrax is still alive. So is Winter.*'

'Where are they?'

'*Somewhere here in this hall.*'

'In the power of the Lilim?'

'*I'm afraid so.*'

The idea that the Lilim had forced the obsidian lion to land or even crash made her heart miss a beat. But the Queen had said he was alive. Merle wasn't going to quarrel with that. Not here, not now.

The circle of Lilim had closed to within a few metres of them. Although the spidery creatures were in the majority, she saw others among them, flat on the floor, or moving on two legs, or without any limbs at all, a whirling, whimpering, whispering chaos of claws and prickles and points and eyes.

All those eyes.

And movement everywhere. Fermenting movement under shimmering surfaces that gleamed with moisture, like a confused mass of seaweed and flotsam in the surf of the sea.

'*There's someone coming.*'

Before Merle could ask how the Queen knew, the wall

of Lilim parted. Those in front fell silent and some bowed their heads – or what Merle took to be their heads – in reverence.

She had expected to see a commander, some kind of general, perhaps a beast larger than all the others, something far exceeding them in power and cruelty and sheer horror.

Instead, she was looking at a small man in a wheelchair.

The wheelchair was being pushed by something that distantly resembled a knot of gleaming ribbons in constant motion, twisting in and around one another, always moving forward. Only as it came closer did she see that this was not a single creature but a countless number of them: a set of snakes moving like a single organism, clinging together and well controlled. Their heads darted watchfully back and forth, their bodies shimmered in unimaginable colours, lovelier than anything Merle had seen since her flight from Venice.

The man in the wheelchair inspected Merle without any emotion. No smile, no malice either. Just blank, empty features – the interest of a scientist examining a new but not particularly fascinating specimen under a magnifying glass.

The chill in his eyes made Merle shiver. It frightened her more than the army of thousands of different monsters.

Could this be Lord Light? Was the ruler of Hell really this little man with his dead features?

'*No*,' said the Flowing Queen.

Merle would have liked to ask what made her so sure, but the man in the wheelchair gave her no time. His voice was old and creaky, like the cracking of hard, well-worn leather.

'What's to be done? What's to be done?' he murmured, more to himself than anyone else. And then: 'I know. I know.'

Well, he's one cup short of the full teaset, thought Merle.

He signed to the nest of snakes behind his wheelchair and immediately they moved out, turning the chair and pushing it back the way it had come.

'Bring her to me,' said the man, with his back to Merle. 'Bring her to the House of the Heart.'

THE ASSASSINATION ATTEMPT

There were seven of them.

Too many, thought Serafin, as he made his way through the dark. Still too many.

Five boys including himself and Dario. In addition, two slender figures, women. Taller than some of the boys — no, *rebels*, he ironically reminded himself — but shorter than Serafin.

Eft had drawn the scarf over her face again, he wasn't sure why. They'd probably see worse tonight than a mermaid's mouth. But she insisted on keeping up her masquerade, although he didn't think she was ashamed of her origins. She was a mermaid and always would be. The human legs that Eft now had instead of her *kalimar*, her fish-tail, were only an outward detail, but the salt sea, the water of the lagoon, flowed in her veins.

The second woman was Lalapeya. The sphinx had assumed human form, and by now Serafin's sight of her in her lion's body seemed to him almost like a bad dream. Every diminution of her beauty, every blemish, however slight, seemed absurd in view of such perfection. He had to force himself to remember that this was just a part of her magic too. It didn't stop at changing her outward appearance; she manipulated the thoughts of all who looked at her, just as she seemed to manipulate everything that went on around her.

And Serafin asked himself yet again whether they were doing the right thing. Why was he obeying Lalapeya? What was it that enslaved him and the others to her?

Not *all* others. Eft withstood the magic of the sphinx. Serafin even suspected that Eft saw Lalapeya prowling along these tunnels in her true form, a being half human, half lion, moving forward on a big cat's velvety paws. He had already noticed that Lalapeya made less noise than anyone else in the party, even less than he did. It might look as if she were walking on human feet, but that was not the truth.

The sphinx was not human and never would be. So why was she interested in Venice and its people? What made her encourage a set of street children to try to assassinate the Pharaoh? The *Pharaoh*! Serafin still couldn't grasp just what he had let himself in for.

'Eft,' he whispered in the dim light of the underground canals.

She looked at him over the edge of the scarf covering her mouth and nodded just once, very briefly.

'Do you feel it too?' he asked.

She nodded again.

'What is it?' He rubbed his right forearm with his hand. The little hairs were standing on end, and his skin tingled as if he had dug his fingers into an anthill.

'Magic,' said Eft.

'Sphinx spells cast by the Pharaoh's commanders,' said Lalapeya, suddenly appearing at the mermaid's side, as if darkness itself had been made in the shape of a young woman.

Eft cast her a sideways glance, but said nothing.

'Sphinx spells?' asked Serafin. He fervently hoped that the other boys didn't notice his uncertainty. But Dario at least immediately saw it and stopped beside him.

Serafin raised a hand to bring the little troop to a halt. He, Dario and the two women were at its head. So far Tiziano, Boro and little Aristide, chosen for his agility and dexterity, had followed them along these secret canals, known only to Serafin and a handful of other master thieves, without a single objection, question or doubtful glance. The canals ran under the squares and streets of the city, but were just above the water level of the lagoon. Their banks were damp in some places; in others water washed over them ankle-high. On the whole, however, these secret paths were dry. Dry enough for a group of murderers.

Murder, Serafin repeated to himself. That was the word he'd been avoiding as a stone lion avoids water. He was a thief, one of the best, but he was certainly no murderer.

'What do you mean, sphinx spells?' he asked, this time turning directly to Lalapeya.

He knew the others ought not to hear, but his conscience wouldn't let him leave them in ignorance. If they were walking straight into a magical trap, everyone had a right to know. They were doing this of their own free will, not out of a sense of duty. They were doing it for themselves and not this damn city or even its citizens, who had never yet shown any concern for the urchins who begged in the streets.

Yes, they were doing it for themselves. For every one of them.

For me, thought Serafin.

And he saw something else in the boys' faces too: they were doing it for Lalapeya. That worried him almost more than the magical tingling of his skin.

'Sphinx spells are cast by –' began Lalapeya, but Serafin interrupted her.

'By sphinxes. Yes, you said so. But what do they actually do?'

Tiziano and Aristide were staring at him, wide-eyed. They had never heard anyone speak so disrespectfully to Lalapeya before.

However, she didn't seem to mind. She looked at Serafin with a smile, kept her gaze bent on him and continued, 'Such a spell may mean all kinds of things. It can kill anyone who comes under its influence, and in more ways than the human mind can imagine. Or it can be harmless and merely warn those who have uttered it aloud.'

'Then they know we're here now?' asked Dario in alarm.

Even in the dark Serafin could see that Dario was sweating profusely. His own forehead was damp and every few steps he had to wipe his face with his hand to prevent the perspiration from trickling into his eyes.

'Yes, they would know – if I hadn't blocked the spell,'

said the sphinx, and her smile grew a little wider. It made her look stunning.

A murmur of relief passed through the group of boys, but Serafin was wary. 'I can still feel the magic on my skin.'

'That doesn't mean anything. It's just the discharges in the air that occur when two spells meet. Mine and theirs. The tingling you all feel is an after-effect of the spell, not the spell itself.'

They went on, but soon, in a pillared vault full of cobwebs and forgotten statues of saints somewhere under the church of San Gallo, Serafin detained Eft for a moment. She was carrying Arcimboldo's mirror mask in a rucksack of hard leather. Serafin didn't like to come too close to that strange relic, so he put his hand on Eft's forearm, not her shoulder. As she slowed her pace he quickly withdrew his fingers. They were now a little way from the others.

'Do you trust her?' he whispered.

'Yes.' At every breath the scarf over the mermaid's mouth stretched and billowed, even more so when she spoke.

'You're absolutely sure?'

'She is Lalapeya.' As if that were reason enough.

'You knew she was a sphinx, didn't you? From the start.'

'I see her in her true form. She can't deceive me.'

'Why's that?'

'The mermaids and sphinxes have been related since ancient times. Not many people remember it today, but thousands of years ago there were close links. We mermaids have lost our importance and power along with our magic, while the sphinxes – or some of them anyway – have always been able to adapt to new circumstances.'

'Like Lalapeya?'

Eft shook her head decidedly. 'Not her. She's been what she is today for a long time.'

'But –'

She didn't let him finish. 'She is older than most other sphinxes, though it may not look like it to you humans. She knows what the old relationship once was and she honours it.' Eft paused for a moment and then said, 'She gave us a secret place for our dead.'

The mermaids' graveyard, thought Serafin, fascinated. An ancient legend. No one knew where it was. Many had looked for it, but he didn't know anyone who had found it. 'Lalapeya gave you your graveyard?'

Eft nodded. 'Long ago. We are in her debt, although she has never asked for anything in return.'

'What's she doing in Venice?'

'She was here before the city was ever built. The question should be: what is Venice doing in a place that has been under Lalapeya's protection for thousands of years?'

'Thousands of years . . .' Serafin felt the words melting in his mouth. He glanced at the sphinx, the girlish figure of a young woman leading the party beside Dario.

'She never tried to drive human beings away, although it would have been her right to do so,' said Eft. 'Many of us even say her duty. Tonight, Serafin — tonight is the first time that Lalapeya has ever intervened in the destiny of Venice. And she will know exactly why.'

Serafin scrutinised the mermaid and found it difficult to withstand her piercing gaze. 'You know too, don't you?'

Eft's scarf quivered as her shark-like mouth smiled. 'Perhaps.'

'That's not fair.'

'There's knowledge that isn't meant for human beings. But you can believe me when I tell you she knows what she's doing.' Eft's eyes narrowed. 'She made some mistakes in the past. Now she is fulfilling her purpose.'

A thousand questions were burning on Serafin's lips, but Eft was walking faster again in order to reach the head of the party. He hurried too, so as to keep in step with her.

'What is she? Some kind of guardian?'

'Ask her yourself.'

'But guarding what?'

Eft pointed forward. Reluctantly, he followed her glance and saw that Lalapeya was looking back at him over her shoulder. She was smiling, but it was a sad smile. He simply couldn't make her out. For the moment, however, he asked no more questions, even when he was walking beside her again and trying hard not to look at her. He sensed that she herself was glancing at him now and then.

He went to the head of the little party and walked on by himself, a few steps in front of the others. Once again he was concentrating on what he did better than anyone, finding the best way to pass through the city unnoticed, as he had done so many times before.

When they came to a certain point he made them all stop under a round hatch in the ceiling, and told them not to make another sound. With Dario's help, he got the hatch open and climbed out. Above it lay a round stairwell leading up through all the floors of the Doge's Palace. The steps were narrow and had makeshift banisters: a few poles supporting an old handrail. Once criminals had been led up this spiral staircase to have judgement passed on them, but today it was seldom used. The thick layer of dust on the floor and the banisters showed how long it was since it had last been climbed.

Serafin felt fairly sure that the Egyptians didn't know about this stairway. So far. The Pharaoh's bodyguards would certainly study the plans of the palace, but he doubted whether they had had enough time yet. That was another reason why the attack had to take place as early as possible – indeed, tonight.

He untied a rope from his belt, flung it up and fixed it round the lowest post of the banisters with a few quick movements, then helped the others to climb it and reach the stairs. He wondered how Lalapeya would come up – perhaps leaping like a big cat – but she climbed the rope like anyone else, using her hands and feet, if a little more easily than the others. When she did it, it looked almost playful, which earned her the boys' admiration yet again. Getting up to the foot of the stairs was more difficult for Eft, who for all her agility had no practice in rope-climbing.

They hurried silently up the spiral staircase. The Pharaoh's apartments were on the top floor, but Serafin was only too well aware that he mustn't look for the easiest option. They urgently needed an advantage and they wouldn't get that by taking short cuts.

He took the group past the top-floor landing and led them on to the very end of the stairs, where the steps reached a heavy wooden door. The wood was dark with age, and rust had attacked the metal fittings.

As Serafin had expected, the door was easily opened. The heavy handle, as long as his forearm, gave way with a creak and the door swung slowly inwards. Without a word, Serafin directed his companions to go through the opening into the dimly lit space beyond.

He had explained their exact route to the others back at the Enclave – although only as far as this stairway. He had kept the final part of his plan to himself.

However, everyone could guess where they were. Only one place in the Doge's Palace lay above the top floor. Up here, in the much-feared *piombi*, the lead chambers under the rooftops, thousands of prisoners had lost their lives in past centuries, penned up in tiny cells, half frozen in winter, exposed to the heat of the sun-drenched leaden rooftops in summer; they might as well have been locked up in ovens.

Everyone, even the most uneducated of street urchins,

knew the tales of the misery of these prisoners. If this had been Serafin's first visit to the higher reaches of the palace he would probably have been as impressed as the others. But at the beginning of his career as a thief, he and a few friends had made a game of exploring the Doge's Palace under the very noses of the City Guard.

'No one can hear us up here,' he told his companions. 'The ceilings are soundproofed because the prisoners used to scream so much.'

'What are you planning?' asked Tiziano.

Serafin grinned, before the dark look that Eft gave him reminded him that he wasn't winding up the City Guard for fun now. 'We're going to come down in the Pharaoh's rooms from above,' he said. 'I'm fairly sure that's the only way they won't be guarding.'

Dario raised an eyebrow. '*Fairly* sure?'

Serafin nodded.

'And you think no one will hear us breaking through the ceiling?' asked Boro. 'What with, by the way? Our bare hands?'

'No,' said Serafin. 'There's a narrow staircase behind the panelling, leading down from the dungeons to the top floor. The Doges used this secret way when they wanted to watch the torture of prisoners without being seen themselves.'

Torture was not a word to make them feel any better, so no one asked questions. They were depressed enough; their fear went deep.

Serafin led them along dusty passages, so narrow that they had to walk in single file. They often passed cells with their doors standing open. A horrible smell came from them, although it was a long time since anyone had been held prisoner here.

Outside, the air was mild and warm as if it were spring, yet it was difficult to breathe up here under the lead roofing. The air stagnating in the *piombi* felt like hot water in their lungs. Only Lalapeya, whose people came from the great deserts, was unaffected. She and Eft whispered to each other once or twice, but Serafin could not make out what they were saying.

Finally they reached an empty room that had once been a torture chamber. Serafin stopped in front of a narrow iron door with a grating let into it. It was barred on the other side, but it took him only a few minutes to unbolt it with the point of his dagger. Beyond the door, narrow steps led steeply down, obviously inside a wall.

'This staircase ends behind the panelling of a hall on the upper floor,' he whispered. 'Not another word from now on! And get ready for the big firework display.'

'Serafin?' Tiziano held him back by the arm as he was about to move forward.

'What?'

'If we make it . . . I mean, if we survive this business . . . how are we going to get out of here again?'

Serafin took a deep breath, not because of the stale air but because he had feared someone would ask him this very question. At the same time he was glad to get it over and done with. He cast a quick glance at Lalapeya, but she only nodded encouragingly and left him to do the talking. And no doubt to take the responsibility.

Serafin sighed. 'You all know that it won't be over when the Pharaoh is dead. His guards will attack us, and only too probably the place will be teeming with mummy warriors within seconds. Not to mention the priests of Horus and,' he added with another glance at Lalapeya, 'the sphinx commanders.'

Boro gave a hoarse laugh. It was supposed to sound tough, but they all saw through him. 'Then we're as good as dead.'

Serafin shrugged. 'Maybe. Or maybe not. Our speed will count for something. If we get a chance to retreat we'll do it the way we came. Up this staircase, through the lead chambers, back down the spiral staircase to the secret passages.'

'Then what?'

'Then we run for it.'

'No,' said Eft. 'That won't be necessary. We shall get help down there. You remember the old moorings below the Calle dei Fuséri? The basin of water we've just passed?' The boys nodded. 'There'll be help waiting for us. We can make our escape from there too.'

Dario let out air through his teeth with a whistle. 'Mermaids?'

Eft did not answer, but everyone knew he was right.

On the steps, they drew their weapons. Each of them had a revolver with six shots in it and a bag of spare ammunition. Serafin, Dario, Boro and Tiziano were also carrying swords. Eft had only a small knife, no longer than her thumb, but it was sharper than any blade that Serafin had ever seen.

Lalapeya, finally, was unarmed. Serafin felt sure she had other means of defending herself. She was a sphinx, a creature made of pure magic. It was she who had brought them all together. And it was she – so he hoped – who held the key to the Pharaoh's downfall.

At the foot of the secret staircase they came to a second door, taller this time, the back of a panel on the wall. There was no bolt or lock. It was secured by a secret mechanism on the outside.

Lalapeya stepped back and moved behind the row of boys. That was what they had agreed. She needed time to turn her magic against the Pharaoh. Time that the others were to give her.

Serafin and Dario exchanged a glance, nodded to each other and then kicked the wood with their combined strength. With a dull splintering sound, the panel broke out of the wall and crashed flat to the floor on the other side. Dust rose and for a moment the thunder of the impact echoed in Serafin's ears.

Immediately mummy warriors faced them, as if they had just been waiting for the intruders. The mummies were posted to the left and right of a closed portal leading to another hall. The two wings of the door were inlaid with gold leaf and shone in the light of several gas lamps. Golden tendrils seemed to be moving over the wood like snakes in a confusing interplay of reflections.

Tiziano was the first to fire at one of the mummy warriors. He hit the creature in the shoulder, but only a second shot in the forehead stopped the warrior in his tracks.

The boys were all firing their guns now. Boro swerved to avoid the stroke of a crescent sword. Its blade glanced off his skull, tearing a piece of skin from his head. Blood instantly ran down his face, but he still managed to spin round, take aim and fire. The bullet missed and struck the gilded portal with a loud bang. Dario was beside him at once, raising his arm, and struck the mummified skull off the warrior's shoulders.

Serafin raced to the next door. They had crossed the first hurdle.

Eft was beside him again, moving like the wind. He was about to push the portal open when he heard a roar. It echoed through the main entrance to the hall, which led out into a broad corridor. Reinforcements were on their way. Priests of Horus, if their luck was out. Or much worse, sphinx commanders.

Serafin waited no longer, but rammed the right-hand side of the portal inwards and leaped through it with his revolver drawn. He wasn't used to guns, but he hoped his natural talent — or his luck — would enable him to hit the Pharaoh and his vizier.

There was a divan covered with jaguar skins in the middle of the second hall. Serafin could see only the ends of the divan; the middle was hidden by four sphinxes glaring at him. They bore mighty crescent swords much larger than those carried by the mummy warriors. Their lion bodies did not move but stood there still as statues, except that one of them was whisking a few flies away with his tail.

He's shooing flies, thought Serafin, shocked, while we're fighting for our lives out here. He doesn't take us seriously. We're only a bunch of blowflies.

At that moment, Serafin lost all hope.

It happened very suddenly and without any warning. It had nothing to do with the danger represented by the sphinxes, or the fact that they had obviously been expecting the rebels — *yes, there was treachery afoot!* — but simply with that single flick of the lion's tail, that one tiny, apparently insignificant movement.

There was a scream behind him, and out of the corner of his eye Serafin saw a dozen more mummy warriors making their way through the broken door. Boro and Tiziano faced them, splitting the skulls of the leading warriors with mighty sword strokes. Grey dust billowed up and settled like a veil of mist over the fighting figures.

A strange sense of timelessness, of unendurable slowness, came over Serafin. He felt as if the battle had shifted to somewhere underwater. All movements seemed to him slower, more difficult, and for a split second he felt sudden elation.

Lalapeya's magic! It was finally coming to their aid!

Next moment he could hardly have felt more keenly disappointed. It was not a spell. It was not a magic trick. It was just himself and his senses slowing down as, for a few instants, his mind went into a state of deep shock. Shock and brutal realisation.

They were fighting a losing battle. Dario struck down mummy warrior after mummy warrior, but he had no chance against such numbers. Sooner or later he would fall to his opponents' onslaught.

Serafin parried the attack of a mummy warrior who suddenly appeared behind him. None of this felt like reality any more. It all seemed unreal, artificial, somehow false, even his own fighting. He seemed to be watching their defeat from the outside, and so, at last, he understood the mistake they had made – he himself, and Eft, and the others too.

They had been betrayed.

And Lalapeya was nowhere to be seen.

Serafin uttered a cry that made even the mummy warrior pause. At the same time he broke through the warrior's defence, shattering first the crescent sword and then the grey death's-head of the skull. Eft brought down another warrior, and now the four sphinxes began moving, came closer. Through the gaps between them, Serafin saw that the jaguar divan was empty. There was no sign of the vizier either.

'Lalapeya!' he yelled furiously, but no one replied.

Dario cast him a glance that seemed to Serafin strangely empty, as if an invisible hand had extinguished every dream, every spark of hope in the boy's eyes.

Eft took Serafin's arm and drew him back into the first hall. Tiziano stood there; he had drawn his revolver and was firing furiously and at random around him, until Dario struck the weapon from his hand with his own fist, for fear the bullets might hit one of them.

No sign of Lalapeya. Anywhere.

More mummy warriors streamed through the main door of the hall, barring their way of escape. Serafin cast a hunted glance around. His eye fell on Boro, who snatched a small bottle from his belt and emptied it in a single draught. His cheeks remained distended; he did not swallow the contents of the bottle. Then he took a matchbox from his pocket, kindled a flame in the hollow of his hand and spat out the liquid over his palm and towards the mummy warriors. His hand turned first red, then black, but he ignored it; he ignored Dario and Aristide too as they just managed to leap back to safety, before the fire licked past above their heads and into the ranks of the advancing mummy warriors.

'Get out of here!' shouted Eft as a wall of flame shot up behind her.

A chaos of staggering, blazing bodies spread the fire until the front part of the hall had become a hissing, blazing inferno.

'Back!' shouted Serafin too, but Boro did not obey. He was still breathing fire towards their adversaries. He stopped only when the flames had almost reached him. Then, with a quick glance, he sized up the situation, saw his friends, saw the door through which they could escape to safety and at last he began to move.

Too late. One of the sphinxes who were striding through the portal, keeping well away from the fire on the other side of the room, reached Boro just as he was turning to the secret door. A crescent sword the size of a small tree came down on him.

Serafin cried out and tried to rush back into the hall as it filled up with enemies again. But he was carried along by the others; together, they raced up the narrow stairs, followed by Tiziano and Aristide. At the top, Serafin looked back and saw the sphinxes standing on the small landing at the bottom, uttering furious roars; the stairway was too low and narrow for them, and their lion bodies would never get through the door. If they had tried all the same, it would have been easy to cut them down from the top steps.

But none of the fugitives thought of doing that. Even Serafin, who had experienced more breakneck escapes than all the others put together, felt nothing but panic and icy horror. He saw himself as if he were a stranger, racing through the chambers under the leads, out into the round stairwell and down the stairs. If anyone had been waiting for them here they'd have been easily picked off: only Dario still carried his sword. Tiziano continued to clutch his revolver, without noticing that it had fallen open and shed all its cartridges. Aristide, finally, was unarmed and held the palms of both hands to his ears as he ran, as if to block off the outside world.

One after another they leaped down through the hatch to the depths below. No one stopped to close the opening; the Egyptians would discover their way of escape anyway.

'To the moorings,' cried Eft breathlessly.

No one asked about Lalapeya. She wasn't with them and they all guessed why. Now that they were running after each other through the darkness, splashing through puddles, trying not to hit their heads on the low ceilings and supports of the tunnels, it occurred to Serafin for the first time that he could have prevented all this. Everything that had happened. It had been in his power to do it. If he had obeyed his instinct and refused the sphinx's request; if he hadn't let himself in for this suicide mission against his better judgement; if he hadn't believed Eft when she said that Lalapeya could be trusted – if he had done as his own feelings told him to do in all this, just once, Boro would still be alive.

It had felt wrong. Serafin had known, deep in his heart he had known, that this was not a game, not one of his thieving exploits. He had been flattered when the sphinx chose him to get them into the palace. And he had fallen for it, for every one of her lies.

He glanced up and looked into Eft's dark eyes. The mermaid was gazing at him, as inscrutable as ever. She took the scarf from her face, baring her shark-like jaws. 'Wait before you condemn her,' she said. Without a scarf or her mask, her voice had more of a hiss to it.

'Not condemn her?' he repeated incredulously. 'You can't be serious!'

But Eft did not reply, just turned and ran after the others, who were now ahead of them.

Serafin speeded up until he was level with the mermaid again. What did she mean by that? How could she ask him not to condemn Lalapeya for her treachery, for the fact that Boro lay dead on the top floor of the Doge's Palace and they themselves probably wouldn't survive the next few hours? Was he *not to condemn her* for all that?

If he had had the breath and strength left for it, he would have laughed out loud. And he felt like shouting at someone, maybe Eft or one of the others, to vent his helpless rage and hurt on someone, anyone, as he had been hurt himself.

'Don't,' said Eft as she bent to pass under a low arch. 'It doesn't help.'

It was a moment before he realised that the same thoughts must have gone through her head too, the same hatred, the same disappointment.

They had all been betrayed. Lalapeya had led them to the slaughter.

With the last of their strength, they reached the underground moorings. A broad canal ran parallel to the path for some way. There was a boat tied up there, rocking on the waves, now and then striking the masonry with a hollow sound. It was curiously shaped, larger and rounder than an ordinary rowing boat, and not to be compared with the long and slender gondolas.

'A turtle,' said Eft. 'Or rather its shell. All that was left of its body after it had been lying on the seabed for some time.'

The turtle shell was drifting on its back. It was several metres in diameter, and hollow, like a gigantic soup spoon.

Eft beckoned them frantically. 'Quick, get in!'

Dario hesitated. 'Into a turtle?'

'Yes, damn it!' Eft's eyes sparkled with rage. 'We don't have any time left!'

In turn, they clambered into the shell, among seaweed and the encrusted remains of earlier sea creatures that had sheltered there, trying to touch them as little as possible.

Eft was the last to climb into the floating shell and sit down in it with them. Serafin felt the knobbly surface of the inside of the shell through his thin trousers, but it didn't bother him. He felt burnt out; everything within him had turned to ice.

Suddenly heads rose from the water around their boat, only up to the eyes at first – large, beautiful eyes. Then the mermaids showed the rest of their faces. In the dark, their teeth shone like splinters of moonlight drifting on the water.

There were eight of them, enough to tow the heavy turtle shell through the labyrinth of canals and into open water. Aristide was talking to himself and couldn't take his eyes off the mermaid closest to him in the water, although there was little of her to be seen in the darkness but her hair fanning out and moving slowly forward. Borne along by her and the other mermaids, the shell began to move too, an unusual but effective raft which took the survivors gliding through the dark. A faint smell of dead fish and seaweed hung in the air.

Serafin looked round for Eft. The mermaid had turned away and was leaning her forearms on the edge of the shell, staring expressionlessly at the dark water. You could see how she longed to be gliding through the cold current like her sisters, with a fish-tail instead of legs.

The mermaids pushed and pulled them round a number of curves and bends, through low-ceilinged tunnels and open waterways that passed blank facades, through secret gardens, and once or twice even along waterways inside abandoned buildings. Serafin soon lost all sense of direction. Not that he wasted much time thinking about that.

He could think only of Lalapeya and what she had done to them. He didn't understand her reasons. Why incite a rebellion only to extinguish it so pointlessly?

Wait, Eft had said, *wait before you condemn her.*

He would have liked to ask what she meant by that, but this was not the time. None of them felt like talking. Perhaps it would have been better to talk; it might have freed them from some of the burden of their grief. But they didn't think of that just now. They were all brooding in silence, with the exception of Aristide, who went on murmuring disconnected remarks quietly and staring, wide-eyed, into the void.

It was one thing to hear about mummy warriors and sphinxes, and what crescent swords will do to a human being — something else entirely to see a friend die, knowing that he was giving his life for yours.

Serafin wasn't sure whether they would defend themselves if they were attacked now. It wasn't like the stories in which heroes give battle time after time, always boldly escaping with a merry quip on their lips.

It was not like that at all.

They had staked everything, and they'd lost. Boro was dead. It would take time for the survivors to recover. Grief was seeping like perspiration even from Eft, the brave, determined, austere Eft.

From the outline of several rooftops, Serafin saw that they were crossing the Cannaregio quarter, going north. If the mermaids intended to get them right out of Venice that was the best way — the mainland lay somewhere to the north. But he was under no illusions: the Egyptians would track them down in open water. Even if the besieging ring was gone now — for, after all, they had captured the city —

there must be enough Egyptian patrols out there to find them very quickly.

However, he raised no objections. He was exhausted, and more than grateful to put his life in other people's hands. Maybe they'd show more responsibility than he had.

Soon he could make out the mouth of a tunnel leading into the open sea. A velvety night sky still hung above the lagoon, but the stars were bright enough to sprinkle pale light over the surface of the water, conveying an overwhelming sense of space. A fresh night wind blew towards them over the sea and made its way into the labyrinth of the tunnel. Breathing was easier now.

The turtle shell slowly moved towards the mouth of the tunnel. Ahead of them, a few hundred metres away, the island of San Michele, Venice's cemetery, rose above the dark expanses of water. The ochre walls around the island looked grey and dirty in the icy starlight, as if they had been built of the bones of those who lay buried there. It had been a place for the burial of the dead since time immemorial; thousands and thousands of names were carved on its tombstones and urns.

A Gatherer was hovering silently in the blackness above the island.

Dario swore hoarsely. He was the only one of them in any condition to utter a sound at all. Even Aristide's conversations with himself had died away.

The Gatherer was a dark triangular shape standing out against the diadem of the constellations. Colossal and menacing, the mighty pyramid hung a few dozen metres above the island. By day, there would certainly have been Barques of the Sun swarming around it, but it was dark now, and the barques could not take to the air without light.

The mermaids were taking the turtle shell eastward, going considerably faster now than in the maze of tunnels and canals. The headwind blew in the faces of the five passengers. Eft took the pins from her long hair and shook it out. It fluttered wildly behind her like a black flag; she looked like a pirate queen on a raiding expedition.

But although they all had to brace themselves, they couldn't take their eyes off the Gatherer above the island cemetery. They guessed its intentions.

'Can they really do that?' murmured Tiziano, badly shaken.

'Yes,' said Dario, sounding numb. 'They can indeed.'

Aristide began babbling quietly again, nonsense that

was the last straw for Serafin and his strained nerves. But he was too tired to snap at the boy. Even the sight of the Gatherer could not rouse him from his lethargy. Just now they had failed to save the living, why should he care about the dead?

'My parents are buried over there,' said Dario tonelessly.

'And mine,' whispered Tiziano.

Aristide groaned, or perhaps there were words in his groan too.

Eft glanced at Serafin, but he ignored her. Don't think about it. Don't look. I don't want to know anything about it.

A shining network of lines and hooks appeared on the underside of the Gatherer, blazing out suddenly in the darkness and then settling into place, a storm of lightning flashes all appearing at once and maintaining the same intensity.

'Here it goes,' said Tiziano.

The first hooks of light came away from the blackness and moved silently down, disappearing behind the wall of the island cemetery. None of the four boys had ever seen a Gatherer at work, but they had heard the stories. They knew what was going to happen.

More and more lines of light moved away from the underside of the Gatherer and dropped down, forming a jagged and angular grating between the flying pyramid and the island of San Michele.

Serafin couldn't bear the horror on his companions' faces any longer. He turned away. His own father had disappeared before his birth, his mother had died in a ferry accident twelve years ago; her body had never been recovered. But he sensed his friends' grief and horror, and it hurt almost as much as if he had friends or relations buried on San Michele himself.

His eyes wandered to the Venetian bank. The coastline of the Cannaregio quarter was moving past them faster and faster as the eight mermaids towed the turtle shell still more powerfully through the dark waves. Now and then one of them came up beside the shell, but most of the time they stayed underwater, invisible in the blackness.

Serafin saw mummy warriors patrolling the walls on the banks and the quays, but they took no notice of either the Gatherer in the sky above the island cemetery or the turtle-shell boat.

And there was something else.

The sky above the rooftops brightened, a narrow rim of

light dancing over the roofs and gables like St Elmo's fire. It was still too early for sunrise and the place where it appeared in the sky wasn't right either. The sky was as black as ever in the east.

Fire, thought Serafin. The fire in the mirror-making workshop could have set the whole quarter ablaze. He did not let the thought come close enough to him to feel really afraid, but all the same he looked at Eft, to be sure that she too had noticed the strange glow.

Glancing over her shoulder, he saw that the Gatherer's network of light was now spun around the whole island. Clouds of dust and soil were rising behind the walls.

Eft wasn't looking at San Michele any more either, but back at the city, and her eyes shone as if someone had lit candles in their sockets. It was only the reflection of a new, blazing brightness.

Serafin spun round. The St Elmo's fire above the rooftops of Cannaregio had spread, becoming a raging inferno.

And yet – those weren't flames. It was not a conflagration. Serafin had never seen anything so beautiful. The angels themselves might have been descending to the lagoon.

Then he saw something else as well.

The mummy warriors were no longer patrolling the walls of the bank. Some were lying motionless on the ground, others drifting in the water. Someone had put them out of action in a split second, fast as a deadly gust of wind sweeping over the bank.

Only a single figure now stood on the path there, not far from the mouth of a canal: its outline was that of a mighty lion with the upper body of a young woman. She had both arms raised to the sky and her head was thrown back. Her long hair drifted in the wind like smoke.

'It's her,' said Eft.

No one but Serafin heard her. The other boys were still staring, spellbound, at the Gatherer and the island.

Serafin felt all the hatred and rage inside him suddenly erupting. He saw Boro before him, standing in the middle of the sea of flames just before the sphinx reached him. And here was Lalapeya, who had caused all this, working some kind of magic to stop the fugitives.

'Serafin!' cried Eft.

But it was too late. He had thrust the sword into his belt, and before anyone could stop him he dived into the waves head first. The water closed over him, sealing his eyes and ears with dull silence and darkness. He didn't give the mermaids in the water all around him more than a brief thought, he didn't think of the Gatherer either, or San Michele, or any of his friends.

He thought of nothing but Lalapeya.

Coming up, he took a deep breath and set off at as fast a crawl as he could manage – remarkably fast in view of his exhaustion, which now fell away from him like a bundle of rags. With blurred vision, he saw the bank coming closer. Only a few metres to go now. He had the feeling that he wasn't alone, that there were bodies to his right and left, even under him. But if the mermaids were really following him they made no attempt to stop him.

His hand met cold stone, slippery with seaweed and slime. The wall on the bank was almost two metres high; he would never be able to climb up it without help. Still full of fury, he looked around, found the body of a mummy warrior drifting in the water beside him and then saw a landing stage a little way to his left. He swam over to it with a few strokes and climbed into one of the rowing boats tied up there. Behind him there was a strong eddy in the water as a mermaid below the surface darted sideways and returned to the turtle shell.

In the boat, Serafin looked around him. He had been

carried to one side in the water and was a good 200 metres away from Lalapeya. The sphinx had now clasped both hands high above her head, and the light creeping down from the rooftops and along the facades of buildings was concentrated on them like a living thing, a glowing, sparkling tapestry of brightness, wavering like a mist illuminated from within. A bright halo surrounded Lalapeya's hands, spread along her arms to her body and finally enveloped her entirely.

Serafin didn't wait to see what might come of all this. He couldn't let the sphinx harm the others with her magic. She had caused enough grief already. And this was probably his last chance to pay her back.

He drew his sword, jumped out of the boat on to the landing stage and ran over to the bank. His steps sounded hollow as he crossed the wood, but Lalapeya didn't notice him. She looked as if she were in a trance, concentrating entirely on the annihilating blow. In the unearthly light, she was like a vision of the Madonna with the lower body of a monster, a blasphemous caricature drawn by some medieval miniaturist, overwhelmingly beautiful and terrible at the same time.

Only once, very briefly, did Serafin look across the

water at the turtle shell. Eft had leaped to her feet and was standing erect in the shell as it rocked violently. She shouted something towards the bank, perhaps trying to attract Lalapeya's attention. But the sphinx took no notice of her.

The other boys had seen what was happening, and their eyes swivelled between the nightmare spectacle on the island cemetery and what was going on here on the bank. Dario waved his sword at Serafin, perhaps encouraging him, why else?

Thirty metres to go to the sphinx. Twenty.

The glow intensified.

Serafin had almost reached her when Lalapeya abruptly turned her head and looked at him. Looked at him with her dark brown, beautiful eyes.

Serafin did not slow down. He merely let his sword drop – against his will? – and then took off, arms outstretched, and ran towards Lalapeya.

Her youthful face twisted. She opened her eyes wide. The unearthly glow was blazing even in her pupils.

Serafin broke through the circle of light, got hold of her upper body and lifted her off her lion's legs. In a confusion of arms, legs and lion's claws they fell to the ground, tumbled over, suddenly fell into a void and splashed into the water. A claw as sharp as a knife brushed past Serafin's cheek, another tore his clothing and perhaps the skin under it – yes, he was bleeding, there was blood in the water – and then he saw Lalapeya's face, heard her utter a shrill scream, now just a young woman with long strands of wet hair, not a supernatural apparition any more, and the light had been extinguished too.

He saw her flailing her arms about and fought the urge simply to force her down underwater until it was all over, to pay her back for what she had done, her betrayal, the death of Boro, the way she had made use of him.

But he didn't. Instead, he suddenly realised that she couldn't swim and would drown if he did not help her. It was tempting to leave her to her own devices, but suddenly he found himself unable to summon up the hatred in his heart that had driven him out of the turtle shell and to the bank just now. His anger was gone as if it had evaporated, leaving nothing but emptiness behind.

'Serafin!' she cried, her voice distorted by the water lapping over her lips. 'Help . . . me . . .'

He couldn't see her lion body below the surface any more and was afraid her claws would tear him to pieces if he came too close to her. But he felt indifferent even to that now. He pushed off, glided over to her and took hold of her from behind. He felt her struggling underwater and kicking against him, with human legs now. She couldn't swim in either human or sphinx form, but the heavy lion's body would have dragged her down faster than her slight girl's figure. He put an arm around her breast from behind and tried to keep them both above water somehow, but guessed that he couldn't manage it for long. In her panic she resisted and threatened to drag him down too.

Hands took hold of them both from below and pulled them out of the water and towards the turtle shell, drifting there in the darkness like half a skull. The mermaids did not show themselves, staying under the surface, but there must have been at least two of them, perhaps more. Serafin floated on his back with Lalapeya pressed in front of him, still with his arm round her. She had stopped struggling and wasn't moving at all now, and for a moment he thought she was dead, drowned in his embrace — and wasn't that what he had wanted when he made for her like a berserker? Hadn't he intended her to die and so pay for a part of her blood guilt?

Now such thoughts seemed to him absurd and he

breathed a sign of relief when she moved and tried in vain to turn her head.

'Why did you . . . do that?' Her voice was pitiful; it sounded as if she was crying. 'Why did you . . . stop me?'

Why?

A dozen answers shot through his mind. But with them, at the same time, suddenly came the presentiment that it was *he* who had betrayed not other people but himself.

While the mermaids dragged them towards the shell of the sea turtle, he finally saw what Lalapeya had already seen before him. And he realised that her spell had never been cast against them, against Eft and the boys, but against the Gatherer.

The network of frozen lightning flashes that linked the underside of the Gatherer with San Michele was now a twitching tangle of straight and crooked rays, hooks, curves, zigzags and loops. But they had not been intended for the dead Venetians buried in their thousands upon thousands in the island cemetery.

They had sought and found something different. Something very different indeed.

The mermaids raised Serafin and Lalapeya from the

water, and Eft, Dario and Tiziano hauled them into the boat. The turtle shell tipped over and would probably have capsized if the mermaids had not steadied it in the water. Only Aristide still crouched in his place, staring at the island cemetery, talking to himself, his fingers curled like claws as if he wanted to scratch his own eyes out.

The others pressed close together in the middle of the turtle shell, and while the mermaids silently resumed their work of towing the shell further east, away from the bank and towards the open sea, the six passengers looked at the island.

Great cracks had appeared in the walls around San Michele. In many places large chunks of masonry swayed and collapsed, followed by uprooted cypress trees that tipped to one side like black spearheads and plunged into the water. The entire island seemed to be breaking up. Rifts opened and sea water flowed into its interior, washing away tombs and chapels, bringing down the bell tower of the church.

Something that had been lying under the island, beneath the tombs and crypts and the little monastery, was hauled into the open air by the hooks of light falling from the Gatherer, and came up in a series of explosions of dust and eddies of disturbed earth. Something almost half the size of the island itself.

The body of a sphinx.

A sphinx larger than any living creature that Serafin had ever heard of. Larger than the whales, larger than the sea-witches in the depths of the Adriatic, larger even than the legendary giant krakens deep in the ocean trenches.

Half lion, half man, although both looked distorted, the arms and legs too long, the face too small, the eyes too far apart. Hands the size of warships with too many fingers, and those fingers too long as well, and lion's paws with claws of yellow horn and bone. The misshapen image of a sphinx, yet absurdly attractive, terribly distorted, almost a caricature, yet grotesquely elegant.

The gigantic corpse lay on its side, face turned to the city, and hovered towards the underside of the Gatherer, carried by hundreds of hooks of light. It *was* a corpse, although it showed no sign of decay; there was no doubt that it was dead, and had perhaps been dead for thousands of years.

What is Lalapeya guarding? Serafin had asked Eft only a few hours ago.

What is she guarding?

Now at last he saw it before him and realised that her attack on the palace, the attempt to assassinate the Pharaoh, had been only a diversionary manoeuvre. Something to give Lalapeya time to destroy the Gatherer and protect the tomb whose occupant she guarded.

Eft glanced across at Serafin and placed her hand on his, but he would not let her comfort him.

Boro had died for a dead sphinx.

Or no, he corrected himself, for a dead god.

A sphinx god.

And with that thought, that realisation, he collapsed and wept in Eft's arms, saw that Lalapeya was weeping too, perhaps for other reasons, and then the sphinx god disappeared into the interior of the Gatherer, and somehow, through a crack in the defences of Serafin's mind, there crept the certainty that their enemies now had a weapon calculated to cast any other weapon ever known into the shade.

But that hardly mattered at the moment. All that mattered was his despair.

Lalapeya sat down beside him and took his hand, but it felt cold and lifeless, almost as if it were dead.

THE HOUSE OF THE HEART

Merle was alone when she woke up.

The first thing she did was to feel for the water mirror in the pocket of her dress. Good. They hadn't taken it away from her. She distinctly felt the oval pressing against the fabric of the skirt, as if it missed the touch of her hand.

She wasn't sure how long she had been lying in the dark, in an unsettling silence, hearing only the beating of her heartbeat and the whisper of her own confused thoughts. The darkness woke with her, breathed with her. Alone in pitch darkness, alone with herself. Thousands of questions, thousands of doubts, and even more fears.

Where was Vermithrax? What had become of Winter?

She was all alone.

Only then did it dawn on her what was so unusual about being alone like this. She couldn't feel the presence of the Flowing Queen any more!

'*I'm here*,' said the voice in her head, and it sounded to her a hundred times louder than usual. '*Don't worry.*'

'You weren't saying anything. I thought you'd gone.'

'*Would you have been glad of that?*'

'Not here.'

'*Oh, so I'm good enough for you when things get serious.*'

'I didn't mean it like that. You know I didn't.' Merle's hands groped about on the ground where she was lying. Cold stone, carved out of the rock and filed smooth. A dungeon cell, she supposed. 'Bring her to the House of the Heart,' the old man in the wheelchair had said. This wasn't how she had imagined it. Well, to be honest, she hadn't imagined anything at all.

'*You've been asleep.*'

'How long?'

'*Difficult to say. I do have certain abilities, but a built-in clock isn't one of them.*'

Merle sighed. 'Since we've been down here . . . in Hell, I mean . . . I've lost all my sense of time. Because it never gets dark. Have we been here one day, or two, or maybe a week?'

'*I don't know.*'

'Then tell me where we are. Or don't you know that either?'

'*In the House of the Heart, I expect.*'

'Oh yes?' In the dark, Merle rolled her eyes.

The Queen was silent for a moment and then said, *'Well, we'll find out the rest any moment now. They're coming to fetch us.'*

Merle was about to ask how the Queen knew when she heard hollow footsteps and then the squeal of an iron bolt. Suddenly there was a column of light in the darkness. It grew broader, opened, and proved to be a doorway. Strange silhouettes, jagged and pointed, appeared there, looking like exotic plants, maybe cacti with many branches, but then appeared to merge and recompose themselves. Or perhaps that was just happening in Merle's head and the first sight of them was an illusion, an image betraying her fear of them.

She had just come to terms with that idea when the Queen said, *'Shape-shifters.'*

'You really do know how to encourage other people.'

'I knew you'd be glad to have me with you some time.'

'In your dreams.'

'I can't dream. Except when you do.'

A hand took hold of Merle, and then she was led through the door into the light, out on to a latticework footbridge leading along a rock face. Steel doors stood at regular intervals on one side of the bridge, on the other an abyss yawned.

The view was terrifying in its extent. They were obviously inside the huge dome they had seen as they flew towards Axis Mundi. The stone wall curved slightly as it continued up. High above Merle, its contours were lost in reddish-yellow vapours. Dozens of ledges ran along it, and more latticework bridges, floating free above the abyss, led down into the glowing vapour, where they met yet other footbridges, crossed them or joined them, thus forming a broad network of iron paths, countless kilometres long, on which you could move about the dome.

A bright red-gold glow rose from the floor of the dome, broken here and there by the vapour that drenched the air, so that the real source of the light could not be seen. It was as if the whole base of the dome were glowing, as if they were standing above a lake of lava. But Merle already guessed that the explanation was not so simple, for the light gave off no heat. Even the mists wafting through the dome felt clammy and uncomfortable. And something else dawned on her: although the dome was made of rock, it had looked from the outside as if it were shedding the light itself. So the brightness of the ground must come *through* the rock, but at the same time it was not strong enough to dazzle Merle. It was almost as if the light in the depths imparted its brilliance to the rock, so that the dome glowed of itself.

It was strange and utterly improbable.

Her new companions suited the scene. The shape-shifters – if that was really what they were – had tried to assume human form. And in a way they had succeeded, except that their shape was not that of just any human being, but of Winter, which was particularly ironic, since he claimed not to be human at all.

However, their faces looked clumsy and somehow unfinished, as if swollen. Their bodies were white, but they had not taken the trouble to imitate the structure or shape of Winter's clothing. And their eyes seemed to have been painted on and were blind, like the eyes of dead fish.

If they had hoped to calm some of Merle's fears by this absurd masquerade, they had achieved the exact opposite.

They escorted her silently along the path, gesturing at every crossing to show her which way to go. They led her back and forth over the footbridges above the glowing abyss, until finally they came to a platform standing where several paths met.

A little house stood on the platform.

It didn't suit this place. Its walls were half-timbered and it had a steep roof of red tiles. A weathercock rose from its pointed gable end. The windows were made up of bull's-eye panes, and to complete the idyll someone had put a bench outside the wooden door, as if the occupants of this little house came out into the fresh air now and then to smoke a pipe at their leisure. It had the cosy aura of a fairy-tale cottage. As Merle drew closer she saw a carved notice above the door: *Come in and bring your heart!* Little hearts and flowers were worked clumsily around the lettering, as if done by a child.

One of her guards pushed her towards the door, while the others stayed behind on the edge of the platform. Someone opened the door from the inside, and Merle was led in under the notice, which now that she read it again gave her goose pimples for some reason that she couldn't quite explain. Didn't this kind of welcoming slogan usually say *Come in and bring good luck*? For a moment she felt as if her heart were beating faster in protest, and so hard that it hurt her chest.

Inside the house they had tried to keep up the romantic appearance of the exterior, but here the attempt had failed miserably. There was more half-timbering, yes, and even a rustic cupboard with an inlaid flower pattern on its doors, but other items did not match the deliberate prettiness of the scene.

The operating table, for instance.

The ground floor of the House of the Heart consisted of a single room that, curiously, seemed larger than the outside of the house suggested. Merle decided that it was an optical illusion.

'*Perhaps*,' said the Flowing Queen.

At the back of the room, half concealed behind a number of beams which stabilised the building, were all kinds of metal shelves with well-scoured surfaces where instruments lay, neatly aligned on black cloth and meticulously polished. Steel flashed in the omnipresent glow of the light falling in through the bull's-eye window panes.

The door closed behind Merle. She spun round and saw who had opened it for her. The snakes that had been pushing the old man's wheelchair in the Hall of the Heralds came gliding smoothly in her direction, and immediately in front of her formed themselves into a pear-shaped structure at least a head taller than she was. This thing leaned forward until its surface was only a finger's breadth from Merle's nose, a shimmering mass of coiling bodies. Finally the nest of snakes flowed out into a broad, flat shape and moved like an ankle-high carpet to the back of the room, where it towered up again, this time into the conical form of a sugar-loaf. The creature stayed there waiting.

Merle would have turned to flee, but the shape-shifter barred her way. It looked even less like Winter now and was turning into something else instead, something too repulsive for Merle to give it more than a fleeting glance.

'*I can't help you,*' said the Flowing Queen.

That's really good news, thought Merle.

'*Sorry.*'

Me too.

'*I know I brought you here, but –*'

Be quiet. Please.

'Is she the one?' said a voice.

If the snakes gave any answer, Merle couldn't hear it. But next moment the voice commanded, 'Bring her down.'

The snakes slithered towards Merle again. She avoided their touch and walked of her own accord towards the opening in the floor from which the voice had come. Although Merle had heard it only once before, she immediately recognised it as the old man's.

'Come here, come here,' he called.

Merle reached the opening and climbed down a spiral staircase into a room with its floor and walls made of steel bars. Light rising from below flooded it on all sides. She could look down at the glowing abyss through the bars at her feet, in the same way that it could be seen through the bridges outside. For the first time she felt so dizzy that she had to stop at the foot of the stairs and hold tight to the banisters.

In the middle of the stairwell there was a round disc that could be winched up by a cable, but the wheelchair for which it had been made was empty. Its occupant was moving around this barred lower room on crutches ending in wooden feet the size of the palm of a hand, large enough not to get caught between the bars.

Along the walls stood a number of tall glass cylinders, many of them almost three metres high. At least fifteen or twenty of them, Merle estimated. Each cylinder was filled with a fluid that shone gold as honey in the light of the dome. And in this fluid, caught like prehistoric insects in amber, floated what had once been living creatures. None of them was human.

Merle had to force herself to look away from these grotesque figures, but she had seen enough to know that they had one thing in common: all showed the mark of a deep incision, usually in the middle of the body, sewn together with thread in cross-stitch. Operation scars, situated in what would be a human being's chest.

The House of the Heart, thought Merle, and shuddered.

'Take a look,' said the old man, shifting his weight to the right and sweeping his left-hand crutch shakily around the room in a gesture that indicated all the glass cylinders and the creatures in them. 'My own work,' he added more quietly, in a whisper, as if he didn't want to wake the beings in the containers.

'Who are you?' asked Merle, still trying to look just at him.

'My name?' He cackled with what sounded to her like assumed laughter, and she couldn't help wondering if he was just pretending to be mad. Playing the part of the mad scientist — but it was a part that he liked, which was at least as worrying as genuine madness.

He said no more, and Merle repeated her question,

realising that he had got her talking just as he did. He had a habit of repeating what he said, as if he had to make sure of its sound before saying it again a second time, and more distinctly.

'Most of them here – or at least those of them who can talk – just call me the Surgeon,' said the old man. 'Just the Surgeon.'

'Are you a doctor?'

He grinned again and his whole face seemed to shift. What she had taken for grey skin was really the stubble of a beard going right up to under his eyes. 'Oh yes, indeed, a doctor, yes, indeed.'

He was trying to scare her. That might mean that he wasn't really as dangerous as he made out – or that he was much worse, a madman who liked dramatising himself.

'These things,' said Merle, pointing to the cylinders without looking at them, 'are they all your . . . your patients?'

'Early specimens,' he said. 'From a time when my technique had not been perfected. Not perfected. I kept them to remind me of my mistakes. One so easily becomes over-confident, you know. Over-confident.'

'Why are you showing me this?' It struck her that neither the shape-shifter nor the snakes had come down the staircase with her. She was alone with the old man. Yet somehow she couldn't believe that this was just carelessness. He felt sure of himself, and certainly for good reasons.

'I don't want you to be afraid of me.'

Ha, ha, she thought.

'*He's playing with you*,' said the Queen.

So I'd noticed.

'*Then play along with him. Make a better move. Checkmate him.*'

I hope he won't take my Queen first.

'*Very funny.*'

'What do you want with me?' Merle asked the old man.

He gave her a warm smile which seemed almost genuine. 'You must have patience. Patience.'

Merle was doing her best not to show how frightened she was. If he gave her a chance she must try to find out as much as possible. 'When the Lilim caught me you told them to bring me here at once, but then you locked me up somewhere else first. Why?'

He waved this nervously away. 'I had things to do.' He repeated, with a grin, 'Things to do.'

Merle instinctively looked round and let her gaze move slowly over the creatures in the cylinders.

'Not here now,' he said. 'Not here now.'

'Where are my friends?'

'Safe.'

'You're only saying that.'

'No harm has come to any of them. Although the lion fought like –' he chuckled – 'well, like a lion.'

'When can I see them again?'

The Surgeon tilted his head slightly to one side, as if he really had to think about the answer. 'Let's wait and see. Patience. You'll soon learn patience.'

'What do you want with me?' she asked for a second time.

'Oh, that's simple,' he said. 'I want your heart. I'll exchange it for a better one. A heart of stone.'

'But –'

'It will be very quick,' he interrupted her. 'My mishaps with the unfortunate creatures here were made long ago. It's no problem today. I may be old, but I still learn more with every new heart. Every new heart.'

Merle's heartbeat was thudding so loudly in her ears now that she could hardly make out what he was saying. She instinctively retreated to the stairs and clung to the banister rail.

'You'll soon forget all about it. Believe me, you'll forget all about it.'

He's enjoying this, thought Merle, with great dislike. That's why he brought me down here: he wants me to see what he does. And he wants me to ask about the details.

He confirmed her fears. 'Just ask, just ask! The faster your heart beats, the easier the operation is. You have a strong heart, don't you? Very strong.'

She hesitated and then said, 'You *are* a human being, aren't you? I mean, a real human being . . . not a shape-shifter or something?'

'Of course I am.'

'Do you come from the world above?'

'Why do you want to know?'

She tried to think of a quick answer that would both satisfy him and keep him talking. 'I've seen lots of doctors,' she said untruthfully. 'And the fact is, there's nothing I'm more scared of in the world above than doctors, honestly.' Perhaps it would help if he thought her a little naive.

'*Good idea,*' said the Flowing Queen.

'I was a doctor in the world above too,' said the old man in self-satisfied tones. 'A doctor in the world above, yes, indeed. Many people were afraid of me, it's nothing for you to be ashamed of. Nothing to be ashamed of.'

'How long have you been down here?'

'Many years. Very many years.'

'And what made you come?' Seeing that he was getting suspicious, she added quickly, 'I mean, were you a criminal or something? Did you do experiments on people? If you did, then at least I'd know why I'm so terrified.'

He looked at her for a moment, then almost imperceptibly nodded. 'Experiments, yes. But I committed no crimes. I was a scientist. I'm still a scientist. Like all of us.'

'Are there more human beings down here?' Merle asked the old man.

He tapped one crutch on the bars of the floor, twice, three times, then smiled. 'Interrogating me, eh? But that will do for now. Let's begin. Yes, let's begin.'

Merle took a step backwards up the stairs, but her feet slipped on something soft and slimy. She lost her balance, just managed to shift her weight forward to save herself from falling with her back against the sharp metal steps and slid full length to the floor.

When she looked up the nest of snakes was forming

again behind her; part of it still covered the stairs like a film of oil, shimmering in all the colours of the rainbow.

'No!' she cried, jumping up and spinning round to face the old man. He was sick, weak, and not much bigger than she was. She would try attacking him sooner than let him give her a stone heart.

'*Too late*,' said the Queen.

Merle felt that at the same moment. Her legs turned cold as the quivering tapestry of snakes made its way up her, faster than she could react. In no time an unbroken layer of gleaming snakes covered her legs, her belly, went on up to her shoulders and then from her shoulders down her arms, until the cool, coiling creatures enclosed her whole body like a close-fitting suit. They left only her head free.

She tried to defend herself, but it was useless. Against her own will she walked forward and began climbing the stairs. The snakes controlled her arms and legs, moving her like a doll.

Merle tried to turn her head, and to some extent succeeded, although her legs were still carrying her up the stairs. 'Stop it!' she shouted at the Surgeon, who was just sitting down in his wheelchair. 'Call these creatures off!'

The old man merely smiled, threw a switch and was hauled up by the winch mechanism in the centre of the spiral staircase, slowly enough for Merle to keep pace with him.

Once at the top, she moved straight to the operating table, lay down flat on her back, and shouted and cursed so wholeheartedly that the Surgeon threatened to order the snakes to crawl into her mouth. At that she fell silent and watched, helplessly, what was being done to her.

Some of the snakes came away from the middle of her body, disappearing to right and left under the top of the table. Merle tried to rear up, but the result was pathetic, little more than a twitch of her torso.

Steel bands snapped shut over her wrists and ankles, and then the rest of the snakes withdrew, crawling and sliding off the table and forming into the pear-shaped nest structure on the floor.

Merle pulled and tugged at her bonds.

'Very good, very good,' said the Surgeon. 'I think we will anaesthetise you first. Is your heart beating fast enough?'

Merle flung a torrent of abuse at him, calling him the worst names she could think of, and she knew a great many after her years in the orphanage. She didn't care whether the snakes crawled over her face. She didn't care about anything now, if only lightning would strike this horrible man dead on the spot.

The Surgeon signed to the nest of snakes, and soon she began to smell something acrid and unpleasant behind her head, like many of the chemicals in Arcimboldo's workshop. The anaesthetic was being prepared.

The acrid smell grew stronger. She twisted her head round as far as she could to look behind her, but out of the corner of her eye she could see only the coiling of the snakes. They were streaming towards her like a dark wave.

Merle's perceptions shifted. Her surroundings began going round before her eyes, merging together.

Snakes were crawling about in the background. Merle's heart was hammering inside her ribcage.

The Surgeon came closer, his face swelled, filled her field of vision, filled the world.

His flesh and the snakes, shining like the colours on a painter's palette.

His grin.

'Stop!'

The world rotated again, a world of yellow teeth and grey skin.

'I said stop!'

The smell became fainter. Merle's surroundings changed. The old man's face blurred and withdrew.

'Let her go at once!'

Not the Surgeon's voice, and not her own either. It belonged to someone else.

The iron bonds on her hands and feet snapped back and suddenly she was free. No fetters, no snakes holding her in place any more.

With the disappearance of the pungent vapour, her real surroundings came back. The white ceiling, the wooden beams, all in place again.

Two voices were arguing in the background. One of them belonged to the Surgeon, the other to the unknown person who had rescued her.

Rescued her?

Maybe.

'*Merle?*' asked the Flowing Queen. She sounded as dazed as Merle herself.

I'm here, she thought, although it felt as if someone else had taken over her thinking for her. But where else would she be?

'*You're all right.*' It was a statement, not a question.

All right. Yes.

The argument broke off and now someone was bending over her face. Not the Surgeon, although this man was at least as old.

A scientist like all of us, the Surgeon had said.

Like all of us.

'Are you Lord Light?' asked Merle faintly.

'Yes,' said the man. He had thick grey hair.

'You're a human being,' she remarked, and thought she was dreaming, was firmly convinced of it.

Lord Light, the ruler of Hell, smiled. 'Believe me, Merle, human beings make better devils than the Devil himself.'

His face withdrew and then she just heard his voice.

'Now get up, please, and come with me.'

LORD LIGHT

The Surgeon stayed behind in the House of the Heart. Merle gave the man in the wheelchair a last glance as Lord Light guided her out on to the platform with one hand on her shoulder, in a firm but not unfriendly manner. The Surgeon had stared first at her and then at Lord Light out of small, narrowed eyes with rage and hatred blazing in them.

'You have nothing to fear from him now,' said her companion, as they stepped off the platform and on to one of the latticework bridges.

Lord Light, she kept telling herself. *This is Lord Light.* Only a man.

'The Surgeon can't do anything more to you,' he added.

Her hand moved to her breast and felt for the rapid beating of her heart.

Lord Light noticed. 'It's still the old one, don't worry. Stone hearts don't beat.'

She gave him a sideways glance and thought he looked

like a scholar — which he undoubtedly was if the Surgeon had been telling the truth.

He wore a black frock coat with a red glass flower in his buttonhole. His trousers were black too, and his pointed patent leather shoes shone brightly. A golden watch-chain hung from his jacket pocket, forming a semicircular loop that seemed to imitate the shape of the rings under his eyes. Merle had never before seen anyone with such rings, as dark as if they had been painted on his face. Yet he did not seem to be tired or exhausted, far from it. He had an aura of vigour that belied his age.

Merle couldn't take her eyes off him. Was this the man who was going to help her free Venice? An old gentleman strolling along beside her in his frock coat as if they were out for a Sunday walk together?

'*Ask him his name,*' said the Queen. '*His real name.*'

Merle ignored her. 'Where are my friends?'

'No one's hurt a hair of their heads. The lion has been raging and roaring ever since the Lilim captured him, but he's in good health. He survived the landing in the Hall of the Heralds without injury.'

They were walking side by side along a latticework bridge, then climbed down a long flight of stairs and crossed more bridges.

'I want to see him.'

'You will.'

'When?'

'Soon.'

'How is Winter?'

Lord Light sighed quietly. 'Is that his name? Winter? A strange fellow. To be honest, I can't tell you how he is.'

'What do you mean?'

'He escaped.'

'What?'

She stopped, one hand on the rail of the bridge. Some way off, several figures peeled away from the swathes of light, figures no bigger than matchsticks but with too many arms and legs. On reaching a crossing, they moved away and quickly disappeared again in the glowing vapour of the dome.

'He escaped,' said Lord Light, turning towards her. She sensed the impatience in his voice, but he was not pressing her to do anything yet. 'I had a long conversation with him, and then he was gone.'

'A *long conversation?*' asked the Queen suspiciously.

'He was weak,' said the incredulous Merle. 'Sick,

I think. When we met him he could hardly stand by himself.'

'Well, at least he was able to escape by himself.'

Merle looked past him and down into the glowing depths. She wondered why she wasn't afraid of Lord Light. 'That's impossible. You're lying to me.'

'Why would I do that?'

'Perhaps you've killed him.'

'For no reason?'

She was briefly taken aback as she tried to find a good argument. She was on the point of saying something stupid, for instance, 'But you're the ruler of Hell! You're evil, every child knows that. You don't need a reason to kill someone.' Then she thought a moment longer and whispered, 'It just can't be true. He was much too weak.'

Lord Light started moving again and asked her to follow him: he wanted to show her something, he said, and it wasn't far to go. Merle asked herself why he didn't simply summon some flying monstrosity to take them both to their destination, but that didn't seem to be his way. He was not at all like the image she had formed of Lord Light.

Shall I ask him now, she wondered, ask if he will help us? But somehow the idea suddenly seemed a bad one. The huge extent of this world within the world made her request shrink to shadowy, insignificant proportions.

But that was what they had come for, wasn't it?

Wasn't it?

Instead of answering, the Queen repeated, '*Ask him his name.*'

This time Merle obeyed before the Queen could take over her voice.

'What are you called?' she asked. 'I mean, I don't suppose Lord Light is your true name – at least, not if you're really a man.'

His eyes sparkled with humour as he looked down at her. 'Do you doubt that I'm a man?'

'I don't know.' And that was true. 'Only just now I saw shape-shifters, and –'

'Then you saw what a poor job they make of imitating a human being.'

'How about magic, though?'

'I'm not a magician, only a scientist.'

'The same as the Surgeon?'

He shrugged his shoulders. 'If you like.'

'Then tell me your name.'

Smiling, he raised both hands as if he had no choice but

to surrender to her persistence. He cleared his throat – and then told her his true name.

Merle stopped. Open-mouthed, she stared at him. 'Are you serious?'

The drifting mists prevented his laughter from echoing in the distance. 'I may have been down here for quite a long time, but believe me, I haven't forgotten my name.'

'Burbridge?' she repeated. '*Professor* Burbridge?'

'Sir Charles Burbridge, Honorary Chairman of the National Geographic Society, Explorer by Appointment to Her Majesty the Queen, discoverer of Hell and its first and no doubt only cartographer. Professor of geography, astronomy and biology. And an old man now, I fear.'

Merle let out her breath between clenched teeth. It sounded like a whistle. 'You *are* Professor Burbridge!'

He smiled, almost embarrassed. 'And more as well,' he said mysteriously. But then he went on, this time without telling her to come too. He knew she would follow him anyway.

Merle trotted along beside him without a word, while he brushed dust from the left sleeve of his jacket with his hand. Shaking his head, he said, 'You know, you can teach these creatures to build everything we have here – cities, steam engines, factories — but you're doomed to failure if you try getting them to understand something as basic as fashion sense. Just look at this!' He held out his sleeve to her and she had to force herself to look more closely. 'See that?' he asked. 'Cross-stitch! They sew a garment like this with cross-stitch! Absolutely inexcusable!'

Merle thought of the creatures in the House of the Heart. Cross-stitch. She shuddered. 'Where are you taking me?'

'To the Stone Light.'

'What's that?'

'You'll soon see.'

'Is Vermithrax there?'

He smiled again. 'He should be, anyway. Provided he hasn't tricked those fools the guards like your other friend.' A grin. 'But I don't think so.'

In silence, they climbed down more flights of steps, followed endless footbridges. But whichever way she looked she couldn't see the curving wall of the vault anywhere; they were still somewhere in the middle of the light-filled dome. The House of the Heart had vanished in the vapours above them too.

The Stone Light.

She had goose pimples and didn't know why.

She still meant to ask him for the help his envoy had offered the Venetians, she meant to carry out her mission – but she had a feeling that this was not what was at stake any more. Not Venice. Not she herself.

Is that *really* why we came here? she asked in her thoughts, and received no answer. The Queen had fallen remarkably silent since the Lilim got Merle into their power, almost as if she were afraid someone might notice her. But was that the only reason?

'The Surgeon,' said Merle after quite a long time. 'Can he really do that? Replace a human heart with a heart of stone?'

'Yes, he can.'

'But why does he do it?'

'Because I told him to.'

Merle's stomach contracted, but she didn't let it show. She had fallen for him and his friendly manner. It was time to remember who he was and what he represented.

'The envoy I sent up to the Piazza San Marco,' he said in a conversational tone, 'he had a heart of stone. One of the first that really worked. And so do many of the others that I trust. The stone makes it easier to control them.'

'You mean they don't have a will of their own any more?'

'Not as you and I do, but it's a little more complicated than that.'

'Why all this? The Lilim seem to obey you anyway. Or do they all have stone hearts?'

'Oh no, control their leader and you control the whole band. Down here, you see, everything works on a huge, immeasurable scale. But in fact the threads all run together into small centres, as they do in a knot. Or a heart. Get it on your side and the rest is child's play.'

He was walking more slowly now, almost strolling, an amiable elderly gentleman who, you would say, wouldn't hurt a fly.

Huh, thought Merle, the devil he wouldn't! Then she remembered that he *was* the Devil.

'But why?' she repeated.

He took a deep breath, looked at his immaculate shoes and then straight ahead into the mist. 'Why did I come here and build all this? Why did I write books full of lies about Hell, so that no one would think of venturing down here? For the sake of science, of course! What else?'

'You became ruler of Hell to explore it?' She remembered that the Flowing Queen had suspected something very similar – and wondered at the same time whether she hadn't even *known* that it was so.

The Queen maintained her silence.

'Several of us came here,' said Burbridge. 'I and a handful of colleagues from many different fields of study. Medical doctors like the Surgeon, scholars of art and aesthetics, geologists and biologists like myself, even a philosopher . . . he made the mistake of arguing about Plato's parable of Hell with one of the Lilim. They could not agree. And *he* didn't agree with the Lilim digestive system either.' He smiled, but almost sadly. 'We had to learn a lot. We had to adjust our ideas and make basic changes – not just to our claims and opinions but to ourselves. Our consciences, for instance. Our morality.'

Merle nodded as if she knew exactly what he was talking about. And at heart she did understand what he was trying to tell her: that whatever way you looked at it he had done the right thing. As if he personally had made the sacrifices that this madness had called for.

Suddenly she felt he was all falsity and deception. She despised him almost more than the Surgeon. The old man in the wheelchair had at least been honest with her and himself.

Whereas Burbridge was a hypocrite.

She had always hated such people when she was still in the orphanage and met more hypocrites than she cared to remember: supervisors, priests, teachers. Even many of the people who came to take one of the children away.

She felt sick. Not from the height and not from fear. Being close to him made her feel sick.

'You don't share the results of your research with anyone. You told the world up there a load of nonsense and kept everything you've really found out down here to yourself. What kind of sense does that make?'

'Merle, tell me, don't you feel curious yourself?'

'Of course.'

'Then imagine that your curiosity is like a glass of water. Now imagine a whole barrel full of it, and you'll know what the heart of a scientist is like. A true scientist!'

Nonsense, she thought. Just talk. He and his scientist friends probably tell each other lies the whole time.

'Are we nearly there?' she asked, changing the subject.

'Look down. You'll be able to see it in a minute.'

'The Stone Light?'

He nodded.

'How can a light be made of stone?' she asked.

He smiled and suddenly looked terribly friendly again. 'Perhaps light always is, and you just haven't noticed before.'

She looked over the handrail of the bridge and down. He was right: the vapour was gradually dispersing. Down there she could vaguely make out something like a dark star: massive grey struts running out in all directions from a bright centre. But only when they had climbed down another long flight of steps did she see that these struts were bridges leading to a round latticework gallery in the middle of them. It had a diameter of about 150 metres and a single bridge intersected it right across the middle, like a solitary spoke.

The circular latticework gallery rose high above the bright floor of the hall, which now, as they came closer, turned out not to be a smooth surface but a mighty concave shape like the upper part of a globe, about a quarter of it, buried in the rock. Its size could not even be guessed at, but it must lie above the base of the stone dome. The gallery was exactly above the centre of this concave form, floating above its highest point; there were no supporting columns or scaffolding, the bridges alone held it in the air.

'That's the Stone Light, down there,' said Burbridge.

'It looks like a piece of the moon.' She imagined someone cutting the moon in slices like a round loaf of bread, then putting one of the two outer slices on the ground and building the dome above it.

Burbridge went on, 'Imagine a gigantic shining globe that once fell from the sky, pierced the outer crust of the earth and plunged into the ground of Hell down here. What you see there is the part of it that still shows above the rock. The Morning Star. Lucifer, the fallen angel. Or the Stone Light.'

'Did you have the dome built over it?'

'Yes, indeed.'

'Why? What does it do, apart from giving light?'

For the first time, the Flowing Queen spoke up again. *'Are you still acting naive, or are you really that innocent?'*

Be quiet, thought Merle. To her surprise the voice obeyed without protest.

As they went on, further and further down towards the glowing light and the round latticework gallery, Burbridge gestured at the entire interior of the dome. 'When I first came here, the Lilim regarded this place as a shrine, one that they feared. None of them would willingly venture near it. They avoided the place as much as they could. It was I who showed them how you can use the power of the light.'

'But Axis Mundi, the city,' said Merle, 'it must be much older! Older than the sixty or seventy years since you found the way down to Hell anyway.' Even as she spoke she realised how old Burbridge must actually be, and wondered whether he owed his age to the light at the bottom of the dome too.

As he went on, the Professor ran one hand over the rail of the bridge, lost in thought. 'There was already a city in this place when human beings were still living in caves. The Lilim once had a highly developed civilisation — not *technically* highly developed, more like our own Middle Ages. But they had a social structure and a culture of their own, they lived in cities and large communities. However, by the time I climbed down into Hell that was all in the distant past. The few Lilim who had survived their decline over the aeons lived alone in the vast expanses of rocky desert here, or some of them in tribes and hordes. But there was no real civilisation left. It had all crumbled and been forgotten long ago. Together with this city.'

Merle was beginning to understand. 'So when the

Morning Star – or the Stone Light – fell here the city already existed?'

Burbridge nodded. 'It was the centre of ancient Lilim culture. The Stone Light destroyed large parts of it and made them uninhabitable for thousands of years. When I came here the Lilim used to tell many legends about the ruins of the city. Many of them claimed that the light made them alter, change shape, turn into distortions of themselves – become human.'

'Is that true?'

Burbridge shrugged. 'Who knows? Over sixty years ago, when I had completed my first expedition here, there was no trace of any such development left anyway. I discovered the light and realised that its energies could be used for all sorts of purposes. But of course I also knew that I would need helpers, countless helpers, and I could not use human beings.'

'Why not?'

'What do you think would have happened if I'd gone back to the surface and told everyone what I had found here? I would have been thanked, of course, I'd have had all kinds of orders pinned on me, and I'd have been sent home. And then others would have decided to exploit this place.

First the kingdom of Great Britain, then perhaps the Tsar. They would have hired experts. But they wouldn't have needed me any more, a simple scientist – a brilliant but also very young scientist.' He firmly dismissed the idea. 'No, Merle, what I needed at the time was a kingdom of my own, with my own subjects and workers. I and some of my colleagues in whom I had confided managed to train most of the Lilim as a labour force by simple means: a few technical devices, toys from the box of tricks used by the old colonial masters of all periods. The Lilim may look to us like animals, but basically they are no different from the indigenous peoples found by the Spanish and Portuguese in South America and the French in Indochina. With a little pressure, they can be manipulated and controlled.'

'By force, you mean.'

'That too, yes. But not only force and not primarily. As I said, a little technology, a few simple games, can work wonders. And once we had brought them to the point of serving us and we could make use of the power of the Stone Light, we were in a position to come up with greater marvels. The flying heralds, for instance. Or other forces that at first sight look like magic, such as the dismantling and drilling of rock on a huge scale. And of course the stone hearts that keep an organism alive *and* control it.'

'Wouldn't you call that magic?'

'Well, it depends how you look at it. There is certainly something of magic about it, and to be honest I doubt whether the Surgeon himself knows what he's doing. The heart – the stone – takes over the real work.'

Merle mopped perspiration from her brow, although it was not really hot down here, even close to the Stone Light. She looked down at the glowing curve of it. 'It's the same thing. Exactly the same thing.'

'What do you mean?' he asked, puzzled.

'The Stone Light. The Morning Star. The globe down there in the ground. It's like a huge heart itself, beating in the middle of Axis Mundi.'

He agreed enthusiastically. 'I'm glad you thought of it for yourself. You've hit it exactly. My own theory is that the Morning Star – wherever it came from – functions like a heart that, for an infinitely long time, was in search of an organism it could drive. Until finally it fell here. The world of the Lilim, like every society, can be compared to a huge living creature. The city on whose ruins we have built Axis Mundi was once the central point of that world. When it was destroyed the culture of the Lilim crumbled because they were not in a position to use the power of the light. Today, however, thanks to our help, the Lilim are better off than ever. I have given their people a new heart with the Stone Light, and now the organism of their society is thriving and growing into something yet larger. And better.'

'Do the individual Lilim see it that way?'

Burbridge's euphoria cooled off. 'They're like ants. Individuals don't count; only the nation matters. The individual may suffer grief or pain or exhaustion, but that nourishes the population, which derives profit from it.'

Merle snorted. '*You* derive profit from it, not the Lilim.'

He looked at her intently for a moment, with sudden disappointment in his eyes. 'Is that really how you see it?' When she did not reply he straightened his back and walked faster. It was obvious that he was annoyed. Without looking round, he went on, 'What profit would I derive from it? Wealth, perhaps? I wouldn't even have an opportunity to enjoy it. What else? Luxury? No. Freedom? Hardly, for my life has belonged not to me but to this world for a long time. Power? Perhaps, but that's not what I want. I'm no megalomaniac dictator.'

'You gave the answer yourself.'

'I did?'

'You do it for science. Not for the Lilim, perhaps not even for yourself, just for science. That's another form of power. Or megalomania. Your research won't help anyone because no one will ever know about it.'

'Perhaps they will. Some day.'

It was no use. He wouldn't understand her, and it didn't matter now. 'You must tell me one more thing.'

'Just ask.'

'Why are you telling me all this? I mean, I'm only some girl.'

'Only some girl?' His left eyebrow rose, but he still didn't look at her. 'Perhaps you'll understand everything soon, Merle.'

Once again she thought of her mission, of help for Venice. But in her mind she saw her own city drifting in the sea like a floating island, going further and further towards the horizon and oblivion.

Burbridge himself showed not the slightest interest in it any more. And there could be only one reason for that. Because he had got what he wanted long ago.

Only some girl . . .

Everything in her felt hostile and confused.

The latticework ring above the Stone Light was now just 100 metres below them. The paths over the bridges grew broader and more and more often passed through pipes and tunnels where mighty machines were working away. Chimneys spewed clouds of smoke and steam that mingled with the ever-present vapours and made breathing difficult. Steel cogwheels the size of houses turned beside the bridges, connecting with each other or operating chains and belt drives which in turn led to other wheels and machines above or below them. The nearer they came to the floor of the dome, the more closely the structures on both sides of the latticework bridges soaring through the air resembled the interiors of the steam-driven factories that had been built on some of the islands of the Venetian lagoon – Merle had become familiar with two of them herself when the supervisors of the orphanage had tried to get her employed there.

She wondered where the Lilim working all this machinery were. She saw no workers of any kind anywhere; it was as if these complexes were entirely abandoned. Yet many of the machines were running at high pressure and the noise in some of the passages was deafening.

Only after a while did she realise that the tunnels

containing the machines were by no means deserted. Sometimes she saw a shadow among the machinery; at other times something scurried at lightning speed over the ceiling of a tunnel. Several hoses and angular pipes that she had thought were machine parts suddenly moved; there were Lilim concealed there, drawing in their limbs at the last moment.

'*They're hiding*,' said the Flowing Queen, but when Merle repeated that out loud, Burbridge only nodded, said a brief, 'Yes', and fell silent again.

They're afraid of him, she thought.

'*Or you*,' said the Queen.

How do you mean?

'*You're his guest, aren't you?*'

His prisoner.

'*No, Merle. A prisoner is put in chains or locked in a cell. People don't deliver lectures on science to a prisoner. He's treating you as an ally.*'

They finally left the tunnels and smoking chimneys behind and reached the lower level. There were no structures now on the star-shape of bridges leading to the circular latticework gallery. Once again, only thin iron railings separated them from the enticing suction of the abyss.

Even from a distance Merle saw that they were expected on the round gallery. The latticework ring rested like a crown above the centre of the light, thirty or forty metres above its great curve. Around it stood figures grouped close together by the railings. Figures of human proportions. They stood perfectly motionless, like statues, and as she came closer Merle saw that their bodies were made of stone.

'*They're waiting for something*,' said the Queen.

They're only statues.

'*No, they certainly are not.*'

Merle had already seen the single bridge leading right across the latticework circle from one side to the other. In the middle of it, and thus at the exact centre of the dome, there was a small platform, just large enough for several people to stand on it at once. At the moment it was empty.

The body of an Egyptian dangled from the platform at the end of a rope.

He wore golden garments that were torn and burnt in many places. His head was shaved bald. A golden pattern covered his scalp like a net.

She had seen this man just once before, and even then only from a distance, yet she recognised him at once.

Seth.

The Pharaoh's vizier. High priest of Horus.

His body turned slightly, showing now its face and now its back to Merle. He had been strung up on a coarse rope that looked curiously archaic in a place like this. She would have expected Burbridge to have more sophisticated methods of executing a man at his disposal.

Seth, the second most important man in the Empire. Burbridge had had him hanged like a street thief. His death was a great relief to her, but it shook her badly all the same.

Whenever the dangling corpse turned its face her way, that lifeless look met her. The same look as when he had stared out from the top of the Gatherer. A shudder passed down her spine, like icy fingertips.

'The Pharaoh sent him to kill me,' said Burbridge. He sounded indifferent, or even slightly surprised. 'One might almost think Amenophis wanted to get rid of him. Seth never had a chance down here.'

'Where did you catch him?'

'Above the city. He got a long way, but not far enough.'

'*Above* the city?' she asked.

Burbridge nodded. 'He flew here. Not himself, naturally.' He pointed up. 'There, look at that.'

Merle's eyes followed the direction of his hand. She saw two cages hanging from a steel girder on long chains high above the latticework ring. The first cage was above the right half of the circle, the other above the left half. It looked as if they were to be let down on their chains at any moment — except that there was nowhere for them to land. Below them only the curved surface of the Stone Light shone.

In one of the cages a mighty sphinx was prowling up and down, back and forth again and again, like a beast of prey deprived for the first time of the freedom of the jungle. Mighty wings were folded on its back. Merle hadn't known there were any winged sphinxes.

In the other cage, looking much calmer, almost relaxed, sat —

'Vermithrax!'

The obsidian lion roused himself from his stillness and moved his face closer to the bars of the cage. At this distance she couldn't make out any details, but she sensed the sadness in his glance.

The sphinx saw Vermithrax moving and snarled at him across the bright abyss between them.

'*Don't reproach yourself*,' said the Flowing Queen, but

even she couldn't keep a tremor out of her voice.

We brought him here, thought Merle. After all those years in the Campanile he was free at last, and now he was a prisoner again.

'*You can't help it.*'

The Queen was trying to reassure her, but Merle wasn't falling for that. They were both to blame for Vermithrax's fate.

Lips quivering, she turned to Burbridge. The twitching of her cheeks showed that she was close to tears, but she still had herself under control. She wanted to shout at him, call him names, but instead she summoned up her powers of reason and sought for the right words.

'Why are you kind to me, but you lock up my friend?' she asked, controlling her voice with difficulty.

'We need him. Even more than we need the sphinx.'

Merle's eyes looked up at the sphinx, half beast of prey, half man, raging furiously in his cage. The steel container swayed back and forth, but the strong chain from which it hung was able to take the weight. Merle quickly turned her attention back to Vermithrax. His long obsidian tail was hanging through the bars of the cage, waving slightly.

We must set him free, she thought.

'*Yes.*' This time the Flowing Queen had no objections. But no suggestions either.

'It's an experiment,' said Burbridge, 'that we have been waiting a long time to make.'

'What . . . what's it got to do with those two?' asked Merle.

'We are going to immerse them in the Stone Light.'

'What?' Merle stared at him.

'I have thought hard whether to show you this, Merle. But I believe it is important for you to understand what is going on down here. And why this world is the better one.'

Merle shook her head in silence. She didn't understand anything. Anything at all. Why did these things have to happen to her?

'What will it do to him?' she asked.

'If I knew that there'd be no need to perform the experiment,' replied Burbridge. 'As you can imagine, this is not the first time we have made such experiments. The first attempts were failures.'

'You burn living creatures just to —'

'The Stone Light gives off no heat, can't you feel that?' he interrupted her. 'It can't burn anyone. Including your friend.'

'So why do you want to immerse Vermithrax in it?'

He smiled triumphantly. 'To see what happens, of course! The light changes every living creature, it *combines* with it and makes it something new. The stone hearts are parts of the light, small fragments, and they deprive bodies of their own will. After that we can do as we like with them. That has proved very useful, particularly with some of the more refractory Lilim.'

So not all the Lilim had willingly accepted his rule. There were troublemakers. Potential opponents.

Merle and Burbridge were now standing by the inner railings of the round latticework gallery, close to the first of the motionless stone figures that flanked the entire circle.

'We tried it with golems,' Burbridge went on. 'Statues, their bodies carved from stone. We let them down into the light by those chains, and when we pulled them out again they were *alive*.'

Merle's eyes passed quickly over the endless ranks of stone figures. They were in human form, certainly, but their proportions were too massive, their shoulders too broad, their faces smooth as eggs.

The corners of the professor's mouth twisted. Then he

spoke a word out loud, in a language that Merle did not understand.

All the stone figures took a step forward at the same time. Then they froze again.

He turned to Merle once more, smiling. 'Stone that comes to life. A great success, one might say. At any rate a persuasive argument.'

Was that meant as a threat? No, she thought, he had no need to scare her with his stone army.

'And now,' he said, 'we come to a new attempt. Another experiment, one might say. Your friend is made of stone that is already alive *before* he comes into contact with the Stone Light. What do you think will happen when we immerse the obsidian lion in the light? What will *he* become?' There was a sparkle in Burbridge's eyes now and Merle realised that it was part of the scientific curiosity he had been talking about. A glitter, a blaze, but it was cold and calculating too. It bore an alarming similarity to the Stone Light itself, and for the first time she wondered if perhaps she was not really talking to Burbridge himself but to something that had got him in its power.

A heart in search of a body, he had said. Like his own? Was that the way the light organised and directed whole societies and nations? By giving its leaders new hearts?

'*We must get away from here,*' said the Flowing Queen.

Really?

'*I can sense something!*'

Two figures were approaching the circular gallery along one of the bridges.

One was a bizarre creature that looked human and moved on all fours – but its chest and face were on top of its body. Thorny tendrils made of steel wound around its head, its eyes and its mouth.

The second figure was a girl with long silver-blonde hair.

Impossible! Absolutely impossible!

And yet . . .

'*Junipa!*'

Merle left Burbridge's side and ran towards the pair of them.

The strange creature took a step back and allowed the girls to fall into each other's arms. Merle stammered something – later, she couldn't remember what. She couldn't hold her tears back any longer.

When they let go of one another, Junipa was smiling. Her mirror-glass eyes shone in the brilliance of the Stone

Light. Deep down inside her, and only very briefly, the sight scared Merle. Then she realised that the shards of mirror glass were only reflecting the wavering brightness that surrounded them all.

'What are you doing here?' she asked breathlessly, asked again and yet again, shook her head, laughed and cried at the same time.

Junipa took a deep breath, as if she had to summon up all her strength to speak. She was holding Merle's hands and her fingers now clung even harder, as if she would never let her friend go again – Merle, who had been with her since those first days in Arcimboldo's mirror-making workshop.

'They . . .' She hesitated and began again. 'Talamar took me away.' With a gesture to the grotesque creature behind her, she sadly added, 'The – Talamar killed Arcimboldo!'

'*We must get away*,' said the Flowing Queen. '*At once!*'

Merle stared at Talamar, saw the steely tendrils that had turned the creature's face into a waste of scars. 'Arcimboldo?' she incredulously whispered.

Junipa nodded.

Merle was going to say something, anything – *That's*

impossible! He can't be dead! You're lying! — when a scream rang out behind her.

A scream of rage. A scream of hatred.

'*We must get away from here!*' the Flowing Queen repeated.

Merle spun round and looked back the few metres to Burbridge and the edge of the round latticework gallery.

At first sight, nothing had changed. The professor was still standing there, his back turned to her, looking at the centre of the circle. The golem guards were as rigid as ever. The sphinx was raging in his cage, while Vermithrax, motionless, was looking down into the depths below. Not at Merle and Junipa, not at Lord Light either.

The lion's eyes were fixed on the narrow bridge that intersected the entire circle and the platform at its centre.

The platform from which the dead priest of Horus had been dangling only a few moments ago.

The end of the rope now hung empty above the abyss. It was frayed, as if it had been bitten off.

Seth was standing on the platform — *alive!* — with both arms raised. He uttered his cry again. 'Iskander,' he shouted into the flood of light that filled the void.

The sphinx's cage shattered as if its bars were made of glass.

And Iskander came down on them.

THE WRESTLERS AWAKE

It all happened too fast for Merle to take in more than a fraction of what was going on at once. Only a little later did she manage to make sense of most of it — a movement here, a vague outline there, accompanied by a cacophony of noise and shouting, and the rush of mighty wings.

In an instant, the sphinx came shooting out of the cloud of iron and steel splinters into which his prison had turned. He dropped faster than the remains of the cage plummeting to the depths around him and reached the platform at lightning speed.

Seth was waiting for him. He leaped nimbly on to Iskander's leonine back and shouted a string of orders in Egyptian. The sphinx immediately took off from the platform again, raced towards the round gallery, and with a single blow of his paw beheaded three of the golem guards who barred his way. Burbridge flung himself to the floor behind them, while more stone warriors moved up from both sides to protect their master.

Carried on through the air by his own momentum, Iskander had to fly in a loop before starting another attack on Lord Light.

When the cage exploded, Merle had instinctively thrown herself on Junipa and brought them both to the ground. She rather expected Talamar to tear her away from her friend, but instead the creature nimbly leaped over her and raced towards Burbridge and the golem warriors, intending to defend Lord Light with its own life.

Unexpectedly, Merle and Junipa were left unguarded.

Not that the chance was much use to them. All they could do was lie there flat, Merle protectively placing herself above Junipa, who was only a year younger than Merle herself, but at the moment seemed to her like a small child for whom she must care.

'*Too late*,' whispered the Flowing Queen in her thoughts, but Merle was not sure what she meant by that.

She raised her head, made sure first that Junipa was all right and then looked back at Burbridge. They were lying about ten metres from the place where the bridge met the circular gallery, and ten metres from where Burbridge was taking cover among a crowd of golem warriors, while the sphinx and his rider – *Dead! Seth had been dead!* – were mounting another attack. Two more stone warriors shattered under a blow from Iskander's claws, while Seth roared further orders in Egyptian, clinging firmly with both arms to Iskander's half-human torso and keeping a watchful eye on the haze of light in the dome.

Merle didn't know how he had managed to survive his execution, and perhaps it was better not to. He was a high priest of Horus, one of the most powerful magicians in the Empire, and he must know ways of rising from the dead. Perhaps that had been his plan from the first: to lull Burbridge into a sense of false security so that he could strike unexpectedly.

And he knew how to strike, there could be no doubt about that.

More of the golems broke to pieces, proving that everything Lord Light had expected of them had been a fallacy. They might offer protection from men, even from Lilim, but not from the anger of a sphinx whose power, strength and cruelty were legendary among the peoples of the world.

For Iskander, as Merle saw at first glance, was no ordinary sphinx. He was larger, stronger, and he had wings as well. His long, bronze-hued hair had come loose at the nape of his neck and was eddying wildly around his head, a network of fluttering strands like the tentacles of some bizarre water-weed. He had claws not only on his lion's paws but on both hands of his human upper body too, and they were long and sharp enough to shatter even stone. Merle didn't like to think what would happen when they met soft flesh, muscles, skin and bone.

She looked for the second cage, where Vermithrax was still imprisoned. The obsidian lion had long since stopped sitting there calmly, and was desperately trying to bend the bars apart with his paws. In vain. Iskander's cage had been destroyed by Seth's magic, not the muscular power of the sphinx himself, and the magic had not affected Vermithrax's prison. The steel cage rocked and shook as Vermithrax prowled around it, flinging himself against the bars again and again and shouting something down to Merle that she could not make out above the noise of the fighting.

Why didn't any of the Lilim go to Burbridge's aid? He had trusted in the strength of the golem warriors, but surely he must have guessed what the sphinx was capable of doing?

Merle remembered the empty tunnel where the

machines stood, and the frightened creatures taking cover from their master behind steel and smoke.

Only one of the Lilim was prepared to die for Lord Light.

Talamar ventured on a desperate manoeuvre. As Iskander came down from above once more to attack Burbridge's stone guards, the grotesque creature took off from one of the sets of railings and flung itself against the sphinx. Iskander collided with it, lost his sense of direction for a moment, crashed into the railings opposite and lost his rider. Seth was flung off the sphinx's back and fell on the bridge, injuring an arm.

Talamar was hanging from Iskander's torso, limbs intertwined. The sphinx carried the creature up in the air, his vision impeded by it, its thin body pressed close to his breast and face. Iskander was disabled for just a moment longer; then he took hold of the creature with both hands, tore it apart and flung it into the abyss. Talamar's remains fell in a red cloud and disappeared into the glow of the Stone Light.

Iskander uttered a cry of rage, licked Lilim blood from his claws as he flew, and did not react to his master's cries. Seth had hauled himself up by the railings with his uninjured arm; the golden network set into the skin of his scalp was sprinkled with wet red. Again and again he shouted orders to Iskander, but the sphinx did not obey.

The winged creature screeched in wild triumph, shot over Seth and flew in a wide arc. As he did so, Iskander's glance fell on Vermithrax and recognised him as a worthy opponent. With violent rage, he raced towards the obsidian lion's prison, leaped at the cage, clung to the bars and tore at them. Iskander was no ordinary sphinx. He was man-made, bred in the sinister laboratories of the Pharaoh and his priests, a cross between several beasts, and it wouldn't have surprised Merle to learn that the genetic heritage of the Lilim was in him somewhere.

Iskander went on shaking the bars of the cage, while Vermithrax struck out at him with his paws from inside it. He wounded Iskander's legs and paws, but the pain only made the sphinx angrier still. The cage danced wildly on its chain in the air, swinging far forward and back, turning and circling, and the creak of iron came down to the round gallery above the light.

Merle and Junipa clung to each other, neither of them able to do anything, and even the Flowing Queen in Merle's mind was frantic with fear for Vermithrax's life.

The injured Seth was still leaning on the railings, looking warily from Iskander to Burbridge. The professor emerged very briefly from behind the wall of his remaining golem warriors to assess the situation, then went back into cover and sent two golems towards Seth. The stone giants set out fast, their footsteps echoing. The priest of Horus was about to hurl magic spells in their direction, but when he opened his lips only blood came out, red and foaming, running down his chin and staining his chest.

'Iskander!' he cried into the omnipresent brightness.

At the same moment the golems reached him and were about to seize him – and then Seth was suddenly gone, and a mighty falcon, staggering through the air, shot past the stone warriors, reeled and turned in a circle above Burbridge, and then soared aloft, disappearing without trace in the haze of light inside the dome.

A metallic grinding and tearing noise was heard, alarming Merle and Junipa and drawing their gaze to the cage.

Vermithrax had succeeded in planting a well-aimed blow on Iskander's face through the bars. In doing so, he had ripped a piece of skin the size of a hand off the sphinx's head like old wallpaper. But even in pain Iskander's roar was the same as the sounds he uttered in mad rage, and he shook and tore at the bars even more violently.

The grinding sound came again, followed by a shrill explosion.

Merle cried out. Junipa's hands dug into her arms like pincers, clinging on with all their might.

The chain broke, and for a fraction of a second the cage seemed to float in the void, caught like a cocoon in an invisible cobweb.

Then it fell.

The roaring of the obsidian lion mingled with the roaring of the sphinx. Iskander took off just in time before the cage could carry him down too. His wings lashed the air and sent eddies through the haze of light in the dome. He swayed and reeled, then stabilised himself and looked down to where the cage was growing smaller and smaller.

Merle tore herself away from Junipa, staggered over to the nearest handrail and looked down into the abyss.

'*Oh no,*' whispered the Flowing Queen again and again.

The cage turned on itself as it fell like a child's building block. Vermithrax could hardly be seen inside it, was only a black outline getting ever smaller as he fell towards the brightness. Then the cage paled in the glowing vapour above the curve of the Stone Light. Finally, the chain that had been falling like an iron tail behind it disappeared too.

Merle could not utter a sound. The Queen was silent as well.

When Merle finally turned, her knees trembling, her hands in no state to hold on to the handrail, Junipa was beside her. Junipa, with her mirror-glass eyes from which the glow of the Stone Light looked out with its own intelligence. That impression did not fade until Junipa leaned forward and the reflection in the shards of mirror shifted.

Now Merle saw herself in them, eyes reddened with weeping, cheeks shining, and she was infinitely thankful when Junipa drew her into her arms, held her close and murmured soft words of sympathy, nothing important, nothing that really meant anything, yet spoken in a tone that was both soothing and encouraging.

An echoing crash. The two girls spun round.

Iskander was not to be halted by the fate of the obsidian lion. Once again he dived down on the bridge, but not to race low above the golems; this time he landed among them. Blows that would have felled mighty trees rained down on him from all sides, and the skin under his pelt was already turning dark red. But he raged on among his adversaries. For every blow that struck him he returned several, shattering golem warriors all around him. Splinters of stone whirled through the air, hitting Merle and Junipa, yet they had no choice but to watch and see what happened next.

From somewhere, more Lilim were now approaching, winged creatures like those that Merle had seen between the two gigantic statues at the gate of Axis Mundi. But they were still a long way off, little more than tiny dots overhead in the brightness.

Burbridge was leaping around among the stone warriors as they shattered, both arms raised to protect his head, bent over, reeling, only a panic-stricken man, fearing for his life.

If the Stone Light had been in him, then it had left him now. Or was waiting to find out for itself what it was like for a human to die. A search for new experience. Knowledge that would make it easier to assimilate the next human being, the next organism – or be assimilated by it, as a new heart, a new centre of everything.

Iskander's powers were failing, but his strength was still terrible enough to put the last golem to flight. Finally Burbridge stood there alone on a heap of debris and stone fragments, some still approximately human, others nothing but splinters and sand.

Iskander was taking aim for the final deadly blow when something shot up behind him from the depths, bright and glowing as a shooting star but larger, and in a shape resembling a lion. A deep roar sounded, drowning out Iskander's cries of rage and echoing back from the distant walls of the dome.

The sphinx turned, his movements slower than before, weakened by the battle and his own anger. And he saw Vermithrax. Saw the light in which the lion's obsidian body was bathed, or rather that pervaded him as if he himself had become light, a light made of stone, not hot, not cold, just different, strange and terrifying.

Vermithrax took Iskander by the head and dragged him off the bridge, raised him into the air, flung him up and broke his neck.

The sphinx's wings fluttered one last time, held him suspended in the void for a moment, and then he would have fallen — if the flying Lilim had not arrived at that very moment. They caught the corpse and carried it quickly away.

Burbridge laughed.

Laughed and laughed and laughed.

Vermithrax took no notice of him, but raced towards Merle and Junipa instead and landed on the bridge beside them. The latticework rattled under his paws as if he were suddenly much heavier.

'Come on,' he called, his roar less thunderous than before. 'Climb up!'

His body was not black now. He was glowing, as if made of lava cast in the form of a lion, and he was larger, his feathered wings were broader, his head heavier, his teeth and claws longer. Amid her relief, Merle wondered if that was all the light had done or if there were other changes too, changes you couldn't see now but might discover later, when no one was expecting them. She remembered the sparkle in the professor's glance and saw a much brighter glow in Vermithrax's eyes, two radiant points of light like stars that had settled in his face.

But she was happy too, so happy, and she embraced the glowing lion's head and patted his muzzle before she jumped up on his back with Junipa and held on tight.

'*He's the same as ever,*' said the Queen in her head, and at that moment Merle believed her. '*Just the same as ever.*'

Vermithrax took off and raced past the crowd of Lilim

that had gathered around the dead sphinx. They came away from Iskander's corpse; there wasn't much left of it. Burbridge shouted orders, and one of the Lilim hurried over to him and waited for its master to mount it, a contorted creature something like a dragonfly but as twisted as a corkscrew, with massive wing-cases like a beetle's, three on each side, and a head that looked like an eddy of teeth.

The creature rose in the air, placed itself at the head of the flying Lilim and took up the pursuit of Vermithrax. Burbridge shouted something, but his voice was so shrill that even the Lilim couldn't make it out, and so they raced after the shining lion, the first living stone creature to have been immersed in the glow of the Stone Light.

'They're afraid,' said the Flowing Queen. 'They're afraid of Lord Light, but just as much afraid of Vermithrax and what he is now.'

What is he, then? asked Merle in her thoughts.

'I don't know,' said the Queen. 'I thought I knew a great deal, but now all I know is that I don't know anything.'

Junipa was sitting behind Merle and had put both arms around her, holding on very tight and trying desperately not to look down at the abyss below. Vermithrax was still rising steeply, and it took all Merle's strength to cling to his glowing mane. Junipa was slender, almost thin, which was lucky, since it was all that allowed Merle to hold the weight of both of them steady on Vermithrax's back.

Vermithrax was faster than before, as if the light had redoubled the power of his wings too. But he lost some of his precious start when he was forced to circle under the highest point of the dome before he found an opening leading out of it, a kind of gate guarded by two winged Lilim. They both gave way in alarm as they saw him coming towards them, a radiant Fury, a living, breathing, roaring comet.

Vermithrax carried Merle and Junipa away from the haze of light in the dome, broke out of the brightness with them, and shot away into the eternal red twilight of Hell. After the blaze inside the dome, Merle found the diffuse lava light of the rock roof above Axis Mundi gloomy and sinister. Her eyes took some time to get used to it.

She imagined what Vermithrax must look like to the Lilim who had gathered in the city's streets and squares: a glowing comet-tail of light in the sky of rock above the city, a being such as had never before been seen, even in Hell.

Looking back, she saw the growing swarm of their pursuers again, shooting out of the dome not 100 metres behind them, and bringing with them thin, hazy wisps of light which soon faded and dissolved into glittering dust.

Lord Light sat astride his mount at the head of the Lilim, his coat-tails flying, his hair blowing around his head, his face twisted; several of the sphinx's blows had caught him and torn red furrows in his skin and clothes.

'*He wants Vermithrax,*' said the Queen. '*More than anything else, he wants Vermithrax.*'

And as if Junipa had heard the words in Merle's head, she contradicted them. 'He wants you, Merle. It's you he's after.' A moment later she added, 'And me too. My eyes.'

'Your eyes?' Merle called over her shoulder, as the towers and rooftops and domes of Axis Mundi passed far below them, and Vermithrax approached the cleft in the wall of rock.

'Yes. It was he who told Arcimboldo to put them in my eye sockets.'

'But why you?'

'Do you remember how I began seeing with the mirror-glass eyes? Just shapes and outlines at first, then people's faces and everything around me. And then how I started seeing even in the dark? I can *always* see, anywhere, any time, whether I want to or not.'

Merle nodded. Of course she remembered.

'It didn't stop there,' said Junipa.

'What do you mean?'

'I can see even further.' She sounded sad. 'Further and further. Through things and . . . and into other places.'

Merle looked back at the Lilim. Vermithrax had increased the distance between them again, but the number of their pursuers had grown too, to fifty or sixty.

'Other places?' she repeated.

'Into other worlds,' said Junipa. 'Serafin told me that you and he saw the reflection of another world in the water of the canals. I can do the same – without a canal, without water. That's why Lord Light needs me. I'm to look into other worlds for him . . . worlds that need a new heart, that's what he said.'

Merle suddenly froze. All at once she remembered Winter, and she immediately felt guilty for not thinking of him all this time. He had escaped, said Burbridge. She silently wished him good luck. He had made his own way through Hell before they met him, and she hoped he would do it again.

'Where are we flying to?' she shouted in Vermithrax's shining ear.

Ahead of them, the cleft now gaped like a great maw in the rocky wall of Hell. 'Out of the city first,' the lion called back. 'Then we'll see where our guide is taking us.'

She was baffled. 'Our guide?'

Vermithrax's mane vibrated as he nodded his mighty leonine head. 'Look there!'

Merle peered forward over the bright head. The cleft was darker than its surroundings and it was difficult to make out anything in it. There were a few flying Lilim, but most of them gave way when they saw Vermithrax coming.

Then Merle saw what he meant: a tiny dark dot, flying some distance ahead of them. She could just make it out before it disappeared round the first bend inside the cleft in the rock. It looked like a bird, like a –

A falcon!

'Let's hope Seth knows how we get out of here,' called Vermithrax.

'*He very likely does,*' said the Queen, finally sounding like herself again. '*Perhaps we really will make it.*'

The walls of the great cleft seemed to be coming towards them on both sides as Vermithrax raced through at breakneck speed. Ledges, cornices, needles of rock, seen out of the corners of Merle's eyes, blurred into a red-brown mist.

They had almost reached the last curve when a tremor passed through the rock walls, a shaking and vibrating, followed by dust and avalanches of boulders falling into the abyss to the right and left of them. The vibrations seemed to be approaching them, as if the structure of the rock were forming waves that rolled their way, crunching and thundering. The falls of stone became more violent; more and more chunks of rock broke away with such force that they were carried far into the cleft before they fell. Several times Vermithrax swooped aside fast to avoid the boulders, but even he could not prevent them from being hit again and again by smaller stones that struck them painfully, like shots fired from a gun.

The end of the cleft came into sight ahead of them, and their worst fears were confirmed.

The gateway of the city was impassable.

The Eternal Wrestlers had come to life, awakened, like everything else here, by the Stone Light.

The two mighty statues were continuing their wrestling match, leaning forward, entwined with each other like two children fighting for a toy. They wrestled so grimly, there was so little to choose between their strength, that they kept matching each other's positions. Again and again they collided with the rock walls in the narrow confines of the opening of the cleft, causing more tremors. Merle saw one of the Lilim hit by a boulder and flung to the depths. Others crashed into the walls; some managed to recover, but others fell.

But those who suffered most were the many pilgrims and travellers who had come between the feet of the stone giants. The endless stream of them began to fray. In panic, those who had reached the interior of the cleft hurried on, falling and stumbling over each other, struggling up, running on two, four, even more legs; many cried out in voices that sounded almost human while others uttered shrill whistles, harsh croaks or sounds for which there is no word and no description.

Although the two stone giants wrestling did not entirely fill the cleft, anyone who ventured between them risked being crushed on the spot. It would be suicidal to fly through the gateway.

'I'm going to try it,' called Vermithrax.

Merle glanced back over her shoulder again, gave

Junipa an encouraging nod and then looked at their pursuers. The Lilim were still after them. As Vermithrax slowed down because of the Wrestlers, they had finally made up a little of the distance behind him. Lord Light still rode at their head. She wondered how he had managed to wake the Wrestlers from a distance. Just now, when it looked as if the sphinx would kill him, Merle had assumed that the Stone Light had withdrawn from Burbridge — but now it seemed to be back and perhaps stronger than ever. There could be no doubt that the light, with its power over stone and rock, had called the Eternal Wrestlers to life. It suddenly occurred to Merle that perhaps this whole place, maybe all of Hell, was possessed by the Stone Light. And she wondered whether it hadn't been a mistake to regard the Egyptian Empire as the greatest of dangers to the world. Perhaps they had been wrong; perhaps it was not the Pharaoh, or Lord Light, or Hell that was the most terrible threat to them all. Perhaps an entirely different war was being waged here in secret. The Stone Light wanted more. First Hell, then the world above. And after that, with Junipa's help, all the other worlds that might exist somewhere beyond the bounds of dream and fantasy.

Vermithrax suddenly folded his wings and dropped. Something gigantic raced over them and crashed into the rock wall with a deafening sound like thunder – the elbow of one of the Wrestlers, as big as a church tower.

Junipa's grip on her waist was so tight that Merle could hardly breathe, not that it mattered, for in the stress of the moment she almost forgot to breathe anyway. Splinters of stone were raining down on them, and it was only thanks to Vermithrax's agility that none of the larger rocks hit them. Suddenly everything else was meaningless. They plunged into the middle of the struggle between the two titanic figures, seeing nothing but towering stone walls and ramparts that were constantly shifting, grinding and crunching against each other, moving towards or away from them sometimes slowly, sometimes at lightning speed. Vermithrax performed hair-raising manoeuvres in flight to avoid the bodies of the Wrestlers, the tip of a wing touching the curve of a muscle here, the top of a rib there.

Then, just as suddenly as the Wrestlers had appeared, they were left behind. Vermithrax carried the two girls out of immediate danger, past the sides of the great cleft in the rock and away into the expanses of the plain, high above the heads of scattered hordes of Lilim streaming away from the battlefield of the stone giants, fanning out and seeking safety in flight.

'Have we done it?' asked Junipa in Merle's ear. The words sounded as if she had merely breathed them, her voice was so tired and weak.

'At least we're out of the city.' Was that any reason to feel relieved? Merle didn't know, and she was sorry that she couldn't give Junipa more encouragement.

Before Lord Light's swarm reached the Wrestlers the two titans froze, as closely intertwined with each other as they had been before. The flying Lilim, led by the one with Lord Light sitting on its back, shot through the gaps between the bodies unimpeded. The Wrestlers had crushed hundreds of Lilim underfoot, and the survivors were still fleeing in all directions; it would be a long time before anyone ventured here again. Merle saw a few Lilim standing on the ground, gesticulating up at the red sky with a wide variety of different kinds of limbs, pointing to Lord Light and his companions. Then Vermithrax beat his wings faster, and his speed became so fast that Merle had to blink to keep the headwind blowing towards them from stinging her eyes.

The falcon had flown past the avalanches of stone in the crevice and the bodies of the Wrestlers much faster than Vermithrax. But now Vermithrax was catching up again, staying just within sight of the bird. It was their only chance. They would never find the way they had taken down into Hell by themselves. None of them had been able to take notice of which way the heralds flew, so they did not know where that entrance was or how long it would take them to get there.

Seth must know another way of getting out of Hell.

Merle had hundreds of questions that she would have liked to ask Junipa, but they were both utterly exhausted. Her curiosity could wait.

The waste land seemed to her even more monotonous now than during their flight with the heralds. The precipitous peaks and crevices, the gaps in the ground, the pointed stone needles and long frozen glaciers of lava went on and on as if they had really been flying round in circles for an eternity. Only small differences, divergent formations here and there, reassured Merle that they were still going straight ahead and Seth was not leading them astray.

At some point, long after Merle had lost all sense of

time and had to take care not to lose her hold on Vermithrax for sheer weariness, an outline appeared against the red glow on the horizon. At first she took it for a wind spout, perhaps a whirlwind. Then she saw that it was massive and didn't move from the spot.

A column. Kilometres high, linking the floor of Hell with the roof.

As they came closer, they could make out openings in it, irregularly arranged but all the same size. Windows.

'That's not a column,' whispered Merle in amazement. 'It's a tower!'

'The falcon's making straight for it,' said Vermithrax.

'Is it the way out?' asked Junipa faintly.

Merle shrugged. 'Seth seems to think so anyway. And he's led us here.'

'*Yes, indeed*,' said the Queen, '*and not just us.*'

Merle didn't have to look back to know that the Queen was telling the truth. The swarm of Lilim was still after them, as untiring as Vermithrax and the priest of Horus.

'This could get exciting,' she murmured.

'And short,' said Junipa, who unlike Merle had looked round.

Now Merle herself couldn't help it; she looked back too.

The Lilim were less than fifty metres away.

She could see Burbridge's smile.

FLOTSAM

The turtle shell rocked on the waves like an autumn leaf sailing down from a tree. Serafin had been having stomach cramps for hours, as if he were falling, an endless fall into an unknown abyss, and something in him seemed to be seriously expecting the moment of impact — or *something* that would bring the monotony to an end.

He had been looking out at the formless sea for so long that he could see it even with his eyes closed: a cloud-covered sky, and under it the grey wilderness of the waves, churned up but not stormy, cold but not icy, as if even the water couldn't make up its mind what it wanted. There was no land anywhere in sight. Their situation was not improved by the fact that the mermaids who had brought them this far had disappeared without trace some time ago. All of a sudden they had dived right down, and he had only to look into Eft's eyes to see that she herself was baffled.

She was sitting between Dario and Tiziano in one of the horn segments of the turtle shell, holding the rucksack containing Arcimboldo's mirror-glass mask firmly pressed to her. Serafin was mourning with her, of course, but in spite of everything he would have been glad if she had put her sadness aside for a while and thought about the future. The immediate future.

It didn't look good. Not good at all.

At least Aristide had stopped talking to himself. Serafin had been afraid that either Dario or Tiziano would throw the boy overboard, but at daybreak Aristide had finally calmed down. Now he was staring ahead of him in a daze, saying nothing when anyone spoke to him, but sometimes nodding or shaking his head if he was asked a question.

Strangest of all, however, was Lalapeya's behaviour. The sphinx, in her human form, was leaning half over the edge of the shell, letting one hand hang in the water up to the wrist. Someone — Serafin thought it was Tiziano — had wondered out loud whether Lalapeya hoped to catch a fish for breakfast, but no one had laughed. It was long past breakfast time anyway.

The sphinx's silence angered Serafin almost more than the situation into which Lalapeya had brought them. Even now, after endless hours on the water, first in darkness and now in broad daylight, she didn't think it necessary to explain the night's events to them. She was brooding, gazing into space – and letting her hand dangle in the water as if she were just waiting for someone to grasp it from down below.

But whoever she might be waiting for, he wasn't going to do her any favours.

'Lalapeya,' said Serafin for the hundredth time, 'what happened on San Michele? How long has that . . . that thing been lying there?'

She's going to say, 'A long time,' he thought.

'A long time,' she said.

Dario shifted back and forth with the horn wall behind him, but couldn't find the comfortable position he was looking for. 'That was no ordinary sphinx.'

'You don't say!' Tiziano made a face. 'As if we hadn't noticed for ourselves.'

'What I mean is,' said Dario sharply, giving his friend a nasty look, 'it wasn't just a *large* sphinx. Or a *gigantic* sphinx. What was lying buried under San Michele was . . . more.' He couldn't find the right word, but shook his head and fell silent again.

Serafin agreed with him. 'More,' he said briefly, and after a pause, 'A sphinx god.'

Aristide, confused and silent Aristide, looked up and said his first words for hours. 'If it was a god, it was a wicked one.'

As if Lalapeya were waking from a trance that had carried her far away from the boys and the turtle-shell boat, even from the sea itself, she responded. 'Not wicked. Just old. Unimaginably old. The first Son of the Mother.' She took her hand out of the water, stared at it for a moment as if it were a part of someone else's body and then went on. 'He was lying there before there was any Egypt – and I mean *ancient* Egypt. At a time when other powers ruled the world, the sub-oceanic cultures and the Lords of the Deep and . . .' She broke off, shook her head and began again. 'He's been lying there for a long time. No human beings lived in the lagoon then, and he was taken there so that no one would disturb his rest. He *was* a god, at least by your standards, even if no one called him that. And they wanted to be sure he would be undisturbed forever. So guardians were appointed to protect him.'

'Guardians like you,' said Serafin.

The sphinx nodded, looking infinitely beautiful in her grief. 'I wasn't the first, but never mind that. I have been watching over the lagoon for so long that I've given up counting the years. I came here when there was no city yet, not even houses or fishermen's huts. But then I saw humans coming, taking possession of the islands and settling on them. Perhaps I ought to have prevented it, who knows? But I always liked you humans, and I saw nothing wrong with it if you were to live where *he* lay buried. I did what I could to preserve his honour and his rest. It was I who made sure that San Michele would be a graveyard for humans too. And I was careful to be a friend to the mermaids, for they are the true rulers of the lagoon – or at least they always were, until men took to making a game of catching them and killing them, or harnessing them to their boats.'

Eft had been listening attentively for some time and now she nodded. 'You gave us the mermaids' graveyard. A place that human beings have never been able to find to this day.'

'I did only what I do best,' said Lalapeya. 'I watched over the dead, just as I have done for thousands of years. And it was simple. At first I had only to be there, waiting. Then it was time for me to build a house, and finally a palace, just to avoid attracting attention, to give no one grounds for suspicion.' She lowered her gaze and for a moment it seemed as if she would put her hand into the water again in an almost melancholy, almost guilty mood. 'When the lagoon was still uninhabited I didn't mind the loneliness. That came only later, when all the others arrived, the mermaids and the human beings. And of course the Flowing Queen. I saw what it's like to have friends, to trust other people. That was why I gave the mermaids a place for their dead, but they avoided me too.'

'We venerated you,' said Eft.

'Venerated!' Lalapeya sighed softly. 'I wanted friendship and got veneration instead. They have nothing to do with each other. I had always been lonely, and so I would have remained, but for . . .' She fell silent. 'Never mind that. When the great war began, when the Egyptians made the nations subject to them, I knew it was time to act. I heard that they had power to bring the dead to life and to enslave them — and then at last I understood that, without guessing it, I had been waiting all those ages for this one moment. It suddenly made sense. If the Egyptians succeeded in making the *god*, as you have called him, their tool . . . if they really succeeded in that, then yes, they would probably rule the world.'

'But where do the sphinx commanders come into it?' asked Dario.

'I don't doubt now that the Pharaoh has long been nothing but a puppet of the sphinxes,' said Lalapeya thoughtfully. 'By comparison with me and some others among my people, the commanders are young, and they no longer respect the old laws and customs. They have understood the power the god will give them. But for the Flowing Queen they would have achieved their aim much sooner.'

Serafin slowly nodded. So that was it. The sphinxes had been working behind the scenes all these years to enslave the old god of their people. For that they needed first the Pharaoh, then the priests of Horus with their power to make the dead obey them. And if the rumours that as of yesterday the priesthood had fallen from Pharaoh's favour were true, then it looked as if the plans of the sphinx commanders had succeeded. Not much longer now and it would be they who ruled the Empire with the aid of the old god.

Lalapeya was continuing. 'So I began to make preparations. All those thousands of years, all that waiting . . . now at last I saw that it had not been for nothing. So I tried everything in my power.' She lowered her gaze. 'And

I failed. So long, and then to be defeated. The Son of the Mother is lost.'

Serafin hadn't said a word. Now, however, he had to admit to himself that she was not to blame for her failure. He himself had prevented her from stopping the Gatherer; he had spoilt everything she and her predecessors had been waiting for over the aeons.

But even that didn't change the fact that Boro had been made to sacrifice his life.

Serafin did not feel guilty. He wanted to but he couldn't. They had both made mistakes, he and Lalapeya, and now they must face the consequences together.

'We're dying of thirst,' said Tiziano, as if Lalapeya had never made her confession. Perhaps he hadn't been listening to her.

Serafin stared at the sphinx and now she returned his gaze. For a split second he thought he had seen those eyes before, but not in her face.

'Land!' Dario's voice broke the silence. 'I see land over there!'

They all looked the way he was pointing. Even Lalapeya.

Tiziano jumped up, and the turtle shell immediately began rocking and tilting. Suddenly water slopped over the side, a whole wave, and then they were up to their ankles.

'Sit down, damn it!' Dario shouted at Tiziano.

The boy stared at him for a moment, still in the grip of euphoria at the sight of the rising land, pale in the distance, as if he didn't understand what Dario wanted him to do. But then he sat down again and kept his eyes fixed on the grey hillocks that had broken through the surface of the sea some distance off, like the hump of a giant whale.

The rise must have been within view for some time before Dario saw it, but its colour was hardly different from the colour of the sea and the sky.

'That's not land,' said Serafin, and no one contradicted him.

For a while there was a tense silence and then Dario said what they were all thinking. 'A fish?'

'A leviathan?' suggested Aristide.

An icy shudder ran down Serafin's back. 'If it is, then it's dead. The thing isn't moving. Eft?'

When she looked at him and he saw the expression in her eyes, he immediately wished he hadn't asked. But it was too late now.

'You don't want to hear this,' she said quietly.

'*I* want to hear it,' said Dario, annoyed.

'So do I,' Tiziano was quick to say.

Serafin said nothing.

Eft kept her eyes on him as she said, 'We're sinking.'

'*What?*' cried the horrified Tiziano. He jumped up again, but was immediately pulled back into his place by Dario.

'It's only a bit of water,' said Dario quickly, letting some of the salt water in the bottom of the shell run through his fingers. 'Not too bad. And I don't know what it has to do with that out there —'

'We're going down,' Eft repeated. 'We have been for some time. Very, very slowly. We can't stop it. And the only place where we can go is over there.' She pointed to the pale mounds in the sea without looking at them herself.

'Why didn't you say so before?' asked Serafin.

'What difference would that have made?'

Aristide looked frantically from one to another of them. 'We're sinking? Honestly?'

Dario closed his eyes for a moment and breathed deeply. 'That's what she said, yes.'

'Hair-line cracks,' said Serafin, examining the water level inside the turtle shell for the first time. They had all been wet through since leaving Venice and no one had bothered about the water at the bottom of the shell. But now it dawned on him that they had in fact been sitting in water before Tiziano almost capsized their boat just now.

'Hair-line cracks?' Tiziano paddled his hand about in the murky water as if he could feel them and close them with his bare fingers.

Suddenly Dario was very calm. 'Right. We're going down. But there's land ahead – or something like it. And Eft, you know just what it is.'

She nodded. 'If I'm not mistaken, it's a dead body. A very special one. The mermaids got wind of it, that's why they swam away. They're afraid of it.'

'A . . . a dead body?' stammered Tiziano. 'But . . . but that thing is at least . . . at least seventy or eighty metres long. Isn't it?' When no one answered he said again, louder this time, 'Isn't it?'

They were drifting closer and closer to the pale grey hillocks now. And gradually, very gradually, Serafin could distinguish an outline.

'The carcass of a sea-witch,' said Eft.

Serafin's heart beat faster.

'A sea-witch,' repeated Aristide, and now it was he who tried getting to his feet. Dario pulled him down so violently that for a moment Serafin considered telling him off.

He let it pass and turned to Eft. 'How much longer?'

She slowly ran her right hand through the water inside the turtle shell. 'Three hours. Perhaps four. Unless the shell breaks up first.'

'Can we reach land in that time?'

'I haven't the slightest idea where we are.'

Serafin nodded. None of all this could surprise him any more. 'So we must leave the shell?'

'Yes.'

'And climb on that thing?'

'She's dead,' said Eft. 'She can't hurt anyone now.'

'Just a moment!' Dario rubbed the palms of his hands over his eyes and then slowly massaged his temples. 'Are you seriously suggesting we move to a dead *sea-witch*?'

Eft sniffed the wind. 'She hasn't been dead long. She'll drift for another few days.'

'Which is longer than three or four hours,' Serafin heard himself saying in support of her, although he could hardly grasp that he was letting himself in for this madness.

'I'm not getting on to that.' Aristide's voice sounded higher now, almost panic-stricken.

'She can't be any more of a danger to us,' Serafin reassured him. 'And she's our only hope.'

Tiziano came to his aid. 'Imagine it's a dead fish. You might even eat it then.'

Aristide stared at Tiziano blankly for a moment, then his features distorted and his voice rose to a shrill howl. 'You're all totally crazy! You're raving lunatics!'

Dario paid him no attention. 'The current is driving us straight towards it. Another few minutes.' When Aristide was about to protest again, Dario silenced him with a glance that would have turned most people to stone. His eyes narrowed as he looked at the drifting corpse of the sea-witch again. 'Is that her face?'

They all stared at the place he meant.

'Yes,' said Eft. She suddenly turned pale and said no more. Only Serafin noticed. But he did not ask any more questions; there'd be time for that when they were safely on the carcass.

The wind turned, and the next breath of air they drew stank as disgusting as the Venetian fish market on a summer day.

The witch was drifting on her back. As far as Serafin could make out from here, she had the body of a gigantic old woman – down to the hips. There her waist joined a mighty fish-tail like the mermaids', except that the witch's tail was as long as a ship. Her floating hair fanned out on the waves like a mat of grey seaweed. They would have to take care the turtle shell didn't get caught in it; if they were forced to abandon the sinking shell in the middle of all that hair they would get hopelessly entangled in the long strands and drown.

Serafin expressed his fear out loud, and immediately they all set to work rowing with their hands to steer the turtle shell another way, down to the scaly fish-tail, where they could most easily climb on the sea-witch. Even Lalapeya helped, although Serafin wasn't sure that she was not just using this opportunity to dip her hands in the water again and feel about there for heaven knew what.

Two more metres.

One more metre.

The shell struck the witch's fish-tail. Its scales were the size of wagon wheels, covered with seaweed and silt and algae that had caught in the cracks. The stench took their breath away. The boys swallowed and fought their nausea before their noses and mouths gradually got used to it. Only Eft and the sphinx seemed immune to the smell.

No one wanted to be the first to put a hand on that scaly tail. Even Eft stared at the dead witch, white as a corpse herself, although Serafin suspected that she had other reasons. Later, he told himself. Not now. Not yet another anxiety.

He plucked up courage, supported himself on Dario's shoulder, balanced in the swaying shell for a moment and then grasped the edge of a scale with his right hand. The scabby plates, which felt like horn, were arranged in the same way as tiles on a roof, overlapping and providing plenty of footholds and handholds. But for the horrible stench, Serafin would have felt almost at home: he had climbed up and down so many roofs in his life that clambering up the fish-tail was child's play.

He reached the top, turned and looked down the curving slope of the tail to the turtle shell. From here he could see even more distinctly how deep it already lay in the water. Eft's estimate had been more than generous. Serafin doubted that they could have kept afloat for longer than an hour.

He couldn't help the others, could only watch them climb over the side of the shell, reach for the scales with trembling hands and try to get a firm footing as best they could on the slippery surface under them. The tangle of dead water-weeds was smooth as soft soap, but somehow they all finally managed to reach the highest point of the bulging tail. Eft was last to leave the turtle shell. Serafin and Dario reached out their hands to pull her up to them.

The shell rocked beside the corpse a little longer; then it was caught by a current that carried it away. Aristide and Tiziano watched it go, but Serafin's attention was now bent entirely on the gigantic body where they were stranded.

He had overcome his nausea, but his sense of disgust remained. He had never in his life seen anything so horrible. Carefully, he got to his feet and took a few steps over the bulging fish-tail towards the upper part of the body.

A hand was laid on his shoulder from behind. 'Let me go first,' said Eft, stepping past him and taking the lead. The others, Lalapeya included, were left on the tail. As long as the carcass lay still in the water, nothing could happen to them there, and for a moment Serafin relished the silence as he stood beside Eft, who herself said no more.

As soon as they had left the scales, the consistency of what they trod on changed. The witch's belly was soft and spongy, and at every step the indentations around Serafin's feet filled with moisture. He had often run over the piazzas of Venice when market stalls were being taken down there and the paving stones were ankle deep in rotten fruit and vegetables – it had felt just like this underfoot.

They walked through the groove between the ribs. Water had collected in long puddles, with all kinds of little creatures darting about in it.

From here Serafin could see the witch's chin, a sharp cone above several broad bulges. Beyond it her nostrils were visible, two cavernous openings below a sharp crest of skin and gristle.

A broad scar divided the chin, with fleshy growths over it. Eft saw it and stopped.

'What is it?' Instinctively, Serafin looked in all directions. There was no danger threatening anywhere, or at least none that he could name.

In spite of their difficult march, Eft's face was not flushed but white as a sheet.

'Eft,' he said urgently, 'what's the matter?'

'It's her.'

He wrinkled his brow, feeling his stomach cramp at the same time. 'Her?'

Eft didn't look at him as she spoke, only at the ugly

scar, as long as a horse and cart. 'The witch who took away my *kalimar*.'

'Your fish-tail?'

She nodded. 'I asked her to do it, and she gave me human legs instead.'

'Why?'

Eft breathed in and out sharply, and then told Serafin the story of her first great love: about the merchant's son who promised her eternal constancy, but then shamefully betrayed her; about the witch's warning that she could change Eft's fish-tail for legs but could do nothing about her broad mermaid mouth with its needle-sharp teeth; about the men who had half killed her while her lover stood by and watched; and how Arcimboldo as a boy had found her, nursed her back to health and took her into his house.

'Merle knows the story,' she said at last. 'After Arcimboldo, she was the first I told it to. You are the second.' Her tone of voice left the words neutral; they were not meant to suggest that hearing her tale was a privilege or a warning, they were only a statement.

Serafin looked from her to the grey landscape of the witch's face. 'And now she's dead. Does that mean . . .?'

'That I must stay as I am forever,' she said huskily. 'Not human, not a mermaid.'

He tried to think of a way out for her, a few hopeful words. 'Couldn't another witch . . .?'

'No. A witch's magic can be reversed only by the witch herself.' The bleak sea was reflected in her eyes. 'Only by herself.'

He felt helpless, and wished he hadn't come with her but had left her alone with her grief.

'There's nothing to be done about it.' She didn't sound really composed, but she was trying hard. 'Let's go back to the others.'

He followed her sadly, imagined the way this gigantic being had once lurked in the depths of the sea, a terrible giantess hunting fishing boats and merchant vessels – and bringing unhappiness to a lovelorn mermaid along the way. He admired Eft's courage: she had left her home, had swum out into the open sea, to unknown regions that must be a mystery even to the mermaids, and had *asked* a witch for something. He knew very well he wouldn't have done it, however much in love he had been.

Not even for Merle?

He quickly suppressed the thought, but it was hard for

him. He still couldn't imagine what had become of her. Uncertainty gnawed at him even when he wasn't really thinking of Merle at all — or other things were more urgent. Survival, for instance.

The others were sitting where Serafin and Eft had left them. Only Lalapeya had risen to her feet and moved a little way apart from the boys, down towards the broad tail-fin that was drifting on the waves like the sail of a capsized ship. She stood there alone, arms folded, looking out at the sea, out at the void.

Dario rose when he saw Serafin and Eft and went to meet them. He was going to say something, perhaps ask what they had been doing, when all of a sudden Aristide let out a yell.

All their faces turned his way. It had not been a call, just an inarticulate sound born of alarm and pure helplessness.

'What —'

Dario fell silent. He saw it too. So did all the others.

The surface of the sea on both sides of the scaly tail was no longer empty. Heads had emerged from the waves, slender women's faces with long hair shimmering as it floated on the water.

Eft took a step forward, hesitated for only a moment and then called out something in the mermaids' language. All the faces in the water instantly turned her way. A strange chattering arose, sounds of surprise as the mermaids looked at Eft's face, saw the jaws full of sharp teeth and obviously wondered why one of their own kind was walking on legs like a human being.

'I don't suppose these are the ones who brought us here?' Serafin's comment was disguised as a question, but he didn't expect an answer.

Eft climbed down the swell of the scaly tail until water was lapping about her feet. One of the mermaids came closer, and then minutes passed as the two of them talked in the language of the ocean, without any gestures at all, only words and notes and strange syllabic sounds.

Finally Eft went back to Serafin, and together they went over to Dario, Tiziano and Aristide. Lalapeya joined them too.

'To cut a long story short,' said Eft, 'there was a fight between two enemy sea-witches. The older one lost – we're standing on her now. The other one, a young witch, although she's older than any of us – apart, of course, from Lalapeya,' said Eft, giving the sphinx a faint smile, 'the younger witch is therefore claiming this part of the Undersea as her own.'

Undersea. It was the first time Serafin had heard the term and it conjured up pictures of the Sub-Oceanic Realms, pictures that no man had ever seen, and yet were known to everyone's imagination. Pictures from legends, from fairy tales, from ancient myths.

'We've intruded into her domain.' Eft looked nervous, although the sound of her voice suggested otherwise. 'And now she wants to talk to us. Not all of us, but she wants two of us to go with the mermaids and explain ourselves.'

A murmur passed through the group. Only Serafin and Lalapeya remained silent.

'To be honest,' said Eft, 'I am rather surprised. Sea-witches aren't known for their willingness to negotiate with humans. They eat them, or much worse. But they don't talk to them. At least, not until now.'

'Eat them,' repeated Tiziano in an undertone, and Aristide was ashen-faced.

'What do you suggest?' asked Lalapeya.

'We do as she says,' said Eft. 'What else?'

Dario looked at the dozen or so heads bobbing on the waves like flotsam. 'They can't come up here, can they?'

'No,' said Eft. 'But they can pull the carcass down to the bottom. Or ask a hungry leviathan to eat it from under our feet.'

Dario turned pale.

'I'll go with them.' Eft had made her decision. 'They have diving helmets with them.'

Lalapeya sighed. 'I'll go with you.'

'No,' said Eft. 'Not you.' And she looked Serafin straight in the eye.

He looked down at the water, then back at his friends — Dario, Tiziano, Aristide, all staring at him — and finally he met Eft's gaze again.

'Me?' He wasn't even sure whether he had asked the question out loud, or if it was just echoing in his head.

And pictures came again: a mighty shadow, eighty or a hundred metres long; a white body gradually emerging from the dark of night; eyes that had seen more than just fish in the deeps; eyes with infinite wisdom and infinite guile in them.

Serafin nodded slowly.

FRIENDS

Tar-scented winds blew around the sides of the tower, raising dust from window sills, whistling through cracks and gaps, singing with the voices of the lost. For the first time it occurred to Merle that perhaps this really was the biblical Hell, and not just a hollow space inside the earth: the truth of myths under a crust of rock and sand and twilight.

The tower had three walls that gradually narrowed towards the top, like a huge spear-point that someone had planted in the wilderness. Its edges were just as sharp. When Merle looked in through one of the windows, she could make out stone steps in the dim light. She wondered how crooked the angles of a staircase on a triangular ground plan must be, and was glad that Vermithrax was carrying her up the tower on the outside.

The obsidian lion kept close to the wall, only a few metres from the dark stone. Merle saw insects scurrying back and forth all over it, and other, larger creatures changing the colour of their skin to match their background, like chameleons, and resting motionless: sunbathing reptiles in a sunless land.

'Merle,' said the Flowing Queen, '*do me a favour and keep your eye on the falcon. I want to know exactly where he's flying.*'

She dutifully looked up. The bird shot up close to the wall of the tower, much more steeply than Vermithrax could fly. The lion had to be careful not to take too vertical a position, or he risked shaking Merle and Junipa off his back. As it was, Merle's arms ached with the strain on them, even more so because she had to support Junipa's weight as well.

For various different reasons, the Lilim pursuing them couldn't fly up the wall at a steeper angle than Vermithrax either. Most of them had broad wings that would carry them forward at high speed, but when it came to climbing they fluttered like the overfed pigeons on the Zattere quay in Venice.

Just now, before they reached the tower, Burbridge had called out something to Merle and Junipa, but she hadn't been able to understand what he said because of the howling winds and the noise of all those wings. His smile both annoyed and frightened Merle more than she liked to admit. It was not a self-confident smile anticipating victory – no, she almost had the impression that he was putting on his show of kindness again.

Stay with me, I'm your friend. Give up and all will be well.

Not on your life!

She could only vaguely estimate how high they had flown by now. The rocky desert had long since blurred to a uniform orange hue. Details couldn't be made out any more. The walls of the tower at this height measured around 100 metres from corner to corner and were only about half as wide as down on the ground. Merle guessed that they had about half the climb behind them, at least two kilometres. The idea of falling off Vermithrax's back at this height was far from appealing, and she felt her hands instinctively dig deeper into his glowing mane. Behind her, Junipa was more silent than ever, but that was all right with Merle just now. She didn't feel like talking herself. Anyway, her breath was coming as fast as if she and not Vermithrax were carrying them up.

'*Merle! The falcon!*'

The Flowing Queen's cry cut through her thoughts like a knife. It would have made her jump if all her muscles hadn't already tensed up into hard knots long ago.

She looked up, just in time to see the falcon flying in a slight curve out and away from the tower, turning and then flying horizontally towards one of the window openings and disappearing into it.

Vermithrax reacted at once, although a good deal more ponderously. He moved away from the wall of the tower, turned in a wide spiral and followed the bird. His wings were too wide to go straight through the window, and he had to make an interim landing on the sill.

'Get your heads down!'

He squeezed through the opening, while Merle and Junipa pressed as close to him as possible so as not to hit their heads. At last they were all through, and the shining body of the lion immediately filled the dark tower with brightness.

There was a staircase inside; Merle had been right about that. It was broad enough for an army and, because of the triangular shape of the tower, was even more crooked than she had expected. The steps were of different heights; some ran at an angle, while others even curved. They were not meant for human beings but for something with more and longer legs. The walls were covered with strange signs: lines and circles and loops.

'*Those aren't signs,*' said the Flowing Queen as Vermithrax took off again and began flying up the stairway, a dizzy ascent that made Merle's stomach almost turn over. Up and down, in a wide curve to the left, interrupted again and again by daring manoeuvres when one of the walls suddenly appeared round a corner and Vermithrax only just managed to avoid a collision with it.

'What do you mean, they aren't signs?' asked Merle.

'*They're tracks.*'

'Of something running along the walls?' She thought of the barbs on spider's legs, remembered the Lilim in the Hall of the Heralds and shuddered. 'How old is this tower?'

'*Very old. It was built at a time when all the Lords of the Deep were at war with the Sub-Oceanic Realms.*'

'It's time you told me about that.'

'*Now?*'

'No.' Merle ducked her head as Vermithrax came alarmingly close to a wall. 'Not now,' she said, 'but some time or other you won't be able to wriggle out of it.'

The Queen fell silent again, but it was a moment before Merle realised why. She heard loud noises behind them as Burbridge and his Lilim followed them up the stairwell.

The buzzing of insect wings and the slow rush of leathery pinions echoed back from the walls, breaking a hundred times on the steps and their edges; it sounded as if Burbridge's company had gained unexpected reinforcements.

'They'll get us.' Although Junipa's remark was directed to no one but herself, Merle heard it.

'No,' she replied. 'I don't think so.' And indeed suddenly the Lilim didn't frighten her any more. As long as she didn't have to see Burbridge's smile, hidden now behind the corners of the stairway, she thought of the Lilim as a set of clumsy monsters who were no match for Vermithrax in strength or skill. It was really only Burbridge that she feared. Burbridge and the Light in him.

The same Light that now made Vermithrax shine too, pervading and filling him, making him bigger, stronger, more dangerous.

More monstrous?

Perhaps.

Seth – or the falcon into which he had turned himself – was not in sight any more, but there was now no doubt that he was looking for the fastest way up, a way out of Hell that had been used all those thousands of years ago by the beings that the Queen had described as the Lords of the Deep. Enemies of the Sub-Oceanic Realms. The ancestors of the Lilim, whose realm had fallen when the Stone Light smashed their city.

The further they moved away from the ground of Hell, the cooler it was. Perhaps that was because of the shadows inside the tower, or perhaps it was the sweat on their skin chilling in the strong headwind that blew through their clothes and hair. A glance at Junipa's slim hands on her waist showed Merle that her friend had goose pimples too. Vermithrax might shine like a huge Chinese lantern but he didn't give off any warmth, any more than the light inside the dome had done. He had bathed in the Stone Light, and no one yet knew what the consequences of that would be for him and all the rest of them.

'*Don't think about it*,' said the Queen. '*Not now.*'

I'm trying not to.

Another corner, another bend in the stairs. Steps in the most peculiar forms, repeated at certain intervals, as if the high ones were made for larger creatures and the lower ones in between them for smaller beings. A picture arose before Merle's eyes of a teeming mass of creatures pushing and shoving on the steps, while others, perhaps with stilt-like

383

legs bent at many joints, stalked over them, and other even stranger forms of life scurried effortlessly along the walls and ceiling.

She shook herself, and not because of the cold this time.

'What will he do to us if he catches us?' she asked the Queen before realising that she had spoken the words out loud.

'What he did to me,' said Junipa.

Merle sensed the Queen's surprise, but the voice in her mind said nothing. Waited.

'What do you mean?' she asked, this time turning direct to Junipa.

'I said he'll do the same to you as he did to me.'

Were the droning and whirring of the wings behind them coming closer? Or was it just a trick of the acoustics, making the sound seem louder and more menacing?

'I understood what you said,' replied Merle. 'But what exactly . . . I mean, if you'd rather not talk about it, I could –'

'No.' The Queen sounded unusually decided. '*Let her tell us.*'

But there was no need for Merle to repeat the question.

'You can feel it if you like,' said Junipa quietly. Her

hand moved away from Merle's waist and was placed on her right forearm, as if to lift it from the lion's mane.

'Feel it?' asked Merle.

Vermithrax suddenly flew sideways. The girls on his back were flung to the left and Merle almost lost her grip. She dug her hands into the lion's mane and pressed her legs firmly against his flanks. Her heart missed a beat.

'Later,' she managed to say between clenched teeth.

Junipa said no more and the Queen remained silent too.

'We ought to be at the top soon!' Vermithrax's words echoed back from the walls, booming in the shaft like thunder. His bright light cast a host of flickering shadows like ghosts on the walls.

They had lost the falcon from view some time ago. If there was a way out up there, and Seth reached it first, and slammed it in their faces . . .

'*Don't think such things*,' said the Queen.

Merle was shivering more and more. The cold was deepening, and not just inside her.

'Not far now!' Vermithrax beat his wings faster and his manoeuvres round the sharp bends were ever more daring.

'They're catching up,' Junipa whispered in Merle's ear.

Merle looked back, but in the light shed by

Vermithrax's body she could make nothing out. The stairway behind her was empty. But the sounds coming up from below clearly suggested that their pursuers had not abandoned the chase.

'They'll catch up.' Again, even more softly.

Merle shook her head. 'I don't think they will.'

'Yes. Soon.'

You can feel it, Junipa had said.

Merle was alarmed, and suddenly not just because of Burbridge and his Lilim.

An icy gust of wind rushed to meet them, making their hair flutter and piercing their clothes with a thousand tiny needles. An angry cry rang out in the depths behind them.

'What was that?'

'*Only the wind*,' said the Queen.

'I mean that cry.'

'*Lord Light.*'

'But why?'

'*Perhaps his Lilim can't stand the cold.*'

'Are you serious?'

'*I don't think it's ever cold in Hell. They're not used to it.*'

The icy wind was blowing down from above all the time now.

'How much further, Vermithrax?'

'It's getting lighter. There's a way out somewhere above us.'

Lighter? All she could see was the light radiating from the lion. It was like riding a shooting star up the dark shaft of the stairwell. His light brushed over the rough walls, cast wandering shadows and woke the furrows and scratches to life; the tracks, like the creatures that had left them, seemed to crawl over the walls on thin, spindly legs.

When Merle looked more closely, she saw that the light was being reflected back as if the walls were covered with glass – or ice.

Yes, there were frost flowers on the stone.

Suddenly the cold seemed to her a good deal keener.

In her mind, she turned to the Queen: I suppose you don't know where this way out takes us either?

'No . . .'

Not into the eternal ice, I hope.

'I don't think we've flown as far as that. Not in such a short time.'

Was she mistaken, or did the fluttering of wings down below sound fainter? Once again she heard Burbridge's angry bellow, but the shaft behind them was still empty.

Junipa's hands clutched tight.

'We've nearly made it,' said Merle, to encourage her.

She felt Junipa nod; her chin came into contact with Merle's shoulder.

The steps below them were covered with a thin layer of ice now. The glow that came from Vermithrax made their surfaces shimmer in rainbow colours.

Junipa's hands held Merle's waist yet more tightly, digging painfully into her sides. She was shivering miserably.

'Not so hard,' Merle called back. 'That hurts.'

Junipa probably couldn't hear her, for the pressure did not slacken and even tightened further.

'In front there!'

For a moment Vermithrax glowed yet more brightly as they left the steps below and behind them, and raced out into a wide hall. Its ground plan was triangular like the base of the tower itself. The sloping walls met high overhead at a dimly seen point beyond the reach of Vermithrax's light.

They had reached the top of the tower.

Rock debris formed hills and valleys on the floor of the hall. There had once been a ramp here, but only remnants of it were to be seen now. They had led to an opening to the outside world which from a distance looked curiously irregular, until Merle realised that it had once been much wider and today was stopped up except for an angular hole. The cold was considerable inside the hall, and ice glittered on the detritus and the walls.

In front of the opening there was a balustrade under a grey, cloudy sky, half ruined and with no handrail. But the space was wide enough for Vermithrax to land on. From there, Merle hoped, they could see what awaited them outside.

The beating of Lilim wings had died away. Perhaps the Queen was right: the cold had forced them to give up. Or it was possible that the sound was simply lost in the huge expanse of the hall.

Merle tried to free herself from Junipa's painful grip, but the girl's hands clung desperately to her sides. 'Not so tight,' cried Merle again, once more without success.

As Vermithrax rose to the balustrade, Merle looked at the access to the stairwell below. From above, it could be seen that a heavy stone slab the size of a Venetian piazza lay over it. A broad crack had split it from side to side; this was the opening through which they had flown out into the hall. Someone, probably a long time ago, had done everything possible to bar the Lilim's way to the world above. In vain.

The crack gaped like a black maw in the floor of the hall. There were still none of their pursuers in sight.

'We've –'

We've thrown them off, she had been about to say. At the same moment Junipa hauled her backwards.

Merle's stiff, frozen fingers lost their grip on Vermithrax's mane, the Queen called something out in her mind, the obsidian lion's back slid away from under the girls, and then they fell.

Fell into the darkness.

For a moment Merle thought they would tumble through the crack and straight back into Hell. But they were much too far from the stairwell. Instead, their fall ended after a few moments of shock on a slope of loose rubble, part of the remains of the ramp and about halfway up the height of the hall. Merle fell full length. Her back felt as if it were breaking to pieces. Then she tumbled to one side, rolled a few metres and was brought up against a flat piece of stone. It was under an overhang in the ruins that sheltered it from view from above.

Junipa landed beside her, crashed against the stone like

a bundle of loose bones. But unlike Merle she did not cry out. She made no sound at all.

You can feel it . . .

Merle looked up through the opening under the overhang and saw Vermithrax, shining like a star in the darkness and much too far away. He was flying in a curve, looking for her. She tried calling to him, but only a croak came out of her lips. There was sand in her mouth, crunching between her teeth. She breathed vapour white as smoke. The ground under her was so cold that she was briefly afraid the palms of her hands would freeze to it. She wasn't used to such cold, not at this time of the year, and certainly not after the warmth down inside the earth.

Junipa.

Merle looked round in search of her friend, meaning to crawl over and help her. She started in alarm as Junipa suddenly got to her feet and looked down on her with indifference. Her mirror-glass eyes reflected nothing but the darkness; they looked like empty caverns.

Junipa was bleeding from an injured knee and the palms of her hands were scraped, but she did not seem to feel the pain.

She just stared at Merle.

Stared with those black shards of mirror glass. With eyes that went through everything. *I'm to look into other worlds for him. Worlds that need a new heart.*

'We must get away from here,' said Merle, scrambling up.

Junipa shook her head. 'We'll wait.'

'But –'

'We'll wait.'

'Don't you understand yet?' asked the Queen.

Of course Merle understood. She just didn't want to. It was impossible. Not Junipa.

'That was no accident,' said the Queen. *'She did it on purpose.'*

The obsidian lion flew another circuit in the darkness, passing the place where Merle could peer out from under the overhang. He'd never find her here unless she somehow crawled into the open.

But there stood Junipa, barring her way.

'Let me by,' said Merle. Her right ankle hurt, and would hardly carry her weight.

Junipa didn't move. She just stared.

'Let me by.'

It was dark down here; the only distant glimmer of light came from the opening high above them and from

Vermithrax. He was calling Merle's name now, and this time she answered him. But she doubted whether her voice would emerge from under the overhang and reach right up to the lion.

Junipa took a step towards her. The darkness in her eyes came closer.

'What have they done to you?' asked Merle.

'You can —'

'Feel it, yes, I know. But I want you to tell me.'

Junipa put her head on one side for a moment, as if she were working out what Merle meant. Then she began to undo the buttons down the front of her dress. Her flat chest, bony like everything about her, had a silvery shimmer as if her whole body had begun to turn into a mirror. But that was just an illusion. Just her smooth, white skin.

'Here,' she said.

In the darkness, the scar was little more than a line, a shadow.

Cross-stitch.

Merle's voice sounded as distant as the rushing of Vermithrax's wings. 'You've been in the House of the Heart.'

Junipa nodded.

'But why isn't there anything to see? The wound . . .'

Junipa buttoned up her dress again. 'A heart of stone will heal all wounds.'

It sounded like something learned off by heart, a line from a bad poem. But then Merle saw that the cut on Junipa's knee had closed up. There was nothing left but a dark mark and a few trails of dried blood.

She tried to feel rage, hatred for Burbridge, for the Surgeon, for the whole damned lot of them. But instead she could feel only grief and infinite pity for Junipa. A blind orphan girl who had been given cold mirror-glass eyes and now a new heart. A heart made of the Stone Light. She was being manipulated and changed as others thought good. And in the process everything was being taken from her that made her what she herself was.

'*You can't help her*,' said the Queen.

She's still my friend.

'*Lord Light is controlling her. Just as the Stone Light controls him. Or both of them.*'

She's my friend. I can't give her up.

'*Merle.*' The Queen's voice was imploring, but sympathetic too. '*You can't tear the heart out of her breast again.*'

I can't, no, but maybe someone else could. We must try.

'*You want to take her with us?*'

Merle did not reply. Instead, she took Junipa's hands and was surprised herself that the girl let her. A good sign perhaps. 'Junipa, listen. You mustn't obey him. Whatever he threatens you with. We'll find a way to help you . . .'

'Threatens me?' Junipa frowned, puzzled. 'He doesn't threaten me with anything.'

Merle took a deep breath. Far away she saw Vermithrax's bright light flickering over the walls of the hall. But she didn't want to call to him for fear of losing Junipa entirely. At least she was talking to Merle now, not trying to attack her. Perhaps there was still more of the old Junipa in her than the Queen thought.

Merle forced herself to smile. 'Let's get out of here.'

'We'll wait,' said Junipa.

'Junipa, please.'

The girl flung her arms back ready to strike, looked blankly from one hand to the other for a moment, and then made for Merle.

With a cry, Merle leaped back, collided with stone, felt Junipa seize her arm and herself managed to grasp Junipa's wrist. Her instincts told her to let go, retreat, run for it and call to Vermithrax, and the Flowing Queen was talking to her too, begging her to give up Junipa, to escape, get herself to safety.

But Junipa was her best friend. And she couldn't help what had happened to her.

Merle avoided Junipa's left hand again. It was not a seriously meant attack, not intended to hurt her. Junipa was trying to hold her up, perhaps only for a few moments, just for a couple of minutes. Long enough for Burbridge to induce his Lilim to defy the cold and catch up with their victim. From here, she couldn't see the crack in the rock and didn't know if Burbridge was in the hall already. But then she saw the glow of Vermithrax again, and told herself he wouldn't be up there if her enemy was already close.

Suddenly Junipa struck her a blow that knocked her to her knees. She leaped up at once and flung her adversary against the rubble. Junipa's head cracked against the hard stone, bounced back like a ball – and then she collapsed and lay motionless. Before she could get up again, Merle had snatched the rucksack from her back, looking for something to defend herself with, scattering the bottle of water, her mirror and the chicken's claw carelessly to the ground. And gave up.

What had she expected? Had she thought she could shock Junipa out of this nightmare with cold water? Slowly, Merle turned towards her, in the certainty of defeat, guessing that Junipa would not give up before Burbridge had got what he wanted. And found out that she was wrong.

For Junipa was still lying motionless on the ground, showing no sign of life. Her mirror-glass eyes were open. They were staring at Merle's little hand-mirror, which had come to rest on the stone in front of her.

Merle bent down to pick up the mirror and the claw and put both in the pocket of her dress, and then she ran, leaping over the pebbles and cracks, finally emerging from under the overhang. She waved both arms, shouted Vermithrax's name as loud as she could, and saw his light move towards her a few seconds later. The obsidian lion shot out of the darkness. His glow lit up her surroundings, creating shadows behind sharp-edged rocks.

'Where's the girl?' he asked as he landed beside her.

'Wait!'

Merle raced back under the projecting overhang and came back a moment later with Junipa, carrying her in both arms like a baby, her breath wheezing and her back hurting. Junipa moved her lips, but Merle couldn't make out what she was saying.

'We must take her with us.' She was going to say something else, but now her mouth opened without her own volition, as the Queen took it over. 'She belongs to Lord Light! She has betrayed us!' Merle could have screamed with rage, but she couldn't even do that as long as the Queen controlled her tongue. She summoned up all her willpower, concentrated her anger like a clenched fist – and freed herself with a wild cry.

She sensed the Queen's astonishment. Her deep insecurity. She felt her retreat further inside her, alarmed by Merle's sudden strength of will.

Don't you ever do that again! thought Merle furiously. Never, ever again.

And she thought: we didn't even ask him . . . for help for Venice, for Serafin and Junipa and all the others. We never even asked. And you didn't really mean to, did you? You wanted to be sure. That's why we came down here. Were you thinking about Burbridge? Or the Stone Light? No, she thought icily, at heart you were thinking only about yourself.

Suddenly her only feelings were contempt and a

deep sense of injury. At the same time she realised that the mystery around the Flowing Queen was much greater, much more incomprehensible, than she could grasp at this moment.

The Queen did not reply, and the surprised Vermithrax allowed Merle to put Junipa on his back. Then she climbed up behind the unconscious girl, wedged her between herself and the lion's neck, buried her hands in Vermithrax's mane and gave him the word to rise.

The obsidian lion unfolded his stone wings, beating them strongly, and flew towards the opening.

Junipa's lips were moving more and more frantically, but Merle dared not put her ear closer to the girl's face in case it was a trick that Burbridge was forcing her to use.

But then, very briefly, she thought she did hear something that sounded like a word. A word that didn't belong here at all.

'Grandfather,' said Junipa. And then, more clearly, 'He's your grandfather.'

Merle went rigid.

'*He is not,*' said the Queen. '*She's lying. He is lying.*'

Junipa's lids slowly opened and Merle saw herself in the

mirror-glass eyes, lit from below by the light of the lion and white as a ghost.

Junipa's features relaxed; only her eyes remained open, looking right through Merle, the shadows and the world. To somewhere else, the land of lies, the land of truth.

'Grandfather,' murmured Merle.

'Don't do that! It's exactly what he wants to achieve. Burbridge is just using her. He's making up lies to sap your strength.'

Merle stared into the mirror-glass eyes a moment longer, seeing her two white reflections, and then shook herself.

'It wouldn't change anything,' she said, although the thoughts were whirring in her head like a swarm of hornets. 'Grandfather or not, he's to blame for what has happened to Junipa . . . and for everything else.'

The Queen must have felt what was going on in her mind, but she restrained herself and said nothing.

Vermithrax had almost reached the half-ruined balustrade when Merle expressed one of her thoughts out loud. 'Why can he control Junipa but not Vermithrax? Vermithrax has much more of the Stone Light in him than she does.'

The lion settled on the broken stone sill, not far from the opening to the outside world. A snowdrift had come in, and was running down the dark stone in white that thinned out like the feathers of a ripped down pillow.

'It does not rule me.' Since his immersion in the Light, the lion's voice was more awe-inspiring than ever. 'It is mine, but I am not subject to it.'

His eyes said: *not yet.*

But perhaps that was just an illusion, gone in a twinkling. Please, please, please, thought Merle.

Behind them wings hummed in the darkness, slowly, ponderously, and as Merle and Vermithrax looked round Burbridge came flying into the dim light on his Lilim mount. The creature's spiral body swayed and trembled, its eyes were glittering more than ever, and Merle saw that they were covered with ice.

You were right, she thought. The Lilim creature is freezing.

'*Of course I was right,*' said the Queen.

The being came no closer but hovered in the air with an effort, not twenty metres from them and level with the balcony.

Burbridge was looking at her alone. All the friendliness

was gone from his features. The rest of his Lilim troop had not come with him. It must be clear to him that he was in danger of being attacked by Vermithrax.

Yet he was here.

'Merle,' he said, 'do you know her name? I can tell you her name . . .'

Whose name did he mean? The name of the Flowing Queen? But what —

A gust of wind scattered the snowdrift. White flakes frozen hard as splinters of glass drifted over the jagged edge of the balcony and down into the dark. The Lilim creature trembled and retreated.

Burbridge said no more, but only shook his head slowly. Merle felt that this gesture had nothing to do with the Lilim, only with her.

Then he dug his heels into the creature's flanks and the slender body turned ponderously, sinking back down to the crack in the floor and through it into the stairwell shaft.

Merle took her eyes off the abyss below and looked back at the unconscious Junipa's face. Her eyelids were closed now, but a shimmer of silver showed through two tiny slits. Merle's hand went to Junipa's breast. No warmth, no heartbeat. For a moment she had the impression that light was streaming out through her fingers, a fan-shape of brightness. But it faded before she could be sure it wasn't an illusion.

She would help Junipa. She'd help her somehow.

What had Burbridge meant? *Her name* . . .

Vermithrax began to move and carried them out into the open air.

Sparkling brightness awaited them, as if the Stone Light had taken hold of the world above too. But it was only the white of the landscape and the white of the sky. Snow clouds covered the sun. The plain that stretched far below them was buried under a deep layer of snow.

'Winter,' whispered Merle.

'*In the middle of summer?*'

'Winter. He's here.'

The Queen hesitated. '*You mean . . .?*'

'He was telling the truth. He got here before us.'

They were high above the plain of ice, and the wind blew in Merle's face, keen and painful. She had been completely frozen for a long time and had thought it couldn't get any worse. But now she felt that the cold would kill her if she didn't warm herself by a fire soon. Her hands pushed into the pockets of her dress as if of their own accord. Her right hand touched the oval frame of her mirror; it too was cold as ice. Only the water inside it was as comfortingly warm as ever.

She had supposed they were on a mountain a few dozen metres above the plain. But now, when she looked round, she saw her mistake. The snow-covered surface underfoot was smooth, but it was not a balcony like the one inside the hall.

It was a step. The slope she was looking down consisted of dozens of such steps, each several metres high.

'Merle!' Vermithrax's voice made her look up. 'On the horizon.'

Blinking, she followed his gaze, dazzled by the endless expanse of snow. Once her eyes had partly accustomed themselves to the brightness, she recognised shapes in the distance. Too pointed and symmetrical for mountains. They were made up of steps just like the one on which they were standing.

Merle turned her head and looked up at what was behind her. The slope of the steps narrowed towards the top and ended in a point.

'*Pyramids,*' said the Queen.

Merle was breathless with the cold — and also because she understood where they were.

Egypt.

And the desert was metres deep in snow.

Merle's hand felt for the water mirror, slipped into it, into the velvety, pleasant warmth. And while her eyes were still wandering across the ice, over to the snow-covered pyramids, slender, feminine fingers inside the mirror took hold of her own, clasped them, stroked them.

Mother, thought Merle in a daze.

The mirror phantom spoke softly, whispered, spoke low.

And in another place, on the tail-fin of a drifting sea-witch, the sphinx Lalapeya crouched by the water, dipping her hand deep into the sea and shedding silent tears.

IRRESISTIBLE FANTASY STORIES

The Flowing Queen
by Kai Meyer

The Flowing Queen has always protected the people of Venice. Till now.

When Merle and Serafin overhear a plot to betray the city to the Egyptians, they are plunged into a thrilling race against time to save the Flowing Queen – and Venice itself.

But can a pair of lowly apprentices get past an entire mummy army?

The first adventure in Kai Meyer's best-selling trilogy.

The Blood Stone
by Jamila Gavin

One diamond – a world of spies, death and deception.

In Venice, the diamond promises wealth and prestige to greedy Bernardo Pagliarin. At the court of the Great Moghul in Agra, it holds the key to the throne itself. For Filippo and his family, the stone is worth far more. It could bring their father back from the dead.

A dazzling whirlwind of a journey, over seas and across the desert, into the very heart of danger.

The Looking Glass Wars
by Frank Beddor

Alyss, born in Wonderland, is destined to be a warrior queen. After a bloody coup topples the Heart regime, Alyss is exiled to another world entirely, where she is adopted into a new family, renamed Alice and befriended by Lewis Carroll. At age twenty she returns to Wonderland to battle Redd and lead Wonderland into its next golden age of imagination.

See **www.egmont.co.uk** for information on these great books and many others!